Scandals

Also by Sasha Campbell

Confessions

Suspicions

Published by Kensington Publishing Corporation

Scandals

Sasha Campbell

Kensington Books
http://www.kensingtonbooks.com

pbk.

ISBN-13: 978-0-7582-6942-3
ISBN-10: 0-7582-6942-0

First trade paperback printing: April 2012

10 9 8 7 6 5 4 3 2 1

Printed in the United States of America

This book is dedicated to G.E.B.
Yeah, boy! That trip is right around the corner. Fo sho.

Acknowledgments

I would like to thank all the book clubs for the love I received for my sophomore book *Suspicions*. Your comments and e-mails made it possible for me to finish this story even when I wasn't feeling creative. Y'all definitely kept it together for me. Now fasten your seat belt and enjoy the ride!

Prologue

Ashes to ashes . . .

I stood off to the far right under a large oak tree, watching from a distance in disbelief. I still couldn't believe she was dead.

Just a week ago we were sitting at a restaurant, talking, laughing, and realizing we had more in common than either of us had ever imagined. That chick had been there for me when I needed help. She had been my friend. Now she was gone. Neck slit. Brutally beaten. Even thinking about it made me sick to my stomach because that could easily have been me lying in that wooden box.

Behind Versace designer sunglasses, I glanced around at the folks who had come to pay their respects and noticed a woman standing in front, hugging a little girl. Both were crying their eyes out. Few were family, but the majority I knew personally. We all danced at Scandalous Gentlemen's Club. And her brutal death could have happened to any one of us.

As I watched them lower her body into the ground, I forced myself to take a deep breath. For the umpteenth time I wondered, was it really worth it?

None of us set out to be a stripper. Hell no. I still don't know how I even allowed anyone to convince me to start dancing in the first place, yet back then I was convinced it was my only option. What was supposed to be a temporary solution had become a way of life . . . a lifestyle. But the money was easy and too damn good to simply walk away from. However, as I watched her body being lowered into the ground, I couldn't help but reevaluate my life. Maybe it was time for me to do something different, because it wasn't just me who mattered. I had a family to consider. I was needed in this world. I was depended on and I couldn't just make decisions without thinking about the consequences . . . not anymore.

While the others stood around talking long after the service had ended, I returned to my car and headed home, still wondering how I allowed myself to get caught up in the craziness of it all. As I looked back over the last few months, once again I asked myself, all that drama, had it really been worth risking my life? And if I had a chance to do it all over again, would I?

1

Monica

Six months earlier

"You want me to do what!"

I was practically shouting and had every reason. I was even seriously considering popping somebody upside their head. The only thing stopping me was I suddenly remembered where the hell we were.

I glanced around CJ's Café just to make sure no one was eavesdropping on our conversation, and to my relief, the only people looking at me all cockeyed was the couple at the next table. Hell, I didn't mean to be loud and even tossed an apology in their direction before I focused my rage on the chunky chick sitting across the table from me. There's no way in hell Reyna had just said what I thought she said.

"I'm serious, Monica. Look at this," she insisted and had the nerve to stab the newspaper with her index finger.

I shifted my eyes. "Reyna, I'm not looking at that! I can't believe you set your lips to suggest something like that to me." My best friend had lost her mind. "Are you fucking crazy?"

Reyna blinked and then had the audacity to act like it was no big deal. "It's not that bad. I even considered it once in college. I know you could do it."

I sighed silently to myself. "I'm not even about to have this conversation with you."

She blew out a heavy breath, then rolled her eyes at me. "Damn, Monica, you act like I asked you to rob a bank . . . like we about to set it off up in here."

"Shiiiit, what's the difference?" I hissed and leaned back against the seat. I should have known when Reyna asked me to meet her for lunch, she had something up her sleeve. And to think I'd been having one hell of a day.

Fridays were the only mornings I didn't have class, and with the girls in school, I decided to finally do something I'd been considering for months—I got a haircut. I let Sonya, a stylist at Forever You, chop off the hair that once hung to the center of my back. For two hours I was practically in tears, certain I had made a big mistake until she swung my chair around so I faced the mirror. Sonya was heaven sent. She had given me a short layered style that took off almost ten years from my face. You're probably thinking, what's the big deal? Well, listen when I tell you, cutting my hair was a hard decision for me. For years my hair was my strength. I was like Samson. I thought I was weak without it. But I realized the only thing that made me weak was my ex-husband Anthony. Too bad it took his sorry ass leaving for me to finally figure it out.

As soon as I left the salon, I went to meet Reyna for lunch and strolled into CJ's Café with my hips swaying. I couldn't help but notice several men checking me out. I guess the black wraparound dress I was rocking looked good hugging every curve on my body just as I had hoped it would. The attention definitely made it worth the money I spent on the outfit. Some dude even had the nerve to try to get my attention, but I blew him off. Not that he was ugly or anything. It's just that the last thing in the world I needed was a man. All I wanted was to know that even though I was a thirty-year-old mother of two, I still looked damn good. The attention was definitely my stamp of approval. When I finally reached the booth at the far back corner, I was feeling sexy, then Reyna had the nerve to fuck everything up for me.

Our waiter returned with our salads and iced teas. Reyna waited until he had moved on to the next table before she tried to rationalize. "Listen, Monica, all I'm tryna do is help you find a job. You're the one who said you weren't asking Anthony for shit else."

Damn right I wasn't. I'd rather clean the floor of the café with a toothbrush than ask that bastard for a dime. I was willing to even get a job standing on the corner holding up one of those stupid *Everything Must Go* signs. I would do just about anything except beg my ex-husband for money . . . and the shit Reyna was suggesting. "You're right. I meant it when I said I'm not asking him for shit, but just 'cause I said that doesn't mean I'm ready to sell my body just to earn a dollar."

Reyna laughed like what I said was funny when in actuality I was dead serious. "Monica, it's stripping, not prostituting," she said a little too gleefully.

"Hell, they're the same damn thing," I snarled at my friend, then stabbed my garden salad with a fork.

"No, they are not," she said nonchalantly, then shrugged. "In fact, Scandalous is a pretty nice club. I've been there a few times."

"A few times?" Lord have mercy. That girl never ceases to amaze me. I shook my head and gave her a pitiful look. "What were you doing . . . auditioning?"

"Noooo," she said like something was wrong with the idea. What's up with that? Apparently it was okay for me to strip, but heaven forbid I assume she had. "It's nothing like that." Reyna gave me a wicked grin and took a bite of her salad before she continued, "This dude I used to mess with had this thing about taking his date to a strip club. Something about it turned him on to have his woman watching the dancers along with him." Reyna had this faraway look in her eyes. Damn! I couldn't believe she was taking me with her ass on a ride down memory lane.

Reyna then leaned in close. I guess she didn't want anyone else to hear what she was about to say. Hell, I wasn't sure if I wanted to hear it either. "They even have a swingers section upstairs, and we went up there and got our groove on. Monica, *girrrrl*, having sex in the balcony while staring down at the strippers on the stage . . . *oh my goodness* . . . it was better than a porno tape. I don't think I ever came that hard in my life."

I leaned back in the seat, trying to put as much distance between the two of us as I could manage. "Nasty ass." I shook my head because I should have known better. My girl gets off on all that crazy shit.

"Monica, you act like you've never done anything freaky in your life," she said with a disapproving look on her face.

"I have . . . at home . . . with my husband." Reyna would never believe the things my husband used to make me do. Hell, I still had a hard time believing it myself.

"Seriously . . . I wasn't trying to piss you off. It was just a suggestion . . . a quick way to make some money . . . that's all." Reyna tried to act like her feelings were hurt, but I wasn't buying it.

I reached for my iced tea and stared at her cocoa-brown face over the rim of the glass as I spoke. "Well I'm not interested in auditioning at Scandalous. I've got two little girls. What would they think if they knew their mother was taking her clothes off in front of a room full of horny men?"

"They won't know. The only two people who'd know are you and me." She shook her head like I was being ridiculous when it was Reyna who had lost her damn mind. "Some weave, false eyelashes, and colored contacts . . . nobody would know it was you."

"Absolutely not." I scowled. She tried to reason with me, but I stood my ground. "Dammit, I said no!"

"Okay . . . fine." Reyna threw her hands in the air in defeat. "Then what are you gonna do about money?"

If anyone had told me a year ago I would be sitting in a café with my best friend trying to figure out how I was going to keep a roof over my head, I would have laughed at them. Back then I was Mrs. Monica Houston, the wife of Anthony Houston, the hedge fund king and one of Richmond's wealthiest black men. I'd been living in a big-ass house in Chesterfield with a maid and a gardener. Back then couldn't nobody tell me my husband was messing around on me. I loved that man with everything I had and was confident he felt the same. So when he announced he wanted a divorce, I swear to you, I didn't see that shit coming, especially since we had just spent a week in Jamaica, screwing like two teenagers on spring break. That bastard waited until our plane landed in Richmond before he broke the news.

After that my life spiraled out of control, and here I was a year later, a black woman with a limited education and almost no work experience trying to figure out how to make everything right in my life for the sake of my two beautiful little girls, Liese and Arissa. The money the courts awarded me was barely enough to maintain the lifestyle we were accustomed to. In fact, if I didn't figure out a plan soon, I was going to find my ass on the street.

"There has to be another way."

Reaching across the table, Reyna touched my arm. "There is. We just have to figure out what it is." I looked at her and nodded even though I was starting to lose faith. "What I don't understand is how Anthony can be so damn stingy. Those are *his* daughters. As much money as that bastard makes, he should be glad to help you out at least until you finish nursing school."

I love Reyna for always having my back, but she should know it was always his way or no way, and now that we were divorced nothing had changed. I couldn't blame anyone but myself, because I had allowed him to control me all those years.

I remember when Anthony and I first met. I was a freshman and he was a junior at the University of Michigan. We fell in love overnight, and when he graduated and asked me to return with him to Virginia, I gladly dropped out of school. I had every intention of continuing my education, but Anthony proposed and promised to take care of me forever. Shortly after we arrived in Richmond, Anthony landed a position with a large hedge fund corporation, then Arissa was born and Liese a year later. I was happy just raising the girls and taking care of my husband. For eight years that was all I knew. Like I said, I never saw it coming.

I snatched the *Richmond Post Dispatch* up from the table and stared down at the help wanted ad. Exotic dancing? Hell no. I cut my eyes at Reyna, then focused on the ad below it. "Look! Mason's needs a waitress to work the evening shift."

"On Crater Road?" Reyna gave a rude bark of laughter. "I guess so. Some dude was shot and killed in their parking lot last week."

Ms. Know-It-All. "Okay, what about cashiering?"

"Puh-leeze, you can't live off minimum wage."

Whatever. "Ooh! JCPenney's is hiring sales associates." My head popped up and I stared across the table and grinned. Reyna knew I loved shopping at that store.

She frowned. "They're hiring for the morning shift, and last I checked, *you* were in school. That is . . . unless you're planning on dropping out."

Reyna knew better than that. Just like the new haircut, enrolling in school was my way of proclaiming my independence. Nursing had always been a dream of mine. After the divorce was final, I enrolled in a twelve-month accelerated LPN program. It was intense and hard work. I had classes in the morning and barely had enough time to study before picking up the girls from their after-school program. But in less than seven months it would all be over.

While I finished my salad, I scanned the ads and saw a few possibilities but ended up feeling increasingly frustrated. "To be honest, Reyna . . . I really don't know how I'm going to juggle school, the girls, *and* a job."

"Where there's a will, there's a way," Reyna said, trying to reassure me. "How about working twelve-hour shifts on the weekends at the hospital?"

I shook my head at the idea. "No. That's the only time the girls and I have to really spend any time together."

"There is always the evenings after they go to bed," she suggested.

I took a moment to think about it. "I would be too tired for class in the morning."

Reyna leaned back on the seat with a sigh. "Okay, then what about Friday, Saturday, and Sunday? You don't have classes on Fridays." She must have seen my frown because she added, "Seriously, Monica, the only option you have is to find something you can do in the evenings or weekends. You know I have no problem watching the girls."

"Mmm-hmm, but how many jobs are out there like that?"

"I already suggested one and you weren't interested," she mumbled under her breath, then had the nerve to stare at her hands like she was looking for chipped nail polish.

That chick better be glad I loved her, which was the only reason why I hadn't reached across the table and snatched those kinky twists outta her head. She was, after all, my best friend.

We met at First Baptist Church of Virginia on Decatur Street my first year in Richmond, and had been tight ever since. She had gotten a degree in business at Virginia Commonwealth University and three years ago opened her own boutique. Reyna was doing everything she had set her mind to, and unlike me, she hadn't let a man stand in her way.

"How about working at UPS tossing packages late in the evening or the early morning assembly line at Kraft?" she suggested.

"Maybe." Neither sounded like something I really wanted to do, but I guess beggars can't be choosers, and with limited skills I definitely didn't have many options. The only job I ever had in high school was McDonald's. Trust me . . . flipping burgers was not even an option. My eyes traveled over to the ad again. *Exotic Dancers needed*. Goodness, was that what my life had come to?

"If I was your size, I would do it in a heartbeat."

As freaky as Reyna was, she was probably right. See, the problem is Reyna's a big girl. When we first met she was probably wearing a sixteen, but over the years, especially during the stress of opening her own boutique, she started packing on the pounds and was wearing at least a twenty-two. Not that it stopped Reyna. She was a strong believer of you're as beautiful as you feel. Well, as far as Reyna was concerned, she was the hottest chick within a hundred-mile radius. Even now she was sitting with her legs crossed, swinging her foot in the aisle. As usual she was dressing her ass off, wearing a blue jean miniskirt complemented by a fire engine red corset, a jean bolero jacket, and matching five-inch pumps. She didn't let her weight stand in the way of looking good. I'll give it to her, style was one thing she knew a lot about, and she wore it well. I guess that's why she owned Reyna's Couture, the hottest boutique in all of Petersburg.

"Monica, you got one helluva body. Men would go crazy over your ass."

I appreciated the compliment, but friends were supposed to say that. "Yeah, right," I said with a laugh. "You know I don't have the guts for that shit." I still couldn't believe that heifer had suggested such a thing. She was the freaky one, not me.

"Hey, it's good money. My cousin Dawn used to strip, and she made a thousand dollars a week."

My brow rose. "A thousand? Just to take off her clothes and shake her ass?"

"Yep," she confirmed with a nod.

Her words went straight to my head, and I took a moment and tried to see myself on stage, doing exactly what she was suggesting, then realized how ridiculous it sounded. I gave her a dismissive wave. "Reyna, puhleeze. I don't even know why I brought it up again. You know I'm not about to take my clothes off for anyone but my man."

"Yes, but you don't have one of those," she teased.

"Thanks for reminding me," I said with attitude. Reaching up, I stroked my fresh new cut just to remember I had something to feel good about. Reyna had a lot of nerve. Hell, she couldn't keep a man.

"Seriously, all jokes aside, you could do it. We can come up with a stage name for you like Juicy or Dimples." Her eyes sparkled with excitement.

"Juicy and Dimples? Mmm-hmm, that would definitely describe my ass."

Reyna chuckled. "Hey, that's what men love. A black woman with a big ghetto booty! And you definitely have enough for the two of us." I couldn't help but laugh because she was right about that. I had plenty of junk in my trunk. "But who in the world wants to watch a woman with little titties trying to dance?" I was flat-chested just like my mama. Reyna had a pair of triple Ds that she played up in corsets and low-cut blouses. It was the one thing I was most self-conscious about. If I could afford it, I would get a boob job in a heartbeat.

"You got enough. What Anthony used to tell you . . . that more than a mouthful is a waste?" she reminded me with a wink.

"That asshole said a lot of things. He also said he'd love me forever, but you see where that got me." I closed my eyes and rubbed my forehead. A migraine was coming, I could feel it. It was all the stress of wondering if I was going to be able to pay my light bill next month. That's when I felt someone standing over me.

"Excuse me, sexy. I couldn't help but notice you when you first walked in. You have the most amazing legs." My eyelids rose and I almost jumped from the seat when I found a dude at our table with bread crumbs clinging to his matted salt-and-pepper beard. "Can I buy you a cup of coffee?" he asked politely.

Is he for real? I glanced over at Reyna and wanted to laugh. I could tell she too was struggling to keep a straight face. "No, I . . ." I couldn't even finish what I was about to say because at that moment he smiled and I noticed his jacked-up grill. "I don't think so."

"Then can I have your phone number?" He smiled flirtatiously as his eyes quickly ran over my body. Did he really think I would go out with him? Instead, I was two seconds away from cussing him out. Even if I was dating, I never would have been that desperate.

"Hey! Didn't my girl tell you she's not interested," Reyna said with attitude in her voice. He took a step back, looking embarrassed. I guess he finally got the message because he walked away and returned to his table close to the front door. Reyna tried to hold it together but as soon as he sat down in his seat, she burst out laughing.

Leaning across the table, I murmured, "Ugggh! He's got a lot of nerve, looking like Grady from *Sanford and Son*." My comment made Reyna laugh even harder and I couldn't help but join in. We had tears in our eyes. I glanced to my left and made sure he hadn't heard us making fun of him. *Puhleeze*. He had already forgotten about me and was standing over another table trying to holler at some light-skinned chick. I watched as her head started moving while her neck twisted, and it was pretty obvious she was giving him straight attitude.

When Reyna finally stopped laughing, she said, "Now *that's* the type of men dancers up at Scandalous have to deal with, but the beautiful thing is you make a brotha pay for wasting your time."

The conversation was right back where it had left off. My girl never did know when to quit. I guess it's my fault for bringing it up. "Reyna, I already told you I'm not working at no strip club." Just the thought of taking my clothes off in front of a bunch of strangers made my stomach turn.

"I could pick you out some really cute outfits from the boutique and teach you how to walk in stilettos." I swear she almost sounded like she was pleading with me. Damn! Was my girl trying to live vicariously through me?

"Reyna . . . girl . . . quit dreaming and listen to me. I am not stripping." I said the words real slow and controlled just so she'd know I meant what I said.

Pouting, she finally leaned back on the bench. "Hooker. I should have known you didn't have it in you."

While we ate our lunch, I noticed Reyna was still looking down at the newspaper. *Exotic Dancers needed.* Something in my gut told me that until I found a job, this wouldn't be the last time we discussed the subject.

2

Robin

I heard my cell phone vibrating in my purse on the floor and released a sleepy groan because I knew what time it was. *Time to get the hell up outta here.*

Slowly, I slid out from under the heavy arm draped across my naked body, then reached down for my purse and carried it into the bathroom with me. While I peed, I pulled out my cell phone and read a text message from my homegirl, Honey.

Treasure, where the fuck you at? Big money at the club.

I was instantly wide awake and shuddering with excitement. Making money was what I do best, and I wasn't about to miss out on a prime opportunity to get paid. Last week I bought myself a brand-new Camaro. Candy apple red and fully loaded. I still had to pay the taxes on that bitch and needed every dime I could get. Trust and believe, I was willing to do whatever it took to make that happen.

I reached for one of the washcloths hanging on the towel rack. It felt hard as hell, but what do you expect to find at a cheap-ass motel that let you rent by the hour? I conducted the sniff test and was relieved that at least it smelled clean. It took almost thirty seconds before the water ran hot. I lathered the cloth real good with that tiny bar of soap and ran it across my entire body. The last thing I needed was to walk into Scandalous smelling like another man. Chris had been wearing Armani Mania tonight. Don't get me wrong, I loved that scent. However, it smelled better on him. I was almost done drying off my body when my phone started vibrating again. I reached down and glanced at the number on the screen before I answered. It was Honey.

"Treasure, where yo ass at?" Her shrill voice came booming through the phone. Honey was trying to talk over the laughter and loud music in the background.

"Ho, I'll be there in a minute. I had to make some quick money." I tried to whisper just in case Chris was on the other side of the door listening to my conversation. Hopefully not, because I was definitely tryna sneak out before this sexy muthafucka woke up.

"A'ight, but hurry the hell up. Everybody's asking for you."

Of course they were. Unlike most females, I knew the power I possessed between my thighs. It was my treasure chest. And I used it to my advantage every chance I got.

"Uh . . . by the way . . . Mercedes is up in here hating on yo ass."

I sucked my teeth rudely in the phone. Honey thought she was slick. The only reason she'd mentioned Mercedes was because she knew I couldn't stand that bitch, and hearing she was hating was only gonna make me break my neck tryna get down to the club.

Mercedes had been trying for months to gain the spot as the baddest entertainer at Scandalous Gentlemen's Club, but so far no one had been able to still my shine. And as far as I was concerned, they never would. "You make sure you let that skank know I'm on my way." I ended the call and tossed the phone back into my purse, then stared at my reflection in the mirror. After a long night at the club I looked like shit, but it wasn't anything a little makeup couldn't fix. *I never leave home without it.* I grabbed the small travel-sized deodorant and Bath & Body Works body mist from my purse along with my comb and everything else I needed to look like the dime piece that I was.

It wasn't that I was stuck on myself. I'm just keeping it real. I had my mother's golden eyes and full lips and my father's good hair. I didn't need weave. Every honey-brown strand that hung to the middle of my back was all mine. Grinning, I turned side to side and took in every luscious curve, especially the beautiful double Ds. When my finger grazed my left nipple, I flinched. "Damn." My breasts were sore because that horny muthafucka lying in the bed had sucked my titties like he was breast-feeding. I figured he was having a childhood flashback or some shit, but who was I to judge. As long as his money was green, I could be whoever the fuck he needed me to be.

Leaning toward the mirror, I applied my mascara carefully, then painted my lips with a deep red shade. I stared at my reflection for a moment longer, then smiled. I had been blessed with looks that most women dreamed of having. In all of Richmond, no one came even close to looking as banging as me . . . except for one person.

That person being my older sister, Deena.

Even after all these years, it was hard bringing myself to say her name. Just thinking about her brought up a lot of unforgettable memories. Shit, I'd rather not remember because I still hadn't dealt with the pain. It had been almost a year since that traitor had found my number on Facebook, and she'd been calling me at least once a month ever since. Each and every time, I hung up on her ass. I didn't know how the hell she expected me to forgive her for the shit she'd done to me. Well, I couldn't . . . I wouldn't, and as far as I was concerned, I no longer had any family. In my eyes, my sister was dead just like our parents. Only they died in a car accident when I was ten.

Deena'd been dead since the day she left my ass at Ms. Ernestine's house and never came back.

Shaking my head, I pushed the thoughts from my head as I put everything back into my purse. I was fishing for a stick of gum when I noticed the wad of money in the zipper compartment. As I put a piece of Juicy Fruit in my mouth, I couldn't help but grin. It had been a good night and, according to Honey, it would only get better.

After taking one final look, I stepped out of the bathroom. That sexy muthafucka had rolled onto his back. I stood there admiring his six-foot-two, two-hundred-forty-pound body. Even sleeping Chris's dick was hard. And Lord knows he knew how to use it. I could still feel him inside me. Just staring at his dick, I was tempted to climb back on for another long ride. But I didn't have time for self-gratification. He and I were strictly business. I was in need of another sponsor, and Chris was a prime candidate.

I met Chris at Scandalous where I danced three nights a week. Now, don't get me wrong. I wasn't no ho; instead, I was a bona fide entertainer. I believed in making sure a man got his money's worth. Chris had been jocking my ass all night—buying drinks, paying for lap dances. He was definitely a high roller, which was what every girl working the club wanted.

I reached down on the floor beside the bed for my pink dress and slipped it over my body. I then retrieved my thong and stuck it in my purse just as Chris rolled over and opened his eyes. *Damn, why the hell he have to wake up?*

"Yo, where you going?" he asked in a sleep-sexy voice.

With a silly smirk, I gazed down at him, lying there stretching every muscle in his body. He was what any woman would call hot chocolate. Dark, sweet, and delicious. "I gotta go."

Chris had the nerve to laugh like he thought I was pulling his leg or some shit. "Whatcha mean you gotta go? I got somethin' here that's worth staying for." He lay there stroking his dick, and I couldn't believe that thing had the nerve to grow two more inches. Licking my lips, I was tempted, but time was money and I had money on my mind.

"Sorry . . . time's up." I took a seat on the end of the bed and slipped my foot into a strapless stiletto. Obviously, Chris was used to getting his way. He moved across the bed and started kissing my neck.

"How 'bout another hour?" he suggested.

Leaning into him, I closed my eyes and allowed myself a few seconds to enjoy his wet tongue running across my cheek. But when he tried to slobber inside my ear, I flinched and moved away. I hated that shit. "You can have another hour, but it's gonna cost you another two hundred." Dudes like him just don't seem to get it. Don't get me wrong. I love me a thug. However, if I was thinking about getting serious with a man, which I wasn't, it definitely wouldn't be with a man who paid for pussy. "Sorry, boo, but time is money."

"See, Treasure . . . that's yo problem . . . It's always 'bout money. Fuck, you already got five and some change outta my black ass tonight!" he hissed, then paused long enough to bat his long, thick eyelashes at me like I was gonna cave in. "C'mon, can't you give a nigga a break?" Chris spoke in a deep, sexy-ass tone that was supposed to turn me on. He obviously hadn't ever met a bitch like me.

I found my other shoe under the bed and reached for it before meeting his gaze. "This ain't no two-for-one coupon." I hardened my voice to convince him I was all about business. The dick was good, but it wasn't all that. Besides, Chris knew when he asked me for some he was gonna have to pay for it. Did he really think after throwing it on me I was looking for a relationship?

"I guess it's nothing but business with you." He had lowered his voice to almost a whisper and then had the nerve to give me this fake-ass look like his feelings were hurt when I knew good and damn well he already had a wifey waiting at home.

"It's *always* business. Seriously, I've got bills, boo." I leaned over and kissed him several times on the lips. "I had a good time. No doubt. How 'bout we do this again real soon?" Like I said, I was looking for another sponsor. "You got my number, so make sure you holla atcha girl," I purred seductively. "But right now I gotta go." I swung my purse onto my shoulder and strutted to the door, leaving him sitting there pouting like a big-ass baby.

I had just turned the knob when I heard him mutter something that sounded like, "a straight-up five-dollar ho."

My head whipped around and I glared over at Chris. "Nah, boo. You got it all wrong. Thanks to you, I'm a five-*hundred*-dollar ho." I grinned wickedly, then patted my purse and sashayed out the door.

3

Monica

"Mommy, that truck's finna run into our car."

My daughters and I were coming out of Food Lion with enough groceries for the next two weeks when Liese spotted a big blue tow truck backing up behind my Lexus. *Oh shit!* I almost had a heart attack as I hurried across the parking lot pushing the shopping cart over to where a short black man, who had to weigh all of three hundred pounds, pried his big butt out of the king cab.

"Excuse me! Excuse me! What're you doing?" What I should have asked was why the hell was he following me. How else would he know I went to the grocery store every Saturday morning?

He glanced over at me with a cocky smirk on his crusty dry lips. "Is this your car?" he asked as if he didn't already know.

"Yes, that's my car." I hit the button, deactivating the door locks, and urged the girls to get inside. There was no way he was taking my only mode of transportation without a fight.

He wasted no time handing me a pink sheet of paper. "Your car payment is past due. I have instructions to bring this car back to the lot . . . unless you got money."

Hell no, I didn't have any money. If I did, he wouldn't have followed me to the grocery store and be trying to tow my precious Lexus away. Shit. I barely had enough money to cover my bills for the month. To make matters worse, last week I needed four new tires, which took what little I had left in savings.

I glanced down at the paper and groaned. I owed Mallory Finance almost half of next month's child support payment. There was no way in hell I would ever be able to catch up. Sure, I'd missed a couple of car notes, but I never expected them to send the repo man.

I stood there dumbfounded, drumming my finger on the trunk of my car as I tried to figure out what to do. Unfortunately, I couldn't think of anything. I had run out of options. Come on. It wasn't like I wasn't trying to find a job. Trust me. Nobody could ever say I was some lazy chick laid up in the house, waiting for my check at the first of the month. I'd been trying to get a job for weeks, applying for almost anything, and yet I hadn't had any luck.

"Ma'am, your kids are gonna have to get outta that car." He glanced down at his watch as if I was wasting his time. "I've gotta take this car in."

I looked over my shoulder. Liese and Arissa were staring through the window. I could tell they were scared. Ignoring him, I hit the remote starter, opened the car door, and turned on the DVD player.

"Mommy, is everything okay?" Arissa asked, her lower lip quivering. She was the oldest at seven, while Liese was six.

"Sweetie, everything's fine. Y'all watch a movie while I talk to this man." I kissed her chocolate cheek, shut the door, then turned around in time to see the crack of the tow truck driver's ass as he reached down for the chain so he could hook it to my back bumper.

"Please, have a heart," I pleaded. "I've got two little girls and a cartful of groceries."

"That's not my problem." I was getting ready to start begging when all of a sudden he looked at me. I mean *really* looked at me like he was staring at the buffet at Herb's Rib Shack. "You know . . . we can always work out some kinda trade."

I had to bite my tongue to stop from saying what I really wanted. Believe me, I was offended, but I was starting to think that maybe the only thing that was going to get me out of this mess was using what the good Lord gave me.

"What do you have in mind?" I asked skeptically. I'd say anything to distract him from hooking my car to the back of his truck and hauling it away. I could already count all the additional charges that would cost me. "Boy, it's gonna be hot today!" I moaned, then reached for the top two buttons of my blouse and popped them loose. In my haste to get to the store before it got crowded, I hadn't even bothered to put on a bra.

Just as I hoped, his eyes lowered to my chest and his bottom jaw dropped, which I found hilarious because I belonged to the itty-bitty titty committee.

"Look, I know I owe you something for wasting your time, sooo . . . I'm open to suggestions." I softened my voice and tried to sound enticing enough to draw his full attention. I guess it worked. He looked around to see if anyone was watching while I glanced over to make sure my girls weren't still staring out the window. The last thing I needed them to see was their mother behaving like a whore. Thank goodness they were busy watching *Toy Story 3*.

Dropping the hook, he signaled for me to follow him into the cab of his truck. I hesitated for a second as I watched him climb inside. For all I knew, he could be some kinda serial killer. Seriously, I didn't even know who this dude was, and once I got in his truck, he could speed off and folks might never see or hear from me again. Just to be safe, I reached inside my purse for a fingernail file and hid it in my sleeve. If he seemed like a psycho, I would just stab his crazy ass in the eye.

I climbed in on the passenger's side, shut the door, then swung around on the seat. He was sitting on the driver's side grinning like a damn fool. "What do you have in mind?"

He slid over on the bench next to me and placed his arm across my shoulders. He then muttered something that sounded like "Just sit back and enjoy" before he reached over and touched my breasts. "Mmmm, I love me some little titties," he purred as he squeezed them like he was sampling melons at the grocery store. While he was moaning and thoroughly enjoying himself, I looked around, making sure none of the customers pulling in and out of the parking lot were looking our way. By the time I focused on him again, his belt was unbuckled and he was reaching for the zipper.

"You don't expect me to do that in the middle of the parking lot, do you?" I asked with attitude.

His gaze darkened. "Yeah, cunt, I do. You got a problem with it? Because if you do, I'll just take your car and be on my way."

I closed my eyes with anger. Any other time I would have cussed his fat ass out for calling me anything other than the name my mother—may she rest her soul—had given me. The only thing stopping me was that he had something I needed. Apparently I had something he wanted as well.

I cringed as he reached inside his underwear and then I was staring at the littlest dick I had ever laid my eyes on. I was two seconds away from laughing. What was worse was his big stomach. I don't know how the hell he expected me to reach his dick if his stomach was in my way.

My eyes started darting from side to side looking for a way out of this situation without losing my Lexus in the process. That's when I just happened to glance into the side-view mirror and noticed the Impala that had been parked in front of my car was backing out of the space. If I could get away, I could pull my car forward and out of the parking spot before someone came and pinned me in again. Time was of the essence and I needed to act fast. I gazed down at a large red slushy sitting in the cup holder. I knocked it over onto his lap.

"What the fuck?" he screamed as I jumped out of the car without a second to lose. "You stupid bitch!" he yelled after me.

I ran past my cart, stopping long enough to grab a family pack of chicken wings and a packet of Kool-Aid, then jumped into my car. I put the key in the ignition and hit the gas just as a car was getting ready to pull in front of me.

"Get the fuck outta the way!" I screamed and pressed my hand hard against the horn like a crazy woman, then gunned the engine. They had sense enough to slam their foot on the brake just in time to avoid a collision, because nothing was stopping me from getting the hell away from Food Lion. The woman in the Saturn gave me the finger while I simply blew her a juicy kiss.

I zoomed out of the parking lot. My heart was beating so hard, I felt like it was about to come through my shirt. I couldn't believe I had just done that. But when a mother's scared, she's likely to do just about anything.

It wasn't until I was a block away that I felt tears streaming down my face. *There goes dinner for the next two weeks.* All of my groceries were sitting in the parking lot for someone else to take home.

"Mommy, are you okay?"

I had forgotten the girls were in the car. I swallowed back tears and glanced through the rearview mirror. "Yes, Arissa, sweetheart, I'm fine," I said and started laughing like I had been playing a game when I was really hurting inside. This was not at all the life I had signed up for. It wasn't their fault we lived from check to check and could no longer do the things they were used to doing. It had broken my heart when I had told them we couldn't go on vacation for spring break like we had done every year. There was no longer money for gymnas-

tics and piano lessons. All the things my girls had been accustomed to were now gone. Not only could I no longer afford
activities for my girls, but their father refused to help pay for it.
Can you believe it? What kind of man denied his little girls?
My ex-husband claimed he was struggling to make ends meet,
but I knew that was just bullshit. After the divorce, he'd sold
our house and bought an even bigger house on the west end
of Richmond. The only reason I knew was because I noticed
the new address on the child support check he'd given me.
Reyna scooped me up and we drove over to his house after
dark. I about shit my pants when I saw the size of it. Broke, my
ass! Anthony was so full of shit. I always knew he had money,
but since he had always handled the finances, there had been
no way for me to prove it.

Since I was already broke and had nothing to cook but a
pack of chicken wings and a pitcher of Kool-Aid, I took the
last few dollars I had, stopped at McDonald's, and picked the
girls each up a Happy Meal, then sent them to their room to
finish their movie. The tension in my shoulders relaxed a bit
knowing I was home safely with my car back in the garage. I
immediately called Reyna. She came right over.

"I can't believe he tried to get you to give him head in the
parking lot!" she screamed, only seconds after I got done explaining what had happened.

I reached for another Kleenex and blew my noise. "Reyna,
I have never been so humiliated in my life. What am I going to
do? He's gonna come back."

She gave me a sympathetic look. "Are you going to ask
Anthony for help?"

I didn't have the heart to tell her I had already called him
when I needed to replace my tires and he'd laughed in my
face. I know I said I would never ask him for a dime, but I was
starting to feel desperate and scared. I realized when you have
kids, you ain't too proud to beg. "No, I'm going to find a job."
Even flipping burgers was beginning to sound good right

about now. "There's no way I can go without a car . . . not with the girls."

We were quiet for a few moments before she said, "I can loan you the money."

I shook my head. "No . . . no way. I know you're trying to keep your own head above water."

"You're my girl, so I'll do whatever I can to help." She rose from the couch and came around and hugged me. I wrapped my arms around her and held on. "You need to take my offer. How are you going to get to school without a car?"

I released her and for once I didn't bother arguing, because I had run out of options. It wasn't like my phone was ringing off the hook with job offers. Just juggling classes and taking care of the girls was more than I could handle. So how was I going to fit working into my already tight schedule?

When Reyna gave me that look, I knew what she was going to suggest before the words even came out of her mouth. "How about we go down Friday night and check out the place and then you can decide. It doesn't hurt to just take a look."

"Okay." What other choice did I have? "I won't make any promises, but I'll go." I'd never admit it, but for some strange reason I felt a shimmer of hope. I was about to step inside Scandalous Gentlemen's Club.

4

Robin

I was straddling Shane's lap, bumping and grinding. "Feel good to ya, Daddy?" I purred in my best little-girl voice.

"Hell yeah! Yo, hold up." I rose and watched as he stuck his hand inside his drawers and adjusted his dick. As big as it was, the head peeked out the top of his jeans. "Okay, now sit on it."

Negros were a trip. Always trying to get something for nothing. *You got the wrong one, baby.* They should know by now Treasure don't do nothing for free.

I took a moment to make sure my crotch was completely covered by the flimsy-ass black G-string. Last thing I needed was for some muthafucka to be saying "oops" when his dick accidently slipped inside my coochie. I had a customer try that shit once before and learned the hard way. I had been so pissed, I picked up a nearby beer bottle and bashed it upside his head, only to end up spending a night in jail. The only reason he dropped the charges was because I threatened to tell his wife his country ass had been at a titty bar tryna get some pussy. His wife was the mayor's daughter. It's a shame how much a muthafucka will tell you about their personal life when you're riding his lap. I always cataloged that information in my memory bank. You never know when you might need payback.

I lowered onto Shane's lap again and rocked my hips to the beat of Usher's "Papers," and within seconds he started moaning and jerking. What can I say? I had mad skills. I know it sounds overly confident, but trust me, it had taken years to perfect my technique. And now I guaranteed I could make a muthafucka come without using my mouth or kitty cat. Trust and believe, I had enough niggas on speed dial who would be more than happy to verify. Brothas liked a challenge. Hell, all I liked was getting paid. In the end, everybody's happy.

I rubbed my crotch directly against the head of his dick, grinding hard, and was certain I was getting ready to double my money. To seal the deal, I leaned forward and licked my lips. It's something about a woman staring at a man while she's riding his lap that turned them on every time.

"Touch it," he whispered.

"What?" I asked even though I'd heard him loud and clear.

"Fuck! Touch it, please." His voice was stressed.

I grazed my lips against his cheek. "It's gonna cost you another bill."

"Shit, whatever you want . . . just make a nigga nut," he said without hesitation. I love it when a guy gets straight to the point.

I looked around and made sure the bouncer and none of the other girls were looking. Scandalous had rules, and there was no way I was letting some baller fuck up my money. He couldn't touch me and I damn sure wasn't supposed to be giving him a hand job.

Reaching down between us, I wiggled my hips and stroked the head of his dick, which was resting against his stomach. Shane started pumping his hips and breathing heavily. I moaned like it felt good to me, then started talking dirty in his ear, and in under two minutes he was shooting in my hand. Sometimes it amazed me just how good I was.

When the song ended, I wiped his cum across the thigh of his jeans—humph, why not? It's his shit—then climbed off his lap, slipped my dress down over my head, and waited while he got himself together.

Grinning, Shane reached inside his pocket and peeled off another hundred. "Pleasure as always, Treasure," he said with a satisfied grin. The pleasure was all mine. Shane was a sponsor who always came off them dollars without hesitation.

I took the money and slid it inside my garter, which was already stuffed with bills, then cooed, "Holla at ya girl again." I blew him a kiss, spun on my heels and headed down the steps of the VIP section and back onto the floor.

The club was hyped. Stages were loaded and muthafuckas were everywhere. I moved across the club, strutting my stuff to the beat of the music, feeling like I owned the world. Shit, I looked good and damn sure knew it. I was rocking the hell outta a gold minidress that was a size four. I normally wore a six, but when I worked, I liked my gear nice and tight enough to turn heads, and this particular dress looked too good against my apple-bottom ass to pass up.

Scandalous was the most popular strip club in southern Virginia. It had a vibe as potent as smoking weed, and smelled drenched in money. I rubbed my hands in anticipation. The deejay was rocking and every night was a list of who's who. The clientele included ballers, athletes, politicians, and plenty of rich wealthy men. There were even old men who came in after popping a few Viagra so they could pass the time jacking off in the corner. You name it, they were up in there. Everybody found their fantasy when they stepped through those double doors. Tall, skinny, white, black, thick, titties, and plenty of naked asses. There was something for everyone, but the star of the show was me. No doubt. Hell, I worked hard to get where I was and I wasn't letting anyone steal my shine.

While I glided through the crowd, brothas were jocking me. But I blew them off. "I'll be back," I sang playfully. I was on my way to the dressing room and didn't need anyone standing in my way.

I stepped into the room. Chicks were running around trying to get ready for their sets. The room smelled like cheap-ass perfume and sweat. I headed back to my locker, opened it, and put my money inside. In less than two hours I had earned three hundred dollars. Not bad, but the night was young and there was still plenty to be made. I reached for my hand sanitizer and cleaned that Negro's nut from between my fingers. Sometimes stripping could be nasty business.

"Hey, girl, how you doin' tonight?"

"Not bad," I said as I swung around and faced Honey. "What about you?"

She twisted her lips, then dropped down on the bench in front of me with her legs cocked open, her bald coochie on display for anyone who wanted to see. "Girl, puhleeze, the night's been slow."

That was a surprise, considering Honey, unlike me, will do just about anything for a dollar. What I just did for a bill, she would have done for half and even slobbed on his knob in the process. Trust me, she made her paper, I just couldn't figure out what the hell she did with it, because she definitely didn't spend it on her appearance.

I looked down at her platform shoes. They'd seen better days. The heels were run over and the toes were scuffed and worn out. The dress she was wearing was as cheap as it made her look, and that's a shame because Honey wasn't a bad-looking chick; not a dime piece, but she had the potential to be great, if she'd take some advice and learn to spend money on her weave. Instead she did it herself. I was a firm believer that you get what you paid for. Well, she paid twenty dollars for her weave, and that's exactly what it looked like. I know I sound like I'm hatin', but I'm just keepin' it real. She needed to step up her game. But despite her lack of class, Honey was cool people and one of the few girls that I even gelled with, because there were some cutthroats that danced at Scandalous. Every girl was fighting to be on top and had no problem taking you down in the process. I was cool with everyone, but I learned growing up never to trust anyone but myself, because ain't nobody else gonna have my back like me. Honey was just an exception to the rules. She was trying to make her money and she probably could make more if she wasn't so damn naïve. Niggas ran game on her and she was stupid enough to believe anything that came out of their mouths. Speaking of niggas, I suddenly noticed she was wearing sunglasses.

"Why you got them dark shades on?" I asked suspiciously. Honey tried to turn away, but I snatched the glasses away from her chocolate face before she could stop me. As soon as I saw the bruise under her right eye, I got mad. "Jordan beat yo ass again, didn't he?"

"Uhhh . . ." She tried to deny it, but I already knew the truth.

I was so mad, I slammed my hand against the locker. "Damn, Honey. Why you keep letting him treat you like shit?"

She lowered her head, trying to avoid eye contact. "It was my fault. I provoked him."

No one could possibly be that stupid, could they? "Who told you that, Jordan?"

She hesitated as if she wasn't sure she should tell me what happened. I knew it wouldn't last, because I was practically the only friend Honey had who wasn't strung out on crack. "He was trying to leave and I was all up in his face. I shoulda just let him go, but instead I snatched his keys off the table and wouldn't give 'em back."

"So he hit you." It was a statement, not a question, because it wasn't the first time, and it damn sure would be the last.

Honey finally nodded and gave me that pitiful look with those big brown eyes of hers. I just don't get her. You would think she would be trying to get her shit together, but instead she allowed Jordan to treat her like she was his own personal punching bag. Then she'd dump his ass for a while but eventually take him back. I was her once until I learned. One thing

I'd never do again was take any shit from a man or female. Been there. Done that. And got the scars to prove it.

I sighed. "So what happened after that?"

"I told him to get the hell outta my crib and don't bring his bony ass back," she said weakly. I noticed her bottom lip quivering. She was trying to act tough but I could tell she was scared of him.

"Mmm-hmm, but how long before you let his ass back in?" I asked as I shifted from one leg to the other in agitation.

She shook her head. "I'm not letting him back in. I had it with him. I've gotta get myself together and focus on getting Sophia back."

Well, it was about damn time.

A couple of months ago, Honey lost custody of her three-year-old daughter. For some strange reason, she thought since Sophia was asleep, she could run down to the bar on the corner and have a drink. By the time she made it back to her apartment, the police and social services were waiting for her. One of the neighbors had found Sophia in the hallway crying. According to him, it hadn't been the first time.

"Did you get to see her on Tuesday?" I said, trying to change the subject before I got mad and went looking for Jordan myself.

A sad smile curled her lips. "Yeah, she's getting so big! Sophia's ready to come home. I told her real soon."

I felt sorry for Honey because I knew in her own way she loved her daughter and wanted her back, but actions speak louder than words, and so far her actions said otherwise. From the things she had told me, it seemed like the foster family that had her was taking real good care of Sophia, and that said a lot. However, speaking from experience, even the idea of my child being in the system would have freaked me out. Thank goodness I don't have any.

"You'll get her back just as soon as you get your life together," I said, trying to be positive. I waited for her to say something, but we were interrupted by a tall blonde with the best pair of boobs money could buy.

"Hey, Treasure, some guy's asking for you."

I nodded at Pinky, then turned my attention back to Honey. "We're not done with this conversation. You stay your ass away from Jordan and focus on getting your daughter back."

She nodded like a little kid does when they've been scolded. "I will, Treasure, watch and see." I stared at Honey in silence for a few seconds, wondering if she really meant it.

No time to be wasted, I reached for a baby wipe and rubbed it across my coochie, then sprayed some mango-scented body spray all between my legs before I slammed my locker shut, spun the lock, and checked it twice to make sure it was secure. If a customer asked for you by name, that meant they wanted to spend some money, and my regular customers were the ones who kept the bills paid at my town house.

As soon as I met the heavy beat of the music, I sashayed across the floor and glanced at the small tables to my right and left. When I realized who was looking for me, I stopped dead in my tracks and cussed. It was my former boyfriend and the only man I'd ever been in love with. Damn. *What the hell does he want now?*

"Well, well, well, if it ain't my little treasure chest."

I was tempted to go back into the dressing room, but he'd already seen me.

I dragged my feet in five-inch heels over to his table and huffed, "What the fuck you want?"

"Came to see my favorite entertainer." Halo smiled like I should be excited to see him. *Whatever.* I tried to turn away, but he grabbed my hand and yanked me back to him. "Now, is that how to treat me? C'mon, all I want is a few minutes of your time." He held up a hundred-dollar bill just like he was giving a dog a bone.

Why can't he just leave me alone? I thought. But what bothered me most was that no matter how much I tried to deny it, Halo still turned me the fuck on.

He was six feet with a medium build and a pair of green eyes that you could get lost in. Not to mention he had curly hair and the smoothest peanut butter brown skin.

Halo was one of the first ballers I had hooked up with. I thought that maybe we had something there for a moment. He kept my hair and nails done and my pockets fat, and invited me to move in with him. But after two years, our relationship started taking a turn for the worse.

I remember the first time he'd hit me. It was a Friday and I'd had a good night. Some rapper had hit the mic and the place was so packed you could smell money in the air. I had over a grand in my pocket and went home feeling damn good. I walked into Halo's house, and the second I saw him sitting in a chair in the corner with the lights off, I knew something was wrong.

He flicked on the lamp and rose from the chair. "What's this?" he asked, holding up a business card.

I shrugged my shoulders and lowered my purse to the coffee table. "I don't know. What is it?" I said because I was too got damn tired to play guess who. *Big mistake.* As soon as I swung around, I was introduced to his left hook. Halo hit me so hard, I stumbled on the heel of my shoe and fell back against the end table, bruising my back.

"Bitch, do you know who ya fucking wit? When I ask you a question, I expect yo yellow ass to answer!" Halo screamed.

"What the hell you hit me for?" I whined. I brought my hand up to my nose and wiped away blood.

"Why the fuck you think? What you doin' wit some other muthafucka's number in your pocket? You think you slick. Thought I wouldn't find it?" He then knocked me to the floor and started kicking me in my head and shoulder.

"Please, stop! I didn't have no number!" I cried, pleading with him.

"You fucking lyin' bitch! I found this in yo pocket!" he screamed, sending spit flying everywhere. I tried to fight back, which pissed him off even more. He reached down and started punching me in the face and chest.

"Please, don't hit me!" But he wasn't listening, so the only thing I could do was curl up in a ball the way I had always done as a child when I was being beaten with an extension cord. I couldn't believe that shit was happening to me. Men handed me their numbers at the club all the time. I took it along with the tip, but I always tossed them out. I guess I forgot to get rid of this one.

Halo was yelling at the top of his lungs and punctuating each word with a punch. I couldn't understand how my man could treat me this way. "Baby, please, I love you!" I was bawling, but instead of him feeling sorry for me, he hit me even harder for being weak, and eventually with one hard blow everything went black. I don't know how long I lay there before I finally managed to get to my feet. When I realized he was standing over me, I flinched and fell back down.

"Let me find out you fuckin' around and I'm gonna kill you." He then spat on me and walked out of the room. I pulled myself to my feet, showered, and crawled under the covers. Hours later, Halo came to bed hugging and kissing me and begging for my forgiveness. When he started crying I felt so sorry for him that we made up. Before I knew it he was between my thighs pumping inside me.

After that things were never quite the same. If I had any sense I would have left then, but I didn't. I put up with his shit for three more months, hoping that if I tried harder he would love me, but the beatings kept coming and got worse. Eventually I got tired of it, and just like I had done at my foster home, I waited until he left, packed my shit, and moved the fuck out.

Even then there was no getting away from him because Halo frequented the club, yet I stood my ground. It was over and no amount of tears was going to make me take him back.

I was staying with Honey at the time in this roach-infested apartment she called home, desperate and too afraid to be by myself. Eventually Halo left me alone and found someone else to control, but he still continued to single me out from time to time just to see if he could get a rise out of me. What bothered me was the way my body responded to him. When he was around, I was aroused and frightened of him at the same time. I was starting to think I was always going to be a victim when it came to Halo, but I was determined not to. I had been beaten and abused most of my life, but back then I didn't have a choice. Now that I was grown and in control, I had choices, and I chose to stay away from men like Halo.

I glared over at him. "What do you want, Halo?"

He gave me a devilish smile that made me nervous as hell. "C'mon, Robin, why you gotta be like that? All I wanna do is take you out."

I wouldn't let that fool take my temperature.

"We can go have crab legs or some shit like that." He grinned, showing me his platinum grill. "I wanna see you again," he said like I hadn't heard him the first time. "How about it?"

What made him think I would be interested in more of his drama? I threw a hand to my hip. "Halo, how many times I gotta tell you that shit's in the past. Besides, ain't you heard . . . I can buy my own crab legs."

"You tryna say my money's not good enough?" He gave me the sexy signature grin of his again, and of course my body—the freakin' traitor—started to feel all tingly inside. He was sexy, sitting there licking his succulent lips like LL Cool J. That was no lie. I missed feeling his touch and I couldn't help but think about them lips down between my legs. That man could eat some pussy. He knew just how to apply just the right amount of pressure to have me screaming out his name. "Aww, c'mon, Robin. You know you wanna." He was talking low in his Barry White voice. *Like I would really fall for that shit.* I'll admit I had in the past, which was why he thought he could get over on me again, but I wasn't having it.

His green eyes traveled from my breasts down to my ass. "Damn, I miss that sexy body lying next to me. You know I used to suck the shit outta them titties. Don't you?" Halo was so damn cocky. He knew I had loved the way he made me feel and the things that man could do to my body when he wasn't trying to whup my ass. "C'mon, Robin. Admit it. You miss Big Daddy. Don't you?"

I rolled my eyes, making sure he knew I didn't have time for his foolishness. "Nah, boo. I'm good. Now please leave me the hell alone." I sharpened my tone, hoping to convince him I was dead serious.

He placed both hands over his face, and when he lowered them you would have thought he had been possessed by Satan. His eyes instantly darkened, the muscle at his jaw twitched as he spat his venom at me. "You a smart-ass bitch. I'm tryna be nice and all you doin' is shittin' on a nigga. One of these days I'ma knock you off that pedestal of yours."

"I wanna see you try," I snapped, then snatched the hundred dangling from his hand and walked away.

I heard Halo laughing as I left. "You know you miss this dick. I'ma get you back. You just wait and see," he said with way too much confidence.

I froze. For some reason his threat sounded too much like a promise, and that made me nervous as hell. There was still some unfinished business between us. I just wasn't sure what it was, but until I found out, I would never be free of him.

5

Monica

"I'm going to grab us some more drinks."

I watched as Reyna's date, Lamont, rose from our table and walked across the club to the bar.

"So what you think?" Reyna asked as she leaned across the table so I could hear her over the music. Her eyes were wide with excitement. The club had an energy like nothing I'd ever seen.

"I think the dancers are beautiful." And that was saying it mildly. The dancers had bodies out of this world. They came in every shape and size. Asian, black, white, you name it, it was there. And with ass and titties for days—but one thing these women had that I didn't was guts.

"Girl, you're just as cute as any other chick in here. Ask Lamont when you come back and see what he says."

If I had her flair and confidence, I just might be able to pull this off.

"Hey, Ma . . . how much for a lap dance?"

I looked up at some short dude with thick glasses, standing over our table waving a twenty-dollar bill.

Reyna glanced at me with a smirk. "See . . . told ya."

I groaned then shooed him away like a pesky fly. The only

reason he had approached was because Reyna had insisted we wear skanky gear. She had on a red minidress and black stilettos. My girl looked fierce. I still couldn't believe I let her talk me into wearing a pink corset and a black spandex skirt that was so short, I was afraid to bend over. Not to mention I was wearing rhinestone heels that were more for looks than comfort. But I have to say I was glad she convinced me to come, because I was definitely having a good time.

There was just as much going on off the stage as there was on. Men acted like they lost their damn minds every time a half-naked woman swung her hips past them. In a way I understood. There were so many women, my head was beginning to spin.

But it appeared everyone's attention was on this redbone chick. When she sashayed across the club, heads turned and followed her direction. She had long silky brown hair that you couldn't buy in a bag and champagne-colored eyes that just stared at you until you turned away. I had been watching her all night, and I'd never admit it to Reyna, but I was jealous. She exuded confidence and had this walk that put Iman to shame. She was tall with perfect breasts, a small waist, and a nice ass. Not that I am gay, but you know how women are. We size each other up, comparing what we got. Well . . . that chick they called Treasure had it all.

"She sure knows how to work a room," Reyna said. I guess she caught me staring.

"Mmm-hmm, she does." I tried to sound nonchalant, then turned away. I pointed up the stairs. "What's up there?"

Reyna stuck a French-tipped fingernail in the air. "The VIP section. That's where they do the *private* lap dances."

I was clearly confused. "What's the difference between the ones they do on the floor and the ones up there?"

"More money, and almost anything goes. Which translates to, whatever you can get away with." She laughed.

I watched Treasure take some dorky dude's hand and lead him up the stairs. The way he was smiling you would think she was leading him toward the gates of heaven.

"You have to admit this place is nice," Reyna said with enthusiasm. I watched her eyes flash like a camera as she took it all in.

I couldn't do anything but agree. "Mmm-hmm, it's a lot nicer than I thought." In fact, I was awestruck by the place.

I guess I had been watching too many movies. I expected the place to be dark, smoky, and seedy, but instead it was plush and sophisticated. Scandalous was large and spacious with dozens of small intimate tables, bars on either end of the club, and three platform stages with a red crushed-velvet backdrop. The deejay was in a booth over in the corner and he was rocking the tunes just like at a regular nightclub. There were cages at opposite ends of the room with half-naked women dancing inside them. I was amazed and intrigued and half-scared out of my mind.

Good girls don't go to places like this.

I jumped because for a second there I swore my mother was leaning over my shoulder, whispering in my ear. Ethel Mae didn't play. She believed in going to church every Wednesday for Bible study and again on Sunday for worship. She had been tough and strict and rarely showed affection, but there was never any doubt in my mind she'd loved me. Two years ago she lost the battle and died of kidney failure. Her last words to me were that she was proud of me and glad I had somebody like Anthony to take care of me. I was glad she never found out how wrong she'd been. It would have broken her heart to see me struggling just like she had, trying to raise me alone after my father had walked away from us both.

One thing about my mama, she had done whatever it took to make sure there was food on the table. I remember the men who used to come over. Almost a different man every week.

When they would show up to the house, she would give me a few dollars and send me down the street to the arcade with strict instructions not to return for an hour. Back then I had no idea why she always got rid of me. It wasn't until I was older that I had come to understand that working as a waitress didn't pay enough to keep the lights on.

I remember one time Mama had to work late and one of her male visitors showed up at the door. I had let him in and told him it was okay to wait. We were sitting on the couch with his hand sliding up my thigh when Ethel Mae finally made it home. She cussed him every which way, put him out, then beat me like I'd stolen something. It wasn't until two days later that she sat me down and explained why she was so angry. At thirteen, that was a lot for my little virgin mind to handle. All I know to this day is if Mama hadn't walked in when she had, there was no telling what might have happened to me. I grew up a great deal that day, and it wasn't until I was much older that I developed a great deal of respect for my mother and what she was willing to do for us. It was because of her sacrifices that I knew it was my turn to do what I could to support me and my girls.

Lamont returned with our drinks and leaned back in his seat, enjoying the show. As I watched him out of the corners of my eyes, I was curious if this was the freak Reyna had told me about who got off watching strippers.

Another dancer moved onto the main stage dressed as a cowgirl in five-inch thigh-high boots, and all eyes were on her. She wiggled her hips seductively to the music like one of those video chicks. She could work that pole, and I could see how my years of taking gymnastics could come in handy. I watched as she climbed the fireman's pole all the way to the top, then extended her legs and slid down in a split. As soon as she rose again, she stripped out of her costume and dropped it to the stage. My mouth few open and I couldn't pull my eyes away. She had the tiniest waist and the biggest breasts I'd ever seen. Moving to the beat of the music she grabbed the pole, bent over, and made her ass cheeks clap.

The deejay hollered into the mic, "Fellas, show Mercedes some love!"

Men and women flocked to the stage and showered her with cash.

All I could say was "Damn."

"Shit, that's one of the baddest chicks up in here." Lamont whistled.

Reyna swung around on her seat with attitude. "And how would you know that?" Avoiding the question, Lamont cleared his throat and focused his attention on the cage to his right.

Chuckling, I figured that was my cue to go and find the bathroom. I rose and followed the sign to the back of the building. I stepped inside and performers were all over the room. It smelled like sanitary napkins and cheap perfume, and one girl was in the corner taking a hit off a joint. Any other time I would have been disgusted and turned around, but tonight I didn't dwell on any of it. All I saw were the ones leaning against the wall counting their money, and my jaw dropped at the size of the stacks I saw. Ones, twenties, fives, you name it, it was all right there in front of me.

"Uh, excuse me, but the bathroom is next door," spat some skinny chick, sitting on the floor with attitude.

"Oops, my bad," I mumbled, then backed out the room and pushed open the next door on the left. As I stepped inside the bathroom stall, I couldn't stop thinking about all that money. If I could make half of what these chicks were earning, I could save my car and catch up on some bills while I tried to finish school. I was a mother who would do whatever it took to raise my girls, and it was time to be true to my words.

6

Robin

I was lying across my queen-sized bed, flicking through the channels trying to find something worthwhile. As much as I loved having my own crib, bedtime was a different story altogether. Every sound put me on edge and made getting sleep almost impossible without the television lullabying my jumpy ass to sleep. I'd lie there thinking someone was watching me, yet I was too afraid to lock my bedroom door for fear there would be someone waiting on the other side. I know that shit sounded crazy as hell especially since one of the first things I had done before I had signed the lease to my town house was ask my landlord if I could get a security system, and thank goodness he had agreed.

Most of my uneasiness was because of those damn cameras Halo had installed at his house. The only reason I knew he had been videoing my ass was because one afternoon I was looking for an umbrella. Halo had this small utility room that he kept locked. I found the key on a ring he kept on his dresser, and when I stepped inside, my mouth fell open. That was some high-tech shit up in there, with monitors that covered almost every corner of the damn house. Over his bed, and even in the bathroom. Hell, I couldn't even take a shit without him knowing about it. On a bookshelf were videos labeled and dated for years. I had this feeling like I had been violated all over again. I forgot about the umbrella and put that key ring right back where I found it. The last thing I wanted was Halo to know I knew he was watching me.

I flipped to *Good Times* on TVOne, then curled under my six-hundred-thread-count Ralph Lauren sheets. I was laughing my ass off at JJ's skinny ass when I heard the doorbell. I jackknifed upright on the bed. No one in their right mind would come to my place at two in the morning. In fact, hardly anyone knew where I lived, and I preferred to keep it that way.

I sprang from under the covers and headed to my walk-in closet. First person to come to mind was Halo. As far as I knew, he had no idea where I lived, but that man always had a way of finding out what he needed to know.

I reached for the aluminum bat I kept in the back of the closet and carried it down to the living room with attitude. I was all set to go upside his head if he even thought about getting physical with me. When the bell rang again, I leaned over and stared through the peephole. That was not Halo standing under the porch light. Instead it was some fine-ass dude with hazel-brown eyes, short wavy hair, and a diamond stud in his left earlobe. I had never seen him before in my life. Trust me, as fine as that brotha was, I would remember if I had.

"Who's there?" I barked.

"Yo, it's Trey . . . is Robin home?"

Damn, so it wasn't no mistake. He was here to see me, but like I said before, I had no idea who the hell he was. "I don't know no Trey."

I heard him clear his throat impatiently. "Could I holla at you for a moment? It's about your sister Deena."

My first thought was to tell him to fuck off, but curiosity got the better of me and inquiring minds wanted to know. I disarmed the alarm, then turned the lock, and with the chain still securely in place, I opened the door slightly and stared up at the gorgeous man. He had a tapered mustache, and eyes so sexy, I felt my body swaying in his direction before I snapped out of the trance. Treasure doesn't fall for the looks, I reminded myself. It was all about the money.

"What about my sister?" I asked suspiciously.

Trey hesitated as if he wasn't sure he should tell me the truth. "Uh . . . would it be possible to come in? This is pretty serious."

I wasn't one for letting strangers into my house, but it was something I saw in his eyes that said he could be trusted. Still, I placed the bat behind the door just in case I needed it. I've been on my own long enough not to be no fool.

I swung the door all the way open, and that's when I noticed the little boy standing beside him, holding his hand. *Who the hell brings a kid out at this time of the morning?* But it wasn't none of my business, so I kept my question to myself and signaled for them to come inside. They moved into the living room and took a seat on my paisley-patterned couch while I preferred to stand.

"Trey, I don't know who you are, but I haven't spoken to my sister in years."

He nodded. "I know. She told me, but unfortunately I didn't have anyone else to turn to."

"Turn to about what?" He was wearing my patience. Even the little kid looked tired. He was resting his head against Trey's arm and had closed his eyes.

"I don't know how to say this, but . . . your sister was arrested for murder."

"Murder!" I shouted even though I didn't know Deena well enough to know what kind of life she was living. The day she walked out of my life was the day I wrote her out of mine.

I had to have been about ten when our parents were killed

in a car crash, and since Grandma Jeanna had died of a stroke the year before, there was no one left to take care of us. Sometimes Deena and I were together and other times we weren't, so when Ms. Ernestine said she wanted both of us, we were so happy to finally be a family. But living in her house was no celebration. She beat us every which way while her boyfriend Floyd stood back and didn't do a damn thing. I remember one time she duct-taped me to a support beam in the basement and beat me with an extension cord. She left me tied up for almost two days before Floyd finally released me. I was so scared of being separated from my sister that I never told anyone. That was before Deena ripped my heart out.

I was sixteen, and a week before Deena's eighteenth birthday, she announced she was leaving. I was scared and screamed at her not to leave me alone and to wait until I was old enough to go with her, but when I woke up the next morning she was gone.

"Listen, I couldn't care less what happens to my sister," I said with enough attitude to make the hairs at the back of my own neck stand up.

Trey shook his head and had the nerve to look disappointed. "Deena didn't kill anyone. She was framed. I'm trying to get her out on bail, but in the meantime she asked me to come over and talk to you."

I took a long deep breath and shifted my body in agitation. "I'm sorry, but there's nothing about my sister I wanna discuss, so if you'll excuse me I would really like to get some rest."

He hesitated a moment longer before finally saying, "Listen, if you change your mind, give me a call." Trey pulled a business card out of his pocket and set it on the coffee table. He would be waiting a long time if he was expecting a call from me.

I watched him whisper something in the little boy's ear. The kid nodded his curly head, then he leaned back against the couch and closed his eyes.

Rising, Trey looked over at me, then smiled. "Kyle's a really good kid. He won't be any problem at all."

"Excuse me? What did you say?" I couldn't have possibly heard him right.

"Kyle. I said he's a sweet kid."

I shrugged because I obviously wasn't following what he was getting at. "I'm glad to hear you've got a good kid, because most of the ones I run across are badasses," I said with sarcasm all up in my voice. "Now like I said before, I'd really like to get some sleep."

Trey nodded, then strolled over to the door while I stood there with my hands at my hips. "Excuse me, but aren't you forgetting something?"

His head snapped in my direction with his brow raised. "Something like what?"

"That little boy in there on my couch . . . your son." Trey may be sexy, but something just didn't seem to be right upstairs.

He gave me a weird look. "That's not my son."

"You brought him here with you." I was sleepy, but I wasn't that damn tired.

"Yeah, I came over to drop him off."

Was I missing something? "Lemme get this straight. You came to drop him off?" Hell, I was two seconds away from going off. "Okay, you need to start over, because I don't know what the hell's goin' on."

Trey chuckled and shook his head, like he too was trying to figure out where this conversation was going. "I am Trey Armstrong, Kyle's big brother . . . or mentor . . . whatever you wanna call it."

I raised my voice. "And who is Kyle?"

Confusion was written all over his face. Even before he opened his mouth, I could tell something wasn't right. "You're telling me you don't know who he is?" he asked.

"I just said that, didn't I?"

"Damn," he said apologetically. The second he paused to take a deep breath, I knew I wasn't at all prepared for what he was about to say. "Kyle's Deena's son . . . your nephew. And while she's in jail, you're his guardian."

7

Monica

"Mommy, Mommy, Daddy's here!"

At the sound of Liese's voice, I closed the *Essence* magazine I was reading and rose from the chaise longue in my master suite. I could hear the girls running down the stairs, excited about spending the weekend with their father. I couldn't blame them. We'd been divorced almost a year, and not once had he kept the girls more than a couple of hours at a time. Anthony had been too busy enjoying the single life. But since last week, things changed. He was suddenly calling the girls in the evening to see how they were doing with their homework and to say good night. I'd heard more from that man in the past few days than I had in all the time we'd been separated. In the past, he would call me and only had to be cordial long enough for me to call the girls to the phone, but this was different. He wasn't being short or saying something condescending. It was weird enough to make me wonder, okay, what's really going on?

I walked down the stairs and Anthony was already standing in the foyer of my 2,700-square-foot home with the girls both yanking on his arms. As soon as he noticed me, his lips crept into that crooked smile of his. I remembered when I thought that shit was sexy as hell.

"Hello, Monica."

"Hello," I said, trying to sound as cool as possible while my eyes rolled over his body. Anthony looked so good it made me sick. Was it really possible for him to have grown more handsome since our split? But oh, he had. Sexy and more distinguished. He was six-one with a medium build. I always thought he had the prettiest coffee complexion. Anthony's been graying prematurely since he was twenty-one, and I remembered all the evenings I spent running my fingers through his salt-and-pepper curls. And he had the most succulent lips. I loved him kissing me. Now the only thing he could kiss was my black ass.

He was wearing a red polo shirt and a pair of loose jeans and brown Ferragamo loafers. I could tell he'd started going back to the gym because his chest looked swollen and his waist was nice and trim, which was a clear indication he had a new woman in his life.

"I've got something for you." He reached into his pocket and handed me my child support check like I had just won the lottery. He was so cocky. I checked to see if he had given me a little extra, but it was the same amount he gave me every month.

"Mommy, can you go to Daddy's with us?" Arissa pleaded. "Pleeeease."

I gazed down at her big, pretty eyes and shook my head. "No, baby. This is your time with your daddy." And even if I could, I wouldn't have dreamed of going.

Arissa crossed her arms and pouted until her father came up behind her and gently tugged one of her ponytails. "Don't worry, we're going to have fun. I'm taking the two of you to King's Dominion in the morning."

"Oooh!"

"Yeahhh! Daddy, you're the greatest!" Liese shouted.

The greatest? Anthony had the nerve to stand there with a

stupid smirk on his face. I wanted so badly to burst his bubble. Where was he all those months I was struggling to pay the bills? Where was he when I was letting some repo man feel all over my breasts so he wouldn't take my car? But as always, I never said anything to make him look bad in front of the girls. I just watched them jumping up and down, kissing their father and hugging him tight like he was the best thing since choco- late mocha ice cream. I was just happy for them because their dad was finally spending time with them. "The girls are look- ing forward to spending the rest of the weekend with you."

"So am I," he said, then sighed. "I need to start spending more time with them."

Something was going on, because this was not the An- thony I knew. "Girls, go get your overnight bags," I said. As soon as they were gone, I looked Anthony dead in his eyes. "What's up? All of a sudden you're taking an interest in the girls. What's really going on?"

"I'm their father." He shrugged a broad shoulder. "I figure it's time I get *something* right in my life."

It was obvious he was talking about our failed relationship.

He smiled and showed off his gap. "By the way, Monica . . . I love your new hairstyle. How come you never wore it like that when we were married?" He batted his incredibly thick lashes innocently.

Was he for real? "Because you wouldn't let me cut my hair, remember?" How soon we forget.

"I guess I was wrong. That style looks really good." He moved closer to me, then reached up and ran his hand across my spikes, and I could tell by the look in his eyes he was being sincere. Too sincere. What the hell was he up to? I stepped back away from his touch because it felt way too familiar and I wasn't even trying to go there. Thank goodness the girls came racing back down the stairs.

"We're ready, Daddy!" Arissa said and started pulling him

toward the door. Now that he'd told them they were going to
the amusement park, there was no way they were going to sit
still for long.

"I'll bring them back tomorrow after we leave the park,"
he said.

I nodded and kissed Liese and Arissa good-bye, then
watched them walk out onto my large wraparound porch. As
soon as I shut the door, I noticed how quiet the house was.
Thank goodness I had something to do otherwise I would
have gone crazy. I probably should have been studying, but
Reyna had invited me over to her house for Mexican food and
her delicious margaritas. I wasn't used to being by myself, so I
went upstairs to grab my purse and keys. As soon as I stepped
into my room, I heard Liese's laughter. I moved over to the
window facing the front of the house, looked down, and spotted them standing at the car talking to some chick. She was
wearing skinny jeans and heels and had long hair. Nothing
worse than admitting a female is cuter than you. Anthony
helped the girls into the backseat, then leaned over and kissed
the woman passionately on the lips before they climbed into
his Jaguar.

As I drove to Reyna's, I found myself thinking about Anthony and his mystery woman. *I wonder if she sucks dick better
than me.*

Trust me. By no stretch of the imagination was I jealous.
Not anymore. I shed too many tears for that man. But you
know how we women do. We always wonder what she had
that you didn't. One of those things was being better at giving
head than I was. It was one of those things that Mama said
good girls just didn't do, and I wouldn't have even considered
it, but after three years of marriage I don't know what came
over Anthony because suddenly he wanted oral sex, and I'm
not talking about sixty-nine and him going down on me. I'm
talking about me dropping down to my knees in the kitchen
or wherever he commanded and assuming the position. At first

it was fun, but after a while it started to feel degrading. I could be on my way to pick the girls up from a Brownie meeting and there he was leaning against the counter with his fly open and his dick standing at attention. Mama married my stepfather when I was seventeen, and they were married eight years before he passed away. She always said a woman should do whatever it took to make her husband happy even if it meant being less than a lady. Anthony wanted a lady on his arm and a freak behind closed doors. The sad thing about it was no matter how often I sucked his dick, it was never good enough because eventually he found other women to do it for him.

But it wasn't like he had ever gone down on me. I used to douche and practically scrub my pussy raw trying to make sure it was fresh, but it didn't matter. Nah, he said he couldn't get past the smell. Can you believe that shit? Said he never liked seafood so he wasn't about to start. And looking back, that was probably the craziest shit I had ever heard. I was young and naïve and so damn in love I would have done anything to keep my man happy.

However, according to him, I couldn't suck or ride a dick the way he wanted me to. Doggy style hurt like hell because my husband had more dick than a woman should have to handle. Reyna used to say I was crazy for complaining because a woman would give anything to get dicked to death. I guess that's why Anthony eventually got bored and found a woman who was able to give him everything I could not.

I don't know why I was even wasting my time thinking about him. I spent enough months crying and wondering what had gone wrong. After a while I had to stop hitting myself over the head because deep in my heart, I don't think anything would have saved our marriage. Anthony wanted out and that's what he did. He got the fuck out.

"Maybe he's serious about this one," Reyna said with a shrug. "Girl, why you worrying about Anthony? I know you're not jealous," she said suspiciously, keeping her eyes locked on mine.

"Hell no . . . just curious," I said, trying to shake the thoughts from my head, which seemed impossible. There was something going on, or maybe I was just being paranoid.

"Just be glad he's spending time with the girls. Maybe *she's* the reason, and if so that's a good thing."

"Mmm-hmm, I guess you're right," I replied, but even as I said that something still bothered me. Call it a woman's intuition, but something just didn't feel right to me. Anthony was way too eager to be with Liese and Arissa.

"Come on, Monica. I've got something to show you."

I followed Reyna through her cute little Cape Cod house, toward the basement. "What's down here?" She knew I hated surprises.

"Just wait and see," she said with a laugh.

Reyna waited until I reached the bottom step before she turned on the light. I liked her place. It was the kind I would have if I didn't have girls. She had renovated the basement a year ago with hardwood floors and a wood-burning stove. I stepped into the room, and it took me a few seconds to realize what she wanted to show me. My head snapped in her direction. "You've got to be kidding." In the middle of the room were two stripper poles. "Where the hell you get those?"

Reyna started laughing. "I bought them at this adult store last night. They're the Carmen Electra brand. I figure if you're going to audition, then you need to practice a routine."

I chuckled and shook my head. She couldn't be serious. "I'm not about to practice in your basement."

"Yes, you are," she confirmed with a nod. "And I'm going to practice with you. I even bought you a present." She walked over to the side of a beige couch, and a pink gift bag appeared in her hand. "Go ahead, open it."

I may not like surprises, but I love getting presents. I was like a kid on Christmas Eve. I reached inside the bag and pulled out a pair of five-inch black platform shoes. I started cracking up. "Whoa! I can't wear these."

"You can and you will. I got me a pair as well, and a DVD."

Okay, she was taking this whole thing way too seriously. Like I've said before, I thought she was trying to live vicariously though me. "Reyna, this is ridiculous."

"Girl, we've got the rest of the weekend to ourselves. The girls are with their daddy, and Shana can take care of the boutique for me. By tonight, we're going to learn how to dance. This video is really good. Watch . . . I was practicing before you got here. Let me show you what I've learned." She turned on the stereo, and while I strapped on my shoes, I watched her do a routine that made my bottom jaw drop. Reyna may be a big girl, but she sure knew her way around that pole.

"Damn, you looked good!"

She grinned and strutted around a bit. "Thank you, mami. I've been practicing all morning."

I was so jealous. With rhythm and grace, Reyna made those moves look easy. She had always been able to pick up dance moves and had this walk that drove men crazy.

"Come on, grab your pole and I'll start the video."

I rose and did as she said and sighed. My mother used to say if you're going to be something, then be the best that you can. I spent years taking gymnastics and jazz classes. I might as well put that training to use.

8

Robin

I had a long night at the club and wished whoever was ringing my doorbell would get the hell off my porch.

We had a porno star on the stage last night and the club was packed. I made a grand in two hours, then met Chris once again at Motel 6. I knew once he sampled my goodies, he wasn't gonna be able to stay mad for too long. I officially added him to my list of sponsors.

I rolled over onto my stomach and was getting ready to doze back off when I heard the doorbell again. "Dammit!" I dragged myself out of bed and went downstairs to the door. When I looked through the peephole all I could do was groan. If I had a choice I would have pretended I wasn't home, but unfortunately he'd know I was avoiding him.

Mumbling profanities under my breath, I disarmed the alarm and yanked the door open. "Could you at least have waited till I got some sleep?" I snapped.

"Listen, I told you I'd give you until Sunday to think about it, but now we need to talk." Trey brushed past me and moved over to the couch. As soon as he took a seat, he looked over at me and grinned. "Damn, boo. You always greet yo men like that?"

He was eyeing me lustfully from head to toe until it finally dawned on me I was wearing nothing but a sports bra and string bikinis. "There ain't no shame in my game," I mumbled. One thing I was confident about was my body. "I'll be right back." I turned on my heels and swung my hips slowly up to my bedroom, making sure he got an eyeful. Hey, what can I say, I'm a naturally born flirt. Everyone wanted me, so why would he be any different?

I grabbed a robe and slid on a pair of pink slippers and went into the bathroom. I looked a hot mess with my hair all over my head and slobber on the side of my face. Damn, I was slipping. I wasn't at all interested in cutie pie, but I couldn't stand for him to see me looking less than fabulous. By the time I cleaned myself up, ran a comb through my hair, and headed back down to the living room, Trey was nowhere to be found.

"I'm in here!" I heard him call from my kitchen. I walked in to find him making coffee. "Sorry, I haven't had mine yet. Thought we both could use a cup this morning so we can talk," he explained with a sexy little grin.

Sighing, I took a seat at the breakfast bar. Friday after he'd showed up at my house with my nephew, I ranted and raved and made Trey take Kyle back home with him after I promised that he could come back on Sunday so we could discuss it. Damn, time flies.

"Where you keep the mugs?"

I pointed to the cherry cabinet near the stove, and while his back was turned, I leaned back on the stool and took a moment to check him out. I ain't gonna lie, Trey was like a well-seasoned pork chop, ready to be sucked. He wasn't just fine, he was succulent. He was rocking a cream shirt and tie and a pair of black slacks that hung low on the hips of a sensational athletic body. He was a little older than me, probably thirty, which was a good thing because I preferred my men older, not that I was planning to date him or anything, but if I were, he would definitely be my type. He carried two mugs to the breakfast bar, then lowered onto the stool on the end.

"So what's up? You give what we talked about any thought?" His gorgeous hazel eyes were locked on mine, waiting for an answer.

It was hard to focus with him looking so serious. "I haven't had a chance. It's not easy to think when I got a G-string flossing my ass."

He chuckled. "And when you planning to do that? I told you I was coming back today to talk."

"I was busy." I rose, grabbed the sugar dish and a carton of milk and carried them over, then returned to my seat. "I've got more important things to be worried about."

"More important than family?" He clearly didn't understand. "Have you even checked on your sister?"

I paused because for a second there he was about to make me say something I might regret. "Why would I do that? Look, Trey . . . me and Deena ain't close. I'm serious. We haven't talked in years."

He nodded. "I understand. But someone has to take care of Kyle."

As far as I was concerned, that person was him. I mean, come on. He had a lot of nerve. Who did he think he was, showing up at my doorstep to drop off some kid I knew nothing about? I'd promised to give keeping the little crumb snatcher some thought. Well . . . I thought about it a full two minutes, and the answer was still no. "Listen . . . I'm not used to being around kids. I work four nights a week and I don't have anybody to watch him."

"Okay . . . how about I watch him for you on the nights that you work?" Trey was being sincere, and that's what made refusing even more difficult. What would Robin Sharice Douglas look like with a kid hanging around? Somebody might make a mistake and assume he was mine. I brought the mug to my lips and took a generous sip. Damn, I didn't think my coffee ever tasted that good before. If that muthafucka could make love as good as he made coffee, someone was gonna be one lucky chick.

"Tell me . . . why you care what happens to him?" I asked when he looked up from his mug at me. "What's a grown man doing hanging out with a four-year-old anyway?"

"I volunteer for the Big Brother/Big Sister program," he said, then shrugged. "I want to make a difference in some kid's life."

Something about the way he said that sounded so damn sexy, it made my coochie clench. "So whatcha do when you're not hanging out at the playground?"

"I see you got jokes." He laughed and I took a moment to take in his pretty dimpled smile. "I manage a soul food restaurant on Jefferson Davis Highway."

"No shit."

He nodded. "Yeah, Mama Lee's. It's been in our family for years." He took a sip and I watched him staring at me, checking out my face and hair. Like I had said before, he wouldn't be able to resist all this sexiness. "So what's up? We gotta figure out how to keep Kyle's life together until his mom gets out. I'm willing to do whatever I can to help."

He was really making it hard for me to say no. The last thing in the world I wanted was a kid cramping my style. Other than catching HIV, motherhood was the other reason I practiced safe sex. "Trey, seriously, I don't do kids. He's my sister's problem, not mine."

"Yo, regardless of what you think of Deena, Kyle is your nephew and you're the only family he's got."

Why in the world is this happening to me? Some people were cut out to be mothers—unfortunately, I wasn't one of them.

"So tell me . . . What's your story?" he asked between sips, changing the subject.

"What do you mean, what's my story?" I didn't like the way that sounded. Why I gotta have a story?

He shifted on the stool and I noticed his large thigh muscles move beneath his pants. "You and your sister . . . I'm trying to understand why you hate her so much."

"That's really none of your business. Just trust and believe, I have my reasons."

He held his hands up in surrender. "Hey, I was just asking."

"Why you care so much anyway?"

He shrugged. "Deena is cool people and I like Kyle. He's a good kid, just got a bad break."

I didn't want to care but I asked anyway. "Bad break, how?"

"You really don't have any idea what's been going on in your sister's life." He gave me a look like he felt sorry for me. Fuck that. The person he needed to be feeling sorry for was Deena, not me.

"I told you I didn't. I haven't spoken to my sister in years." I didn't mean to have an attitude, but damn. What's it gonna take for him to understand?

"That's a shame," he mumbled under his breath, then took a sip of his coffee while he stared at me over the top of the mug. His sexy eyes met mine and I felt my nipples getting hard. Thank goodness I was wearing a thick robe. "One evening, about two years ago, Deena and Kirk was on their way back with Kyle after going to get ice cream. Someone pulled up beside them, shot Kirk in the head, and blew his brains out. They haven't caught the dude yet. Anyway, Kyle saw everything. He's been seeing a counselor ever since. Deena said he hasn't been the same since he lost his father. So she'd hoped by having a male role model in his life, he would get over losing him."

Hearing that my sister cared about someone other than herself was hard for me to believe. She didn't care enough about me, so why would she care about someone else?

"Anyway, he and I hang out once a week. I take him swimming . . . out to eat . . . sometimes we just go to the park and toss the ball."

Trey was so fine. It was weird to think of him giving up his time to spend with a kid that wasn't even his. "Why? I'm sure you got better things to be doing with your life."

"Sure I do, but like I said, I'm giving back. My father died of a heart attack when I was ten years old. That was the hardest thing . . . growing up without a father. No one was there to show me how to become a man. My mother tried to fill both shoes, but there are just some things a woman can't teach a boy. Anyway, I hate to see Kyle grow up without a positive male role model."

I leaned forward on the breakfast bar and stared him dead in his pretty eyes. "And you think you're positive?"

"Hell yeah, I do." He licked his lips and I felt my lower region quiver. Goodness, that dude was hazardous to my health. He was probably right about being a positive role model because he was definitely doing positive things to me. "What do you do at the restaurant?" I asked, trying to get my hormones under control. Like I said before, he was cute, but I wasn't looking for a relationship.

His brow rose. "What you mean, what do I do? I throw down in the kitchen," he replied with his chest stuck out proud.

"Really? You don't dress like any chef I know."

"What's a chef supposed to look like?" He laughed. "I cook, but I mainly handle the financial end of the business. My sister and mom do the majority of the cooking, and my brother is the king of the ribs."

Shit, I was getting hungry. "Damn, so it's like that? Some all-in-the-family type shit."

"Trust me . . . we bust our asses and the hours are long, but we've been in business for almost twenty years. You need to come down and check us out."

I had to smile. "I guess I will."

Trey stared at me for a moment and my mind started racing with possibilities. "So, what's your story? What's a sexy female like yourself do for a living?"

Any other time I would have thought a brotha was throwing me a line, but something about his eyes said he was keeping it real. "I'm a stripper." I waited to see if he batted an eye. Trey barely blinked.

"Hey, whatever it takes to pay the bills, and looking at this place I can tell it pays quite well."

Tilting my head at him, I replied, "You're different. Most men either try to fuck me or act like I got herpes when I say I'm a stripper."

Trey threw his hand up. "Nah, handle your business, Ma. I'm in the business of making money."

I liked him. I didn't want to, but I did.

"So, what's up with Kyle? You gonna take him or not?"

I released a heavy sigh. "Trey, I don't do kids," I whined. "Never have. Also, he'll cramp my style. I sleep all day and work all night."

"Like I said before, I'll watch him on the nights you are working. I live over in Glen Allen, so I'm not that far away."

He was trying to make it hard to resist. But I just couldn't imagine myself with a kid 24/7. What in the world would we talk about? And then I would have curfews, bath time, and grocery shopping. Who the hell wanted to do all that?

I drummed my fingers against my lips like I was seriously thinking about the bullshit situation my sister had put me in. "Listen . . . I have men over at all hours of the day and night. That's not the type of environment a kid should be around." One of my cardinal rules was to never shit where you sleep, so I never brought a nigga back to my crib, but Trey didn't need to know that.

He took a deep breath, probably growing annoyed. "So what you saying?"

Hello! Is he not hearing me? "I'm saying I don't know how I'm gonna do it," I answered quickly in defense.

"Do you have any other family that can take him?"

I rolled my eyes because he already knew the answer to that. "You know I don't."

Trey rose from the stool and carried his mug over to the sink. "Then I guess I'll have to call DFS and see if they can find somewhere for him to stay until his mama gets outta jail." He cleared his throat. "I don't mind helping, but I can't do it all on my own."

While he rinsed out his mug I thought about what he said, and just thinking about Kyle going to foster care made me sweat. I wouldn't wish that kind of life on anyone. Nobody at all. I still had scars to prove it had been a painful life. As much as I didn't want a little kid hanging around, there was no way I could let my nephew go into the system. Been there, done that shit, and I'd be damned if I let someone else's head get fucked up behind it.

"Damn," I mumbled under my breath and cussed my sister for getting me in this mess in the first place. If her ass wasn't out doing who knows what, I wouldn't have to keep her snotty-ass kid. "I'll keep him, but like I said, you need to take him off my hands from time to time because I'm not about to change my whole life for him."

Trey moved around the counter shaking his head. "Yo, chill. Nobody asked you to change up your whole routine. I'll keep him the nights that you work and get him off to day care in the morning." From the smug look on his face, as far as Trey was concerned it was settled. I forced a smile and nodded even though deep down I was already starting to regret my decision.

9

Monica

"Monica . . . you can come out now."

Was Reyna for real? I was never coming out, not after making a fool of myself. But hey, I couldn't blame anyone but myself. I knew from the jump this whole stripping shenanigan was a bad idea but, *noooo*, I had to let Reyna convince me to do it. And now here I was in a bathroom stall at Scandalous, hiding.

I had come in tonight all set to audition. Reyna tagged along for moral support and also because if she wasn't there pushing me through the front door, I probably would have turned around and taken my ass home. Now I wished I had.

I pushed a frustrated tear away as I remembered changing into my costume and stepping out onto the floor in a short lime green micro-miniskirt, a matching bikini top, and those damn platform heels.

"Awww sookie, sookie now," Reyna complimented me. With my head held high and my shoulders back, trying to stick out what little the good Lord had given me, I strutted across the dressing room floor. I had in green contacts and a long bootylicious blond wig, and enough makeup to give Tammy Faye Bakker a run for her money. I was suddenly Deja. We had come up with the stage name Saturday night while drinking margaritas and pole dancing in Reyna's basement, which, by the way, I'm quite good at. Not good enough to be hanging upside from the ceiling, but good enough to swing and dip and draw a man's attention.

The whole idea of auditioning during happy hour on Tuesday arose because it was supposed to be the slowest time. Men got off from work, still in their suits, wanting a drink and to see some ass before going home to whatever boring routine they were accustomed to.

Reyna had given me a gentle push and I stepped out of the dressing room and had barely gone ten feet when the men started catcalling and throwing compliments, making me feel sexy as hell. I swung my hips feeling confident that I could pull off the new persona. As soon as the manager gave me the cue, I climbed onto the platform stage. Reyna tipped the deejay twenty dollars to play Ciara's "Ride." I closed my eyes and let the music take over, and before I knew it I was gyrating my hips the way Ciara had in her music video, then I strutted over to the pole and swung around, landing in a split. I don't know what it was, but I felt swept up by the atmosphere of the club. I was gyrating and dipping and dancing all across that stage, and when men flooded to the front seats, waving money, I eagerly greeted them one by one, giving them a peekaboo of my crotch. Everything was going so well I was laughing and practically skipping to the next man. That was until I noticed someone sitting at the far end of the stage.

Mr. Jason Biggs.

Arissa and Liese's principal. I jumped off that stage so fast I didn't even bother using the steps and landed like Catwoman. Then in my haste to get away, I tripped on them damn shoes and fell flat on my face. Of course the itty-bitty-ass skirt didn't hide a thing, and my bare ass in a thong was on display for everyone to see. I had never been so humiliated in my life. As soon as some man helped me to my feet, I dashed into the bathroom and been hiding ever since.

"Monica, did you hear me? You can come out now."

"No! I'm never coming out. I wanna go home!" I wailed. This whole situation was a hot mess. I knew I sounded like a five-year-old, whining and shit, but how else was I supposed to act? If Jason had noticed me, I didn't know what I would do.

Reyna knocked and I jumped. "Monica, he's gone."

I took a deep breath. "How do you know?"

"Because I went over and talked to him before he went out the door."

"Talked to him!" I yanked open the door to the stall and gave her an incredulous look. "You went over and talked to him?" Goodness, what was she trying to do, get me recognized?

When a smile curled the corners of her lips, I could tell she was trying not to laugh. "Yes, the second I sat down and hiked up my skirt, I had his full attention. He told me he was a principal and gave me the entire spill on no kid being left behind. Goodness, his ass was boring! Then when the conversation changed to a more personal level, I asked him if he knew any of the dancers here, and he said no, he just liked to come in on Tuesdays to unwind."

I'm sure my eyes were practically bulging outta my head. "Damn, y'all had time to talk about all that? Have I been in here that long?" To me that whole ordeal had happened in a matter of minutes but there was no telling how many times I stood there flushing the toilet.

Reyna shrugged like I had no reason to be tripping. "Anyway, he's gone. So you can go back out there."

In all that excitement, I had lost the nerve. Those men saw me fall on my ass. "There is no way in hell I can go back out there and show my face."

Reyna gave me an impatient sigh. I'm sure she was getting sick of my whining. Well, too bad. I didn't see her trying to climb on a stage and shaking her ass.

"Fine . . . let's go home." She put on a sad face and signaled for me to lead the way. I stepped out of the stall and glanced at my image in the mirror. I had to do a double take. Was that really me? Because I didn't even recognize myself. What were the chances that Mr. Briggs had recognized me? I was starting to think little to none. Maybe not at all.

Reyna reached into her jeans pocket, then held out her hand. "Here, this is yours."

I looked down at the wad of money. "What the—"

She cut me off. "When you went flying outta there like a running back for the Baltimore Ravens, you left your money on the stage. One of the chicks was nice enough to get it for you."

I looked at all the ones, fives, and even a twenty, and was already counting and thinking about what I would do with that money. A tank of gas. Some groceries. I smiled and looked up at Reyna. "I guess I can do this."

Her large brown eyes sparkled. "I know you can. The proof's right here. Just think when you give a man a lap dance . . ." She started humping the trash can.

Oh yeah. My mind stared racing and I was suddenly thinking about catching up on my bills and finally having money to spend on the girls again. It would be so nice to take them to Busch Gardens next month and not worry about which bill wouldn't get paid in the process.

"Monica, you can do that shit. You should have seen yourself. All those years of gymnastics . . . and let's not forget the weekend practicing in my basement. Girl, you looked damn good out there!"

"Really?" I was starting to believe her, but it didn't hurt to hear it again.

She was nodded and grinning. "Monica, you had them men's mouths wide open. You should have seen them when you did that dip and made your ass clap. This one dude dropped his drink."

"You lying!"

Smiling, Reyna shook her head. "Nope. I'm serious. You had all them horny muthafuckas on lock."

I don't know if she was just saying that to make me feel good enough to go back out there, but whatever it was, it worked. I moved over to the mirror and fixed my wig, which was sitting lopsided. I looked at my reflection as a beautiful caramel entertainer stepped into the bathroom, and smiled at me.

"*Hola, chica*, you ripped that stage!" she said.

"Thank you." I cut my eyes in Reyna's direction and she gave me an I-told-you-so grin.

The Hispanic chick stood at the mirror beside me and started fixing her hair but I noticed her eyes kept dropping to my ass. At first she was discreet but then she was openly checking me out. I heard Reyna mumble *what the fuck?* under her breath before I swung around with my hand to my hip.

"Can I help you with something?" I had attitude for obvious reasons.

She licked her lower lip shamelessly. "I need a *chica* to go on stage with me. I got some dude that's willing to pay us a hundred each to do a sixty-nine."

Was this chick for real?

"Just think about it and I'll see you out front. By the way, my name is Lourdes." She winked, then swung on her heels and exited the bathroom.

Oh, my God. I turned to Reyna, who was cracking up with laughter. "*Ohmygoodness!* Can you believe that shit?" I exclaimed and glanced at the door, making sure she wasn't coming back.

Her eyes crinkled with excitement. "I know, right? She wants to eat your pussy."

"What the fuck? I couldn't believe how bold she was!"

Reyna shrugged. "Hey, she liked what she saw," she said, then sashayed over, imitating the look she had given me. "Damn, baby, you thick."

"Shut up, Reyna!" I said and playfully pushed her away.

"Monica, girl, you might as well get ready because all of them bitches are gonna want some of your thick ass. There's a new sheriff in town! And her name is Deja."

I gave her a fist bump, then headed back into the dressing room to change into my jeans and T-shirt. I'd had enough for one evening. Friday night would get here soon enough. And for some crazy reason, I was suddenly looking forward to it.

10

Robin

I had the feeling someone was watching me.

Slowly, I rolled onto my back, opened one eye and then the other. That was when I heard the giggling and cartoons blasting from the flat screen television mounted on the wall above my dresser.

Dammit, the little rugrat had invaded my space.

"Kyle, what're you doin' in my bed?" Not only had he climbed in my bed, but he managed to change the channel. Last night, I'd sat up watching a movie on Lifetime until I drifted off to sleep. Now it was blaring with some talking yellow sponge who lived at the bottom of the sea.

"I'm hungry, Aunt Robin."

I was seconds away from throwing the pillow over my head and screaming, but there was something about the way he said "Aunt Robin" that always seemed to melt my heart. I guess I never thought about being someone's aunt. I never thought about being someone's guardian either, but you see how that worked out for me.

It had been five days since I agreed to take Kyle into my home, and let me just say that boy wore me out faster than a night of lap dances. At first I was resistant to getting to know him any more than I needed to. I figured what was the point?

Deena would be out on bail soon and my life would be back to normal. However, the judge denied her bail, and Kyle was not a kid to be ignored. He demanded attention. I mean all the damn time. At first I found him annoying as hell, but then I noticed how much he looked like my sister, and as much as I hated her right now, I didn't have any reason to feel the same way about him. Kyle was really a good kid, just nosy as hell.

I expected him to be shy and to need time to adjust to living with a stranger, but instead he stepped into my crib and acted like he'd known me all his life. It was crazy and such a big relief all at the same time because I was definitely dreading the awkward period, wondering what the hell the two of us had to talk about besides his jailbird mother. But apparently Deena had told him all about his aunt Robin with the ashy knees who could outrun everybody in the neighborhood.

I glanced over at the clock. Damn. It was barely eight o'clock. Did the kid ever sleep? I rolled out of bed, put on my slippers, and moved down to the kitchen. Thank goodness I had gone shopping yesterday. I grabbed a bowl and filled it to the rim with the sugar-crack cereal and covered it with milk. "Kyle, your cereal's ready."

"Coming!" he screamed as he came flying down the stairs in bare feet.

"Where the hell's your socks?"

He shrugged and gave me this irresistible grin. He was missing two front teeth. "I don't know. I think Mr. Kermit ate 'em." Mr. Kermit was his stuffed green frog and his best friend who he blamed everything on to keep from getting in trouble.

"Well, you need to tell Mr. Kermit to buy his own pair."

He laughed then moved over to the breakfast bar and climbed up onto a stool, which took some effort. "Sit down Aunt Robin."

Damn! I was planning to crawl under the covers and go back to sleep. He could eat the whole freakin' box of cereal for all I cared. I moved over to the stool beside him and watched

as he shoveled food into his mouth. He was such a cute kid. I
didn't have any idea who his father was, but he couldn't have
been half-bad-looking. Kyle had long lashes and the biggest
brown eyes. They were so innocent. Like I said before, it made
it hard for me to stay distant from him. His skin was the color
of the inside of a Reese's Peanut Butter Cup and he had this
mass of sandy brown curls on top of his head. I sat there with
my elbow on the counter and my hand propping up my head
because I was seconds away from falling asleep.

"Aunt Robin, is my mommy ever coming back?"

We'd had that conversation every day since he arrived. I
was starting to think that maybe he didn't believe me. "Yeah,
Kyle. Your mother's comin' back. She just has to stay in that
place just a little bit longer."

"Why? Was she bad? Is that why the police took her away?"

Damn, for a little person, he sure asked a lot of questions.
"The police think that she did somethin' bad, but she didn't do
anything. She'll be home soon. I promise."

I knew that wasn't the right thing to say. Hell, I didn't give
a damn if my sister ever got out of jail. The only reason it mattered was I was stuck with her kid until she did. A week or two
I could tolerate, but longer than that would seriously cramp
my style. I'd gotten a call the other day to make some quick
easy money. It wouldn't have been more than a few hours in a
hotel, grinding on top of one of my regulars, but I had to turn
him down because I'd have to find someone to watch Kyle
while I was gone. Trey kept him enough so it wouldn't be fair
to ask him for any more than he was already doing. Shit, there
was nothing worse than being on lockdown. Nope, I didn't
have any room in my life for a kid. Even if he was family.

After his cereal, we went back to my room and I had to
bribe the kid just to shut him up. I promised him McDonald's
for lunch if he let me sleep while he watched cartoons. That
lasted about an hour before he was patting me on the shoulder

and complaining he was thirsty. I've said it but I'm going to say it again. I don't see how women have two or three kids, because one was way too much.

I grabbed him a glass of juice, then crawled back under the sheets with him propped up on the pillows beside me. I must have dozed off because when I finally woke up, the clock said noon and Kyle wasn't in my room.

"Kyle!"

There was no answer. I rose and slipped my feet into my slippers. I went into the spare bedroom that was supposed to be my walk-in closet but that I had made into a room for him. It meant pulling out the futon.

I stuck my head inside and he wasn't in there. "Kyle," I cried again, but still there was no answer. Suddenly I got scared. There was too much shit on the news about kids being kidnapped. I was racing down to the kitchen to grab the phone when I stopped in my tracks. Kyle was standing on a chair in front of the sink, elbow deep in bubbles.

"What are you doing?"

"Auntie, I'm washing the dishes for you."

I lifted him down off the chair and pointed a finger at him. "Boy, don't you ever scare me again!"

"I was trying to help," he said, and his bottom lip quivered and I couldn't stay mad at him even if I wanted to.

I sighed. "My bad. Just next time you hear me calling your name, you answer me, okay?"

He nodded his little head and pointed those big eyes of his in my direction. Damn, I'm a sucker for this kid.

"Can I have McDonald's now?"

I sighed and threw my hands up in surrender. "Sure, let me get dressed."

We end up spending the entire afternoon out at the mall. That boy had so much energy he wore me out, running up and down the aisles. We went to the Chesterfield Town Cen-

ter after we left McDonald's. I went to Victoria's Secret to get
a red G-string and Gap Kids for a new pair of jeans for Kyle.
As I was coming out, I spotted Trey. I tilted my Rocawear
tinted glasses and gazed across at his sexy ass for a few seconds,
mesmerized.

"Trey! Trey!" Kyle dashed across the mall. Mr. Sexy turned,
saw him and smiled wide.

I took my time walking toward him and was glad I took
extra care in my appearance. I was rocking red skinny jeans, a
white and red Deréon blouse, and five-inch red pumps. The
higher the heel, the sexier my legs looked. As I sashayed toward
him, I didn't miss the women staring him down and doing
what they could to get his attention. But the only person Trey
seemed to have eyes for was that little shorty jumping all
around like a ping-pong ball. And now he was smiling at me.

"Hey."

Damn. Did I mention how sexy he was? "Hey."

"Y'all got plans for dinner?" he asked.

I shook my head, loving the way my hair brushed across
my back. "Nope, I gotta work, remember?"

"I remember. How about you coming over early, eat and
chill at my place until you gotta leave?" he suggested.

I brought a hand to my hip and stuck out the twins for
added measure. What man can resist a pair of double Ds? And
sure enough his eyes were drawn to my generous cleavage. I
don't know what suddenly came over me but I wanted Trey to
like me. I mean really like me. The way a man is feeling a
woman he wants to get to know better. After the drama Halo
put me through, call me crazy, but there was just something
about Trey that made my entire body salivate. My coochie was
practically speaking in tongues. "Can you cook?"

"I see you got jokes." He laughed. "I guess you'll find out
when you get there."

I guess I will.

★   ★   ★

I climbed onto the stage, put my money pouch and a glass of Hennessey and Coke in the corner where I could see them, then moved to the center of the stage and allowed the music to take over. The second I started swinging my hips, niggas started flooding the seats surrounding the stage, waving money in their hands. I smiled because I loved the attention and reached for the pole and pulled myself up to the top and slowly swung around until I landed in a split. Brothas were hollering and even some of the other dancers had stopped what they were doing to watch me. From the mouth of Tupac, *All eyez on me*. Most of the chicks just stared with their playa-hating asses. Others watched, hoping to copycat my moves. They just don't get it. You can't duplicate perfection. I twirled around that pole so fast they could only shake their heads in amazement. Each and every time, I made sure everyone knew why I stayed on top and everybody else needed to fall back.

In six-inch purple platforms, I sashayed to the first man on the left and made my booty clap, and his mouth dropped. One by one I took their money and tossed it to the center of the stage while doing nothing more than shaking my ass and rubbing my titties across their cheeks. By the second song I lowered my dress onto the stage and stood there in nothing but a black G-string that left little to the imagination.

"Shiitt, baby. Can I get a lap dance?" shouted some dorky-looking dude on the end.

I leaned in close and made sure he smelled my sweet, hot breath as I whispered, "Absolutely." I allowed my lips to graze his ear and felt him shiver.

I finished working the stage, trying to give as many of them my undivided attention as I could until the end of the last song. Brothas were trying to cop a feel and spitting game, but I wasn't having any of it. You wanted some of me, you needed to pay for a lap dance; then we could talk about taking things to the next level. I was selective in the men I chose because I didn't have time for games. After that bullshit with Halo, I typically picked the married ones as sponsors, or in other words, the ones that had something to lose. That way I eliminated some of the psychos.

I gathered my money and stuck it in the pouch, then grabbed my drink and came off the stage to find dorky boy standing patiently at the bottom of the stairs. I smiled at him like I had been waiting all my life to meet him, then took his hand and led him up to the VIP section. I set my price, waited until I got my money in my hands, then went to dancing in his lap. To my right, I spotted a new chick trying to work some brother's lap. She looked like she didn't know what the hell she was doing, but most new chicks didn't. She was older but pretty just the same. Ms. Size Nine had toned legs and a big chocolate ass. It wasn't jiggly either; instead it was nice and tight. Just the way men liked them. She was packing a power-house. Bitches were gonna be hating, especially the skinny ones with flat asses. She was obviously wearing a long black wig with bangs, but it didn't take away from her beautiful face. She was definitely a looker and had staying power, which was important in order to survive in this game. I was gonna have to keep my eye on her.

Ms. Size Nine was long gone by the time I got finished working up dorky dude. He promised to come back and see me again, and for an extra twenty I even let him touch my breasts because he wanted to know if they were real.

I finished my drink and by the time I made it to the dressing room, I heard loud screaming. As soon as I stepped into the room, Ursula, our house mom, looked over at me and shook her head. I pushed my way through the crowd and spotted Mercedes standing in front of Ms. Size Nine going off.

"Bitch, don't you ever step to him again or I'll fuck you up!" she shouted at her.

The other dancers were changing costumes or standing

around watching and laughing. Nobody seemed to care enough to come to her defense. Why should they? It wasn't their fight. Mine either, but there was something about Mercedes that always seemed to rub me the wrong way. Maybe it was the way she tried to hate on me whenever she got the chance.

I remember one time she had spotted me in the drugstore buying a pregnancy test. Before I had even had a chance to pee on the stick, rumors had already been flying that I was pregnant with Halo's baby. He called me, going off, claiming I was trying to abort his unborn child. I had to show him the negative stick just to prove it. Trust and believe, I cornered the bitch at the club, and while Honey guarded the door, I beat her ass like she'd stolen something. Now, you would think after that incident she would have learned not to fuck with me, but some women just never learned.

"What the hell's goin' on in here?"

Mercedes rolled her eyes in my direction. "I'm trying to school this new bitch that she can't be coming up in here tryna step on folk's toes." Her head started moving while her neck twisted with straight-up attitude.

The new girl looked like she was bored by the entire conversation, and I must say I was glad to see she wasn't no punk. "Listen, chick . . ." she began with a calm that was almost scary. "I already told you I didn't know he was your regular. It's not my fault he liked what he saw."

Mercedes look like she was about to burst a blood vessel. And I couldn't help it. I started laughing my ass off. She wasn't used to anyone challenging her ass. Most folks knew she didn't fight fair and was quick to pick up a bottle and try to slice and dice your ass when you weren't looking.

Mercedes glanced at me, then back angrily in the direction of the new chick. "Do you know who the fuck I am? Huh? Do you?" she screamed and actually raised her hand when she said it. After that it became a shouting match.

At that point I should have just stepped back and let new girl handle her business. After all it was her problem, not mine, but unfortunately I couldn't help myself. It probably had something to do with Mercedes going out on stage tonight with the same pink nurse's outfit I had bought last week. I told you that chick's always trying to steal my shine.

Mercedes lunged toward Ms. Size Nine, but I grabbed her bony ass just in time and pulled her out of the chick's face. "Just leave her alone."

"Excuse me?" Mercedes swung around yanking free. "Treasure, you wouldn't be saying that if she was fucking up yo grind!" she barked, then had the nerve to move up in my face like she was about to do something she would later regret. Trust me. I was looking for an excuse to mop the floor with her weave.

"I know that's right," chimed in her sidekick, Sunshine. "You betta than me, Mercedes, 'cause if she tried to steal one of my regulars, I would shoot first and ask questions later." That Olive Oyl–looking bitch needed to shut up before someone huffed and puffed and blew her ass down. Sunshine was lucky if she had two men who came and saw her on a regular basis.

"Hold up! I'm not interested in stealing your clients. Next time ask him to wear a sign on his forehead," new girl snapped back.

"Keep talking shit and I'm gonna knock you the fuck out!" Mercedes moved in close and stood there in Ms. Size Nine's face screaming, and spit started flying everywhere.

I moved between them. "Hey, I say every *wo*-man for herself. If she's got what it takes to steal one of my regulars, then I say let the best bitch win. It's too much money to be made to be trippin' off one." Mercedes turned her evil eyes on me. I crossed my arms over my chest and gave her a I-dare-you-to-fuck-with-her look. "Mercedes, quit trippin'. All of us are up in here to make money not start drama. Just 'cause you got shortchanged a few measly-ass dollars, you wanna act a fool when you know good and damn well you'll make that shit back before the night's over."

"She's right. It ain't even worth tripping over," Sunshine mumbled from over on the couch. I should have known her instigating ass made sure she got a front-row seat.

Realizing it was now safe to intervene without getting punched in the process, House Mom came over and stood beside me. "I agree, Mercedes. You need to chill before the manager takes you out the rotation and sends you home." Hearing that she was about to have her ass booted out of the club defused the situation. Money always spoke volumes.

I looked over at the chick. "New girl, go do your thang." I motioned with my hand like a mother shooing her kids out of the kitchen.

Ms. Size Nine released a sigh of relief then nodded and moved into the locker room and the drama was over. Mercedes was so pissed that she stormed back into the club without saying another word. Others were talking and whispering while I walked to my locker. Most of them chicks had nothing better to do than try to start some shit just because they weren't making no money. That wasn't my problem.

As soon as the new chick changed her costume, she walked up to me. "Hey, thanks a lot back there," she began with a shaky sigh, revealing how nervous she was. She glanced around before speaking again. "That bitch's been testing me all night."

"Don't mention it. But you gotta watch your back around here. Unless you're used to this shit, you can't be coming up in here stealing regulars."

"I didn't mean to." And the expression in her large brown eyes said she was dead serious. "I was walking across the floor and he approached me."

I smirked at the innocent look. "Mmm-hmm, I saw you up

in the VIP tryna work it. Just watch your back. Mercedes ain't one to mess with."

She got quiet and for a moment, neither of us said anything. I figured she was thinking about what I had said. I was just keeping it real. She needed to watch her back. Like I said, there's some cutthroats in this place.

Finally, she held out her hand. "By the way, I'm Mon—I mean Deja."

I shook it. "Whassup . . . I'm Treasure."

I guess she took my introduction as an invitation to sit and stay awhile. "I've seen you dance. You're really really good. You ever trained as a dancer before?"

I shook my head.

"Except for gymnastics and jazz as a kid, neither have I," she admitted with a sigh. "I just let the music move me."

"That's all it takes. The dudes up in here just wanna see that big ass shake anyway," I said jokingly, tryna help her relax. "Where you from anyway?" Just hearing her talk, I could tell she was better than this. She seemed educated and smart.

Deja crossed her legs. "I'm from Michigan, but I've lived here for almost ten years."

I changed costumes and watched the way she dropped her eyes when I stood naked in front of her. She was going to have to get over being bashful if she was gonna make it in this game. While I changed I took in her outfits, which screamed slut. She definitely had a lot to learn, but I couldn't say the same about her stilettos. They looked expensive and brand-new. I believed in keeping it cute. The second my shoes become scuffed and run-down, it was time to dump that shit at the nearest Goodwill and keep it moving. You can tell a lot about a woman by her shoes, and hers told me she had class, which was a good quality if she was gonna survive in the game. She had potential, and that said a lot, because I'd seen many wannabes get run out of the club.

Honey came around the corner and paused when she saw me talking to Deja. "What's goin' on? I hear y'all up in here starting shit."

"Nah, not hardly. Just finding another way to piss Mercedes off."

The new girl looked at me long and hard with worry in her eyes. Like I said before . . . if she's gonna make it, then she's got a lot to learn.

11

Monica

You just don't know how happy I was when the deejay finally shouted, "last call for alcohol." At the end of my set, I hurried back to the dressing room to my locker and changed into a running suit and tennis shoes. I had brought shower shoes, but after seeing the globs of hair in the cruddy shower, I decided to pass until I got home. I dressed quickly because I had seen the way some of the women had been eyeballing me. I don't know if they were jealous or gay. Reyna had warned me that there was going to be a lot of that lesbian shit going on around here.

"Hey, how'd you do?"

I looked up as Treasure stepped into the locker room. "I made over three hundred dollars," I announced proudly.

She frowned and peeled off a red dress. "*Is that all?* As hard as you were working, you should have made more than that."

I didn't know what to make of her remark. Was she laughing at me or disappointed because in her opinion I hadn't made much? Shit, as far as I was concerned I was walking out with more than I had come in with, and to me that said a lot. "I guess I'll work harder next time." I felt like a kid who had just gotten scolded by her schoolteacher.

Treasure shook her head. "You need to learn how to work smarter, not harder." While she slipped into a pair of slim shorts and a white T-shirt, I finished getting dressed and listened to her talk about the first night she stripped. The entire time she was talking, I couldn't help but noticing how beautiful her body was. She had perfect breasts that sat up high on her chest. They could possibly be fake, but if they were, she'd spent a hell of a pretty penny on them. Treasure also had the littlest waist, yet for a slim chick, she had enough ass for two people. She reached in her locker for a pack of baby wipes and rubbed one across her body. I would have to remember to bring some the next time I worked. I already felt dirty as hell and I was sure it was from sliding around on that nasty stage. I watched Treasure, taking in her every move, and listened as she schooled me on being the new girl. After she'd taken up for me with Mercedes, I had mad respect for her. Well, that was before she'd started putting down how much money I'd earned. It was my first night of work, and I was plenty proud. If Treasure said I needed to stand up for myself, then dammit, that's what I'd get ready to do.

"I don't think three hundred is bad for my first night." I didn't mean to have attitude, but damn, I worked hard for that money. Do you have any idea how many laps I had to grind? One dude smelled like he'd peed on himself. On top of that my feet hurt and my legs were sore from all that twisting and turning. I was going to have all kinds of bruises from swinging around that damn pole. Stripping was more of a workout than any zumba class I'd taken, hands down. I couldn't even begin to imagine how sore I was going to be in the morning.

"Three hundred would be cool if you were really going home with that much."

Was she calling me a liar? I felt myself getting defensive. "Yes, I am. See?" I held up a wad of bills. I knew exactly how much was there because I counted it every time I climbed off stage. I don't know why I felt like I needed to prove something to her but I hated for anyone to think I was lying.

Treasure laughed. "C'mon. Let me show you what I'm

talking about." She closed her locker and swung her bag over her shoulder. Curious, I followed her through the dressing room where everyone was changing and getting ready to go home. Treasure switched her hips over to a middle-aged black woman sitting behind a long table covered with personal items such as tampons, breath mints, and even baby wipes.

"Hey, sweetie. Thanks for breaking up that fight earlier," she said and glanced over at me for a quick second before smiling up at Treasure again. "You have a good night?"

Treasure shrugged, then reached inside her pocket and handed her a ten-dollar bill. "About like any night. Mom, let me introduce you to our newest chick, Deja. Deja, this is our house mom, Ursula."

She looked over at me with a soft grin. Earlier when Mercedes had jumped in my face, she'd tried to break it up, but Mercedes wasn't having none of that until Treasure stepped in.

Ursula's bleach-blonde hair was in long dreadlocks that she wore in a beehive at the top of her head. She had ashy dark skin that made her look like she'd had a hard life. There were heavy bags under her eyes and the insides of her lips were pink from years of smoking.

"Nice to meet you."

"Our house mom's here to hem a costume if you need it. She's got supplies if you left your own. She's here to service the girls."

I nodded. That was good to know if I ever needed anything.

"As entertainers it's our job to take care of our mom, which means we pay her ten dollars at the end of each night regardless if you use her stuff or not."

"What?" My mouth hung open. Who the hell came up with that stupid rule?

I looked at Ursula, who was staring down at her hands. Her nails were chipped and worn down to the meat.

Treasure nodded. "Yep, it's one of the house rules."

So in other words, pay up. I reached inside my pocket and peeled off a ten and handed it to the woman. Ursula took the money and grinned. "Thanks, sweetie. I'm always here on the weekends if you need me." Need me? Even if I didn't need her I still had to pay her. There were almost fifty girls here tonight, which meant she would clock $500 a night without even having to take her clothes off. Damn, can I be the house mom?

We left the dressing room and headed through the club. As we walked, Treasure talked about the club and how the back offices were off-limits to dancers. It was weird seeing the place after it shut down. The lights were up and the large room was quiet. No loud music was blasting from the speakers.

"Did anyone tell you you also have to tip the bartender and the deejay?"

"What the hell?" This was getting ridiculous. "How much do I have to give both of them?"

"The bartender gets five percent and the deejay ten."

"Why do we have to do that?"

Treasure sighed, lowering her head, then lifting it to look me in the eyes. "Deja, you've got a lot to learn. The deejay keeps the music rocking so the club stays packed. If you got a favorite song you wanna dance to, just request it early and he'll make sure you get it. Quincy knows Nicki Minaj is how I get my night started, and he makes sure to make that happen. The bartenders make sure the drinks are strong enough so these muthafuckas in here keep spending their money. And trust me, don't even try to stiff them 'cause they know how much we make."

I didn't like it but I knew what she was talking about. I washed their hands, and they washed mine. By the time I got done paying everyone, I had less than $250. Damn. "I guess I didn't have such a great night after all." After I paid my electric bill there would be just enough to fill my tank. We waved at the bouncer on our way out to the parking lot. A few feet away, Treasure stopped in front of a brand-new Camaro. Damn, obviously stripping paid her well.

"I hope we didn't scare you off tonight."

I smiled and shook my head. "Nah, I think I can handle it. I'll just stay clear of Mercedes."

"She's just hating." She hit her remote starter and within seconds the engine purred and I could hear Beyoncé's "Ego" thumping from inside. Treasure lit a cigarette, then looked at me for a long moment. "You're really pretty, but . . . you wanna work on your costumes."

"What wrong with my costumes?" Reyna had picked out most of them for me.

She pointed her cigarette at me. "They scream cheap."

"Cheap? I bought most of them at Victoria's Secret."

Treasure tilted her head as she released the smoke from her lungs. "What I mean is cheap . . . like slutty. Everybody can jump on the stage in a nightie. That's the way the ho's do it. You don't wanna come off as a ho. You want people to know you're a classy bitch. I'm sure you're here for the same reason as me . . . to get paid, right?"

"What other reason is there?"

"You be surprised how many chicks work here to meet ballers and to make money so they can get high. Our clients can tell the different between the low-rent bitches and the chick up in here with class." She took a long drag on her cigarette, then blew smoke in my direction. "It's all a game. And that's something you have to remember. Every time you step up in here, you need to leave who you really are at the door and step up inside as the most confident bitch up in here."

I nodded as her words started sinking in.

She leaned back against the hood of her car with her ankles crossed. "Stripping is attitude. And if you have the right attitude you can make some serious money. Make them tricks come to you. Don't be one of them hos hopping across every customer's lap begging for a lap dance."

"So what should I do?" I asked, digging for more details. Hell, if I was going to learn, it might as well be from an expert.

"For starters, that shit on your head looks fake as hell."

Goodness, talk about embarrassing. This chick definitely didn't believe in holding punches. I reached up and slowly removed the long black wig from my head. I had found it at a beauty supply shop close to Reyna's Couture.

"You need a nice lace-front wig. Platinum blond would look damn good against your skin color. I know just the hair store to get it." The way she said it you could tell my hair had been on her mind all night. "Also, you need a wardrobe with class. You wanna look sexy and sophisticated at the same time. I play up my assets and give a man something to fantasize about. Make them wonder what's underneath without revealing everything before you get on stage. You need costumes . . . not pajamas."

I couldn't help but laugh at the analogy. "Okay, I agree. I loved everything you had on tonight."

I saw a flash of pride cross her face. "Thanks. A friend of mine has a shop off Leigh Street in Richmond. I'll take you there if you want."

I would love to go, although I was sure I wouldn't be able to afford half the shit she'd been wearing. She had all kinds of costumes. Tonight she was a genie, and I about freaked when she came out dressed like Catwoman with tail and whiskers. Wherever she got her costumes, I definitely wanted to know. Unfortunately we wouldn't be able to go any time soon. I needed a few more good nights at the club before I would feel comfortable splurging on clothes when I had already bought some.

"I think with a little grooming you could be one of the hottest chicks up at Scandalous . . . besides me, of course." She laughed and I joined in with her. "Just keep telling yourself it's all about attitude, Deja, and you'll start to understand what I'm saying."

"My real name is Monica." Every time she used my stage name, I felt she was talking to someone other than me.

"Whassup, Monica, I'm Robin."

"Nice to meet you, Robin."

While she smoked, her eyes traveled the length of me and I figured she was sizing me up. Oh God! I hoped she wasn't into that lesbian shit, because it seemed like almost everyone else was.

"You got a man?"

I quickly shook my head. "No. That's the last thing I need."

"I know that's right," she said with a laugh, then asked the one question I was dreading. "You ever been wit a woman?"

"Hell no. I'm strickly dickly," I said with attitude because I wanted to make sure she heard me loud and clear.

Treasure held her hands up innocently. "Hey, all I gotta say is don't knock it till you try. Hell, if the price is right, I'll do anything. Although I prefer a stiff hard dick myself." She laughed.

That was a relief.

"You ever fuck for money?"

Goodness, was she serious? "*What?* Never."

"Well, you need to think about it, because in this business you're gonna be propositioned."

I swallowed. That was not at all what I signed up for. I just had to ask, "Have you ever had sex for money?"

Her eyes sparkled mischievously. "Shit, all the time. I know how powerful my pussy is. She's worth millions. That mutha-fucka pays for this car and keeps money in my pocket. I got several niggas on speed dial who'll agree, she's one bad bitch."

I laughed. She was too much.

She tossed her cigarette on the ground and put it out with her foot, then looked at me with those amazing looking cat eyes of hers. Robin had a beauty that I couldn't even begin to describe. She kinda reminded me of Stacey Dash back in the day, only more exotic-looking.

"I think I'll stick with just stripping. Sex for money is just something I'm not interested in."

She looked like she didn't believe me. "I used to say the same thing until I started getting my ass kicked every day. I will do whatever I have to keep a roof over my head and never have to depend on another muthafucka."

Didn't I just say that the other day? If it ever came down to it, I would suck a dick in the middle of Cary Street in downtown Richmond if that's what it took to provide for my girls. "I know what you're saying."

"I'm serious . . . you need to figure out what you're worth. You'll be amazed at how much a man is willing to pay just to smell yo shit." She wagged her eyebrows suggestively and burst out laughing, and I joined in with her. We talked a little more about work, and I must admit, Treasure is cool people.

I heard tires crunching on gravel and I turned around to see a heavily tinted black Infiniti QX56 pull up beside us. The window lowered and some dude in dark shades stuck out his head and his deep voice boomed, "Yo, Treasure . . . Halo wanna holla at ya."

Her body tensed up angrily. "Shit, whatever," she mumbled under her breath and waved a hand at him in disgust. "Girl, I'll see you tomorrow." She walked around her car, climbed behind the wheel, and slammed the door, then shot out of the parking lot. Whoever was driving the QX56 didn't looking too happy at being dissed. I quickly moved to my car, which I had parked at the other end of the lot, and headed home. Life at Scandalous was about to get quite interesting.

12

Robin

I climbed out of my car and looked over at the dingy beige building and cringed. The last place I wanted to be was the county jail, especially after working until the wee hours of the morning. Not that I'm complaining. I'd made a killing. A local rapper rocked the mic, then I met some baller from Newport News at a Holiday Inn on Iron Bridge and rode his ass to sleep. The only reason I had gotten out of bed was because I didn't wanna miss visiting hours.

My nephew was fucking up my routine. I figured the fastest way to get Kyle out of my house was to hire Deena a damn good lawyer and get her ass out on bail.

I walked into the building and over to the desk, signed my name on the visitors list, and waited for what felt like forever before I was escorted to a room in back. When I finally reached the door, I paused and took a deep breath before I stepped inside and walked toward the first plastic chair. A woman was sitting on the other side of the glass in a brown jumpsuit and it took me a few minutes to realize that was my sister. Damn. I hadn't seen her in years, and time had not been nice to her. Her face was so thin her cheeks looked almost sunken in and her hair was a short, hot mess.

I don't know how long I stood there staring blankly at her

before I lowered onto the chair. As soon as I picked up the phone, she sighed heavily into the receiver. "Thanks for coming to see me."

I rolled my eyes. "It wasn't like I had much of a choice."

Deena seemed surprised by my response. After all these years, I couldn't figure out why she would expect any less from me. "How's Kyle?"

If I was her, my son would be the least of my worries. "He's cool. Trey said he'll bring him this weekend to see you."

Deena looked disappointed. "I was hoping you would have brought him with you."

"No, I wanted to come by myself." Did she think all of a sudden we were going to become one big happy fucking family? She just didn't get it. I hated her ass.

"Robbie, I didn't do it," she blurted out like it mattered.

"I don't care if you did it or not," I snarled and leaned as far away from the glass as I could get.

She looked around in shock before she whispered, "I'm serious. I was messing with this dude and he was into some shit. I know . . . I shouldna been fucking with him, but I'd lost my job and he paid the rent and kept food on the table." She tried explaining to me but I just glared through the glass at her. "Robbie, I love my son. I would have done anything for him."

"You need to save the explanation for the jury." If she thought I was going to sympathize with her ass, she was wrong.

"Robbie . . . you know I wouldn't have anything to do with the shit they're talkin' about. Please, ask around. *Someone* has to know what really happened."

Uh-uh. There was no way she was pulling me back into that life. I left that shit behind when I stop fucking with Halo. "I don't know nothing about that. All I know is that you need a lawyer and I'm going to get you one."

Deena stared at me with tears streaming down her cheeks. "Thank you. I appreciate it."

I felt a tug at my heart, and there was no way I was allow-ing myself to feel sorry for her. "Don't get the shit twisted. I'm not doin' it for you. I'm doin' it for Kyle. I couldn't care less if your ass rots in here, but he wants his mother at home with him." I squeezed the phone, shaking with anger.

She leaned back in the chair and grew quiet. I guess she knew it was best to leave well enough alone. It was bad enough I had to get my ass up outta bed and come down to this dirty place with bitches dragging their kids down to see their baby daddies in jail.

"I really want us to talk," Deena said, jilting me out of my thought.

"Talk about what? Because there's no us. You left me in that house and never once came back." I became one big atti-tude.

"That's not true!" she whined. "Robbie, I tried to get someone to listen to me, but no one would. I went to social services. I even reported the abuse to the police, and they said they checked into it but when they came out to Ms. Ernes-tine's house, you told them no one was abusing you."

I raised an eyebrow in confusion. She'd done that?

I remembered the day the police came to the house, asking questions. The second Ms. Ernestine saw them pull into the driveway, she threatened if I said anything, she would kill me, and I believed her and lied when the police questioned me. Had Deena really sent the police? I shook my head. I wasn't sure if it was because I was confused or because I didn't want to believe her.

"I even spoke to our caseworker and tried to find out what I needed to do to be your legal guardian and she kept blowing me off. At first she told me I needed an apartment and a job, but when I did all that she still wouldn't put us together. By then I had heard you ran away and had been placed in a differ-ent foster home. I tried to reach out to you but I didn't know where you were and the caseworker refused to tell me. Hell, I even went and saw Ms. Ernestine and asked her."

"You went and saw her?" I waited for an answer.

She lowered her head, avoiding eye contact, and nodded. "I was messing with this big dude at the time, so I took him with me. Ms. Ernestine was so scared when she realized he was packing a pistol she told me where you were staying. I went to the address and she told me you had moved out."

She was talking about Ms. Melba. I stayed at her house for almost a year, sharing a room with three other girls before I finally got the hell out and moved to this tiny-ass furnished room I had rented. To me it was heaven because it had gotten me emancipated from the foster care system. I was working at Kmart, making just enough to keep a roof over my head and food in my stomach. It was about then that I met this stripper who used to come into the store all the time. I saw she always had on the hottest clothes and her hair stayed laid. When she told me she worked at Sapphires and I should come and audition, I took her advice and auditioned, and the rest was history. I'd been dancing ever since. It took me two years before I made the money I needed to get the hell out of Petersburg and I've been gone ever since. Around that time, Scandalous had opened up and became my new home. I'd come a long way all on my own.

I looked at my sister and could see the remorse in her eyes, but it didn't matter—at least I wanted to believe it didn't matter. I'd gotten far without her, so what the hell did I need with her now?

"Look, I didn't come here to travel down memory lane. I just wanted to let you know I was hiring you a lawyer."

"Thanks Robbie. I'll pay you back." She gave me a pitiful smile.

"Of course you will," I spat sarcastically, then rose from the chair and walked out without saying another word.

13

Monica

"Can I get you anything else?"

I jerked on my seat and was staring directly at my waitress when I realized I must have dozed off. "Uh, yeah, sorry. Another caramel macchiato would be great."

"Coming right up, sweetie. Can I suggest an extra shot of espresso? Looks like you could use it."

I chuckled. "Yes, that sounds great."

I was so tired that if I didn't have a big test on Monday I could have spent the entire morning in bed.

Since I was the new girl at Scandalous, that asshole of a club manager had a rule that I had to dance Tuesday night as well as the weekend. So much for thinking I had a flexible schedule. The last week was a bitch. Although after I got past that nerve-wracking first night dancing on center stage with thousands of people watching, by week two, I was fine.

"Here ya go."

I looked up at the waitress and thanked her as she sat the piping hot mug in front of me. "You might as well keep them coming."

Last night, I worked until two, then had to crawl my ass out of bed, get the girls to school, and make it to class at nine.

Luckily we were seeing a film and I was able to sleep through most of it.

I pulled my anatomy textbook closer and reached for my highlighter. The test on Monday was major, and flunking after making it this far was not an option for me.

I had read the first couple of pages and was feeling pretty good about how things were going so far when I looked across the coffee shop and noticed someone was staring at me. "Damn, it's him again," I mumbled under my breath, then went back to studying, only it was hard to do considering I was being watched.

I'm not going to try to lie, dude wasn't fine, he was *fine* in an Idris Elba kind of way. He had to be about six-three, dark skin with a medium build. He had curly hair and in the very front was a patch of gray waves that added character to his look. But what impressed me the most was the suit he was rocking. You could tell from across the room it was expensive. I'd been seeing him coming into the coffee shop for over a month, and twice he'd even had the balls to come over and ask me out to lunch, although both times I declined. For one, I don't know him from the man in the moon, and who just walks up to a woman they don't even know and asks her out to lunch? I mean yeah, he's fine, but so were a couple of those serial killers. I peeked over in his direction again and caught him blatantly eyeing me from head to toe. I tried not to quiver, but it was hard to do. Like I said, he was sexy.

My cell phone chirped, thank goodness, because I needed a distraction. I glanced down at the screen and noticed a text message from Reyna.

How much we make last night?

I laughed. We? I don't remember seeing her shaking her ass on that grimy stage last night.

"Excuse me."

The first thing I noticed was his cologne. I knew it was him because it was what he wore every time I'd run into him. Sure enough, I looked up and Mr. Sexy was standing over me.

"You mind if I sit down?"

"If I tell you no, will you go away?" I said and struggled to keep a straight face.

His dimples deepened. "Yes, but we'll go through this same thing all over again next week."

He was persistent. I'll give him that. I nodded and he lowered into the chair across from me, then leaned back confidently.

"What are you reading?" he asked curiously.

I closed my book and pushed it out of his way so he would have room. "I'm studying for a big test that you won't let me study for." I rolled my eyes and reached for my coffee.

"Sorry, but I see you here every Wednesday, and every Wednesday I can't resist coming over and speaking to you."

"Why is that?"

He leaned across the table and looked at me in a way a man hadn't in a long time. "I think you're sexy, for starters."

I heard them same lines every night I worked at the club. Dudes talking about can they drink my bath water or wanting to suck my toes, yet when he said it I almost believed he was being sincere.

"I'm starting to think you're stalking me."

He gave a hearty chuckle. "No just trying to get to know you. I'm—"

I cut him off. "Haven't you figured out by now I'm not interested in anything but these books?"

"Everybody has to take a break. Even me."

Okay. Shoot me. I was curious. "What are you taking a break from?"

"I'm an attorney. I usually have court on Wednesday afternoons, so I like to drop in here first, have a couple of cups of coffee and clear my head before I step into the courtroom."

I didn't at all take him for a lawyer, but as persistent as he was, he was probably damn good at it.

"How about starting with your name? Hello, I'm Tremayne Collins."

Mmm, a name as sexy as the man. "I'm . . . uh . . . Monica Houston." That fine man had me so shook that I almost forgot my name.

"Pleasure meeting you, Monica."

It just didn't make any sense for a man to look that good. Since the divorce I hadn't thought twice about getting involved with another man, but there was something about this dude that made my stomach feel all tied up in knots. And I wasn't sure if I like having that feeling at all.

"So what can I do for you, Mr. Collins?" I asked, giving him an awkward smile.

"I already told you. Have lunch with me."

I couldn't resist his smile, which was just as attractive as his dark chestnut eyes. "Okay, get the waitress and I'll order something."

He laughed, and I loved the deep robust sound. "I mean an actual lunch at a restaurant, not a coffee shop."

"I really don't have time for dating. My schedule is busy enough as it is." No point in beating around the bush. I barely had time to spend with the girls, so how in the world did he expect me to find time to share with a man?

"Then I'll just settle for coffee," he said like he was happy just to be sitting at the same table with me. "So tell me . . . what do you do when you're not studying? Do you work?"

"Uh . . . yeah, I do," I stuttered and suddenly realized I should have said no because now I had to tell him what I did to earn a living, and I sure in the hell wasn't going to tell him I was a stripper. "I work at reception in the emergency room." I couldn't believe how easily that lie flew from my tongue.

"That's wonderful. Which one?"

Oh goodness. The Lord is sure to strike me down for lying. "John Randolph Medical Center."

"My cousin Lena works there. You know her? She manages the cafeteria."

I quickly shook my head and dropped my head back to the book. Things were starting off on the wrong foot, and that was definitely not a good sign.

"So tell me something else about yourself." Goodness, he was just sitting there staring at me. It should have made me feel uneasy; instead the attention had me crossing my legs tightly, trying to calm that ache between my thighs.

"Why?"

I could have sworn there was a twinkle in his eyes when he said, "Because I want to learn everything there is to know about you."

"I am a divorced mother of two." There, I said it. Nothing runs a man away faster than the thought of dating a woman with two kids. Unfortunately, for some reason he looked intrigued.

"Really? Boys . . . girls?" His question seemed sincere.

"Two girls."

"Man, you have your hands full!" He chuckled. "My mother raised me and three sisters, and as soon as they hit puberty she was about to pull her hair out. Good thing I was the oldest, because as soon as the boys came sniffing around, I kicked them off our front porch."

I laughed just thinking about it. "Mmm-hmm, my ex-husband said the same thing. Luckily he's around, so as soon as I have problems I can call him to deal with it."

"That's good to hear. I have a lot of respect for men who take care of their responsibilities. Nothing worse than a dead-beat dad."

A couple of weeks ago I would have been saying the same thing about Anthony, but he'd been doing everything he could

to spend time with those girls and I had a newfound respect
for him. The girls seemed happier too, and that was what was
important. It actually made me feel less guilty about having to
leave them every weekend to work at the club knowing they
were with Anthony.

"Do you have any children?"

"No, I haven't met the right woman yet." He winked at me.

"That's strange, because most men your age already have
one or two different baby mamas."

"Not me. I'm waiting until I get married first. In the
meantime, I have plenty of nieces and nephews to keep me
wearing condoms for a long time."

I laughed, and as we sat there chatting and sipping coffee, I
found him so easy to talk to it was scary. "You know what?
Lunch doesn't sound like a bad idea."

The comment caused him to give me a coochie-clenching
grin. I told you, I'm a sucker for dimples. Suddenly, I was definitely looking forward to seeing him again.

14

Robin

"So you gonna do this party with me or what?"

I swung my Prada purse farther onto my shoulder and reached for my rolling backpack as I followed Honey out of the club. I was ready to shower and go to bed. The night had been long and I'd swung around that pole one time too many, trying to show off in front of this music producer who frequented the joint, and I thought I pulled a muscle or some shit.

"Treasure . . . are you listening to me?"

No, I was ignoring her. I had something on my mind that was more important than some damn party. The week had been slow and so far I hadn't even made close to the money I normally made, and I had rent due next month. Don't get me wrong, I had decent savings, but why spend my own money if I don't have to? "What kinda party?"

"Have you been listening to anything I said? It's for Lil D. He might be getting outta prison next month and Dollar wants to throw him a huge party at Halo's joint. They wanna few girls to come and mingle with the crowd."

We walked across the parking lot and I waited until we had almost reached my car before I looked over at her. I liked to be in control of my environment, and at private parties you had no control. "You know good and damn well I don't wanna have shit to do with Halo or Club Swag."

"C'mon, Treasure," she whined. "Dollar's just holding it at Halo's club. He's willing to pay for top shelf." She rattled off an amount that made me do a double take.

"Damn! It's like that?"

She nodded, grinning. "Said he wants me, you, and one other girl."

"And who's gonna be the third chick . . . Mercedes?"

Honey sucked her teeth. "Nah, she don't believe in sharing the wealth. I need someone else. So will you do it? Pleeeee-assse." She was practically begging. I bet you Dollar told her she was out if I wasn't in.

"I'll let you know next week." It wasn't the answer she wanted, but it would have to do for now. I wasn't sure if being around Halo even at his hip hop club was a good idea. Just like his home, that paranoid fool had video cameras everywhere and had this thing about people watching. Just the thought of him sitting in that small room in the back, watching me while I worked the crowd, gave me an uneasy feeling. I knew Honey needed the money so she could get her life together, but she was asking a whole helluva lot.

I noticed her walking over to a black Charger. I wasn't even surprised. "I see you and Jordan are back together."

She swung her weave away from her face, grinning. "Girl, you know I'm a slave to that dick."

That ain't all she is. The chick just didn't get it. Men like Jordan never changed. He was going to keep beating on her ass because as far as he was concerned, every time she took him back, she was telling him it was okay to beat her again.

I glanced around, making sure Halo wasn't anywhere in sight. For the last three weeks, I'd found him sitting in his SUV waiting. Every time he tried to get out and talk to me, I jumped in my car, then drove around in circles until I made sure I wasn't being followed.

As soon as I ensured the coast was clear, I hopped into my beautiful red devil and peeled out of the lot. I loved driving fast and my amazing new car made that possible. The moment I turned onto my block my entire body relaxed and I felt a comfort that I couldn't begin to describe. Pride was one explanation. I lived in Richmond's prestigious West End, where everyone knew you had to be somebody. It was close to shopping and the interstate.

Reaching for my sun visor, I pushed the button raising my garage door and slowly pulled inside, then climbed out. As soon as I did I lowered the garage door, stuck my key in the side door, and went inside.

I stepped into the kitchen, lowered my purse to the counter, and looked around in admiration. I'd been living in my town house for six months and still couldn't get over how far I had come. I looked at my chocolate granite countertops, stainless steel appliances, and the cherrywood that covered all the floors. I had French doors out onto a private balcony, two bedrooms, and two baths. But the best part about it, the place was all mine.

I moved upstairs to my bedroom and immediately changed out of my clothes. The first thing I did whenever I got home was take a shower. I let the water run for about five minutes, then stepped into the walk-in shower and let the grime from the night run down the drain. I scrubbed my body until it was almost raw. We had showers at the club, but everybody and their mama used them and there ain't no telling the last time they'd been cleaned.

Thirty minutes later I stepped out of the bathroom feeling completely refreshed. I climbed under the covers and had just turned on the television when my cell phone rang. I smiled when I recognized the name that flashed on the caller ID.

"Yo, Robin . . . just checking to make sure you made it in."

"I did. How's Kyle?"

"Knocked the hell out. We sat up and watched *Shrek* one

through four while we fed our faces. He's out for the count." I just loved the way Trey's voice sounded over the phone, like he had been sleeping and just woke up. Real deep and sexy.

"Well, good, maybe I'll get to sleep in late."

"No problem." He chuckled, then the phone got quiet for a few moments. I thought maybe Trey had dozed off to sleep. "So did you make that booty clap tonight, or what?"

"You know I did." I had to laugh. Trey is too much.

"You know I'm gonna have to come and see you in action, right?"

I wasn't sure how I felt about that. It was one thing to strip, but to have him see me—I don't know. I guess I was afraid his opinion might change about me, and for some reason his opinion mattered.

The last few weeks with Kyle and Trey were something else. To keep Kyle on a sleep schedule, either Trey dropped by to pick him up on his way home from the restaurant or I came by his apartment early enough to have dinner and take a nap before heading to the club. It was cool for me because that sexy dude could cook his ass off. After we ate, I'd play with Kyle then curl up on the couch and doze off while Trey got Kyle ready for bed. Some evenings I woke up early enough for the two of us to talk until it was time for me to leave for the club. It was nice. Just us sitting on the couch shooting the shit with each other. It's crazy, but on those nights when it was the three of us together, watching television or playing Xbox 360, I felt like a family. I know, that's weird, right? But it's true. I had this feeling that this was what having a real family was all about. Like I said, Trey is good people and I was really feeling him. I didn't want to but I did. But I wasn't looking for a relationship, and as far as I knew he wasn't either.

"Robin?" I heard him say and realized I had zoned the fuck out.

"What?"

"You should have come over here when you got off."

I sucked my teeth. "Why? You only got one extra bed, and except for naps, I don't do couches." We've been flirting back and forth for weeks.

"Who said anything about you sleeping on the couch? You would have got right up in this bed with me."

"Oh really?" I said, trying not to smile. Like I said . . . I was really starting to feel this dude.

"Oh yeah . . . no doubt."

I rolled over onto my side, giggling. "You sure are cocky."

"Nah, boo. I'm just confident. You know you're feeling me, so why don't you stop playing?"

"Who's playing?" I barked with laughter and he joined in with me. Did I mention I loved his laugh? I even noticed the other day he had a deep dimple on the left side.

"What're you wearing?" he whispered into the phone.

I glanced down at the sports bra and bikini panties and grinned as I whispered, "Nothing."

"Damn, why you wanna hurt a brotha like that?" he groaned.

He was too funny. "You asked."

"Yeah, I guess I need to be careful what I ask for." We were quiet for another few moments before he finally said, "How about breakfast at Cracker Barrel tomorrow. Say . . . ten o'clock?"

Pancakes sounded really good. "I'll see y'all there."

We talked a few more minutes, then I hung up with the biggest grin on my face. I really liked Trey. And for once it wasn't at all about the money.

15

Monica

It was Friday afternoon and I was on my way to his house. We'd been dating for three weeks now, and I must say I really liked him. He was funny, considerate, compassionate, and always found a way to include my girls in any decisions that we made.

Tremayne lived in a three-bedroom home five minutes from the coffee shop. I pulled into his driveway and parked, then looked at my reflection in the mirror. I ran my fingers through my short spiky hair, still loving the look, making sure everything was in place. Lipstick. Hair, even checked my nose for any lurking critters. Just as I expected, everything was in order, but, hey, it never hurt to look. I climbed out and straightened my chocolate sundress and glanced down at my new gold sandals. I looked as fabulous as I felt.

The front door was open, so I knocked, then stepped inside. "Hey baby. I'm here."

"Come on back."

I walked through the Colonial-style house. I loved the earth tone décor. The house had been decorated by the last owners with dark wood floors and cream walls, and Tremayne liked it so much, he'd left it that way.

"Man, something smells good," I purred as I walked into his small kitchen.

He swung around and gave me one of his sexy smiles, showing off all his straight pearly white teeth, then lowered the spatula and came over and wrapped his arms around me and pressed those juicy lips to mine. I could taste coffee on his breath. I closed my eyes and gave in to the wonderful feeling I got every time he touched me.

"Damn, baby, you look good."

I loved when he complimented me. During the last year of my marriage, Anthony broke my spirit telling me I had gained too much weight and complained about how much my breasts sagged after giving birth to Liese. What breasts? I used to ask him. I never had much to begin with.

"Sexy, why don't you go into the living room and make yourself comfortable while I finish cooking in here." He playfully patted me on the butt and shooed me into the other room.

Smiling, I went into the living room and flopped down on a comfortable overstuffed couch and watched *The View*. I slipped off my shoes and was snuggling in the cushions when my cell phone rang. It was Anthony.

"What's up?"

"Hey, I wanted to know if I could have the girls again this weekend?"

Every time he called it amazed me because he'd been spending so much time with the girls lately. Maybe he was finally growing up and realized the girls were just as much his responsibility as they were mine, or maybe it was because of Rosa. According to Liese, Anthony's girlfriend was very nice to them. She was so nice she had been taken the girls on shopping trips. Last weekend they came home with bags from Saks Fifth Avenue. It seemed that every weekend they shared, she was always a part of their outings. But now that I was working at the club, every moment I had with the girls was important to me. I wasn't planning on working Saturday night so that I could spend some quality time with them. "Anthony, I planned on spending the day at the spa with the girls."

Anthony released a heavy sigh. "At the last minute Rosa got her hands on front-row tickets to the Justin Beiber concert. She thought the girls would love to go."

He knew damn well the girls were both in love with Justin and would be devastated if they knew I had told him no. "I guess you can have the girls again."

"Excellent. Thanks, Monica." He cleared his throat. "Have you gotten your car taken care of?"

The concern in his voice was surprising to hear. "Mmm-hmm, I caught up on my payments."

He cleared his throat again the way he does when he's up to something. "Listen, I've been, um . . . thinking. And I'm going to increase my child support." He then rattled off a number that made my jaw drop.

"Okay, Anthony, you're up to something and I wanna know what it is."

He quickly denied it. "I'm not up to anything. I just realized the girls are a lot more expensive than I imagine."

"Ya think?" I'd been trying to tell him that for months. I was glad he finally figured it out, although I was sure Rosa had a lot to do with that. I hadn't even met the woman and I liked her.

"I appreciate it, Anthony. Really I do."

"No problem. The girls mentioned you're working on the weekends?"

My heart started pounding wildly in my chest. "Uh, yeah, I'm working as a receptionist on the night shift at the hospital."

"Really, which one?"

Damn, why does everyone always ask that? "John Randolph Medical Center," I lied. It didn't matter. There were enough floors that he would never find out the truth anyways.

"That's good. I'm proud of you, Monica. Really . . . I am."

That meant a lot coming from him. It's been a long time since we'd been at this place where we could have a civilized conversation without getting into a fight.

"The girls really like Rosa," I teased. I wanted him to know I was okay with him having another woman in my girls' life. "Sounds like she's a really nice lady."

"Thanks. She's really special. I can't imagine her not being in my life."

At one time I would have felt jealous, hearing him talk that way about another woman, especially since the reason we had gotten a divorce was because he wanted the freedom to see who he wanted when he wanted. But now that I had gained my independence and had a wonderful man in my life, I was happy for him. We talked a few more minutes and scheduled a time for him to pick up the girls on Saturday and then I hung up.

"Baby, I hope you got an appetite, because your man was working up a sweat up in the kitchen," Tremayne said as he stepped into the room carrying two plates of food.

"Ooh, it looks good."

He took the seat across from me. "Okay, test it and tell me what you think."

I took the fork from his hand and brought the omelet to my lips. "Mmmm, crab . . . delicious." I wasn't just saying that. It was good.

"Good. I was hoping I got the recipe right."

"You did good."

He looked pleased with himself. That was one thing I liked about Tremayne. He catered to a woman.

I had barely eaten my omelet when we started kissing and touching. His kisses were thorough and gentle. I hadn't had any in over a year, so my body was on fire. There was no way I was going to deny myself a second longer. When he pulled my panties down over my hips, my stomach stared to quiver with anticipation. I couldn't wait to feel him inside me. However, it suddenly dawned on me that the only person that was naked from the waist down was me.

"Aren't you going to get undressed?"

"Not yet. Now open your legs," he said, standing over me.

The way he was looking had me squirming against the cushions. I was nervous and self-conscious at the same time. I preferred having sex with the lights off. But it was the middle of the afternoon and the sun was shining outside and I was lying back against the couch with my coochie on display.

"Damn, your pussy is pretty," he moaned and lowered onto his knees, then reached out and started touching me down there. My eyes closed on contact, and when he slipped a finger inside, I think I came right then and there.

"Oooh."

"You like that?"

"Yes," I purred. "That feels wonderful." That was an understatement.

He slowly pulled his finger out and my eyes slid open. And that was when I saw him do what I never could get Anthony's tired ass to do—he lowered his mouth to my kitty cat. I kid you not, I had an out-of-body experience. I don't know where I was floating to, but it had to be somewhere close to heaven. His tongue found my clit and I about jumped off the couch, it felt so good. He licked and sucked and slipped his finger inside again and found my G-spot and I was crying out his name.

"Tremayne . . . baby . . . *yes* . . . *YES!*"

"That's it. Come for me."

He didn't need to tell me twice. As soon as he applied a little pressure to my clit, I came so hard I think I threw my back out. He waited until my breathing slowed before he lifted me into his arms and carried me back to his bedroom. I was more than ready for whatever he had in store.

He settled me at the center of the bed and I watched with half-lidded eyes as he lowered his pants and his boxers. His dick wasn't small by any means, but he had nothing close to Anthony's big dick. I was starting to think maybe that was a good thing, considering I always felt like he was ripping my insides out.

I watched as Tremayne rolled a condom on, then walked over to the bed and moved between my thighs. "Baby, wrap your legs around me."

I followed his lead and within seconds he slipped inside and was moving at a steady rhythm. I never knew sex could feel that good. He grabbed onto my hips and pumped deeper. I opened my eyes and found him staring down at me. All I could do was breathe hard and stare back.

"You like me being inside you?"

Like was a fucking understatement. I loved what he was doing, and the way he made me feel—I couldn't even begin to put it into words because there were none, except that Anthony had fallen short all those years in the pleasure department.

"Monica, look down. I want you to watch my dick slide in and out of your pussy."

I raised up on my elbows and looked down between us. Oh. My. Goodness. I was wet and my juices were coating his chocolate goodness. Tremayne reached down between us and started playing with my clit again, and that's all it took.

"I'm . . . finna . . . come . . . again. *Aaawgh!*" I cried. And no sooner was I done than he came right behind me. We lay there for a while holding each other before Tremayne got up, warmed our plates, and carried them into the bedroom. Like I said, he was thoughtful like that.

"I was hoping we could catch a movie tonight."

He looked so happy I hated what I was about to tell him. "I've gotta work tonight."

"Oh damn, I forgot about that. Maybe I can drop by the hospital on your break and bring you an early breakfast or something."

I gazed down at my plate, purposely avoiding eye contact. "Since I only work six hours, I only get a fifteen-minute break. Not long enough to do anything but swallow down a sandwich and get back to my desk."

"Okay, what about tomorrow?"

This time I looked up at him. "You know I work Saturday nights." I don't know why we went through this every weekend. I hadn't planned on working, but since Anthony was going to have the girls, I might as well go in and make some money. That way I could take off next Saturday.

Tremayne rubbed a hand across his head and grew quiet as he finished his food. I felt so guilty that I had to say something.

"Listen . . . as soon as I graduate I'll have more time. I'm sorry, but I gotta work."

He nodded and looked sincere. "I understand. It's just I wanna take my woman out on the weekends and show her off."

I grinned, loving the way he called me his woman. "Eighteen more weeks and it will all be over."

I thought about Anthony asking about my job. Graduation couldn't come soon enough.

16

Robin

I was up watching reruns of *The Bernie Mac Show* when Trey called.

"I thought you were bringing Kyle home at noon." Can you believe? It'd been six weeks and I already considered my casa his casa. Like I said, the boy had grown on me. I didn't know how he managed to wiggle his way into my heart, but I wished I knew because I could have packaged that shit and made a fortune.

"I was on my way, but I had an idea I wanna run by you first," Trey began in that panty-dropping voice of his. "I'd like to take you to dinner tonight."

"On a date?"

"Yeah, a date. Just you and me . . . no Kyle." I could hear the smile in his voice. Thank goodness he couldn't see the big shit-eating grin on mine.

I couldn't remember the last time I had gone out on a real bona fide date. I let most men take me out because they had already paid for the evening or because I was determined to take everything they had in their wallet before the night was over, but a date with a man who so far didn't seem to have a hidden agenda—now, that was new for me. "Who's gonna watch Kyle?"

"My sister will."

Sundays were my open invitation night. I had sponsors I met on the regular at hotels around the city for a little romp in the sack. I had one regular, an overweight white guy who only wanted to watch me play with sex toys while he sat in a nearby chair and beat his meat. That was the easiest money, and then there were the clients who just simply wanted to fuck. My number one rule was I brought my own condoms and I always picked the hotel. I was supposed to meet Deke, one of my regulars, around nine for a little foreplay, but to hell with that. I could get up with him tomorrow or the day after. "Yeah, that sounds cool."

As soon as I got dressed I headed to Dillard's at Shore Pump Mall and found something to wear. Trey hadn't said where we were going and I wasn't about to call and ask. I figured jeans were always the safest way to go.

I bought a pair of bad black BCBG pumps and paired that with skinny jeans and a white blouse that plunged in the front and back. Honey had called looking for me, so I told her to come and help me accessorize my gear.

We had barely been in Macy's five minutes before she asked, "So who's this dude?" Curiosity was written all over her face.

I made sure I focused on the jewelry at the counter and played it nonchalant with Honey. She's my girl and all, but she has a tendency to ask too many damn questions about my personal life, and some things I just believe in keeping private. "A friend of a friend. No big deal."

I guess my answer wasn't good enough because she sputtered with laughter. "Bitch, he's gotta be something if you out buying shit to look good for him."

"Honey, I don't know what you're talking about. I *always* look good." I glared in her direction, daring her to say otherwise. She just rolled her eyes and picked up a pair of earrings

with way too many rhinestones for my taste. I turned up my
nose and reached for a gold pair of hoops.

"Have you decided yet about doing the party with me?"

To be honest, I hadn't even given it a second thought.
"Nope."

"C'mon, Treasure! Girl, it's gonna be so much money up
in there I might finally get Sophia back."

I sighed. "Do you even *know* when he's getting out?"

"Sometime next month . . . I think." She looked at me
with those large eyes of hers, looking pitiful as shit. I hated
feeling sorry for her. Honey lived in a one-bedroom apartment with less furniture than you found in a motel. Part of me
thought her daughter was probably better off without her, but
the side of me who spent years being abused in the foster system believed otherwise.

"I'm still thinking about it, but if I agree, tell Dollar I need
half my money up front or no deal."

"I know that's right." She was grinning like a damn fool,
like I had already agreed.

"I said I'm still *thinking* about it."

Chuckling, Honey gave me a dismissive wave; then for the
next hour she spent so much time talking about the party and
how much money she was planning to make that I hurried up
shopping and headed back to my town house, alone.

Trey ended up taking me to the CineBistro at Stony Point
Mall. I had never been there before but I actually enjoyed it. It
was a dinner/movie theater where you got to eat a three-
course meal and watch a movie at the same time. Folks had
been raving about the new Tyler Perry movie, so we saw that
while we ate. Afterward we went to a coffee shop and just
talked. I asked him all kinds of questions about running a
restaurant, and he asked me about my life as a stripper. I flirted
like crazy and made sure my answers were as sexually arousing
as the woman sitting across from him. "When's the next night

you work?" he asked after he pulled into my driveway and
turned the engine off.

"I'm working Friday night."

"I wanna come watch you."

"You're kidding." He'd said it before, but I figured at this
point he was just joking.

He shook his head. "Why would I kid about something
like that? I wanna see you in action."

We grew quiet then and I felt awkward, which was crazy
because I am always in control of the situation, but with Trey, I
didn't know which way to go. "Would you like to come in for
a few minutes?"

Trey stared like he was thinking about my question before
he finally shook his head. "Nah . . . I better get home. I've got
a busy day tomorrow."

I nodded, not quite understanding. I guess I wasn't used to
a man saying no to spending time alone with me. "You got a
girl?"

He laughed. "Nah, what made you ask that?"

I tried to shrug like it didn't matter to me one way or another, but I was lying. I wanted Trey to be available and at my
disposal. "I've heard you talking to her on the phone."

"I don't know who you heard, but it wasn't my girl. I
haven't been serious with anyone in almost a year. The last
chick I was kicking it with . . . I was looking for something
long term and she wasn't."

If he wasn't seeing anyone, then what was his deal? I wondered. He hadn't tried to touch me or anything. And I knew
he wanted to because I could see it in his eyes, and when we
weren't hanging out he would call me out of the blue just to
flirt. If that didn't mean he liked me, then I don't what did.
Men usually broke their necks to try to get at something as
fine as me. Trey was hard as hell to figure out, and I was starting to wonder if maybe he might be gay.

But then he did something that erased that idea from my

mind. He kissed me. And not just any old kiss. He leaned over and wrapped his arms around me and slipped his tongue between my lips and stroked my mouth with confidence. The brotha had mad skills, and my kitty was purring for some undivided attention. I put my arms around his neck and leaned into the kiss, making sure he felt my hard nipples against him. He was feeling me, that much was a given. It was in the way he kissed.

After kissing for what felt like forever, I figured if we were ever going to get this party started, then I was going to have to initiate it. I reached my hand down between us and unzipped his jeans, then reached my hand inside. I needed to know what he was working with before I wasted my damn time. You gotta watch them pretty muthafuckas. They might be fine as hell but coming up short in the dick department.

In a matter of seconds I had slipped my fingers inside the opening in his boxers and had my hand wrapped around his dick—correction—almost wrapped around, because Trey was packing a baseball bat. He moaned when my thumb grazed the head and I couldn't wait a second longer. I just had to see it for myself. I pulled it out and feasted my eyes on all he was working with. Let me just say Trey was fucking blessed. He had width, length, and a lip-smacking delicious-looking dick.

"You know you wrong for that, right?" he said with a shaky breath.

"Why?" I said all innocently. "If anything, I'm wrong for what I am about to do next." Before he could respond I had wrapped my lips around his dick. It was crazy but I had this overwhelming need to taste him, and yes, he tasted finger-licking good. I slobbed on him like I was sucking a cherry lollipop. One thing that can't ever be said about me is that I don't give bomb-ass head. In under five minutes, I had Trey moaning and speaking in tongues. I could tell he was seconds away from coming in my mouth when he did something that blew my mind. He pushed me away. What the fuck?

"I better stop and let you take your fine ass inside."

Was he for real? What man turns down getting his dick sucked unless he's gay? "Why don't you come in with me? I'll make it worth your while." I was licking my lips, reminding him how good I'd made him feel.

He looked like he was weighing his options before he finally shook his head. "It ain't that kind of party."

All he did was piss me off. Trey didn't seem to have a problem with me unzipping his jeans and wrapping my lips around his dick a few minutes ago. I rolled my eyes and reached for the door handle. "Whatever." He obviously had no idea how many niggas would kill to get a piece of me. Before I could even get out of the car, he grabbed my wrist and kissed me again.

"I got mad respect for you, but I can see you don't know nothing about a man respecting you. Yeah . . . I could take you inside right now and fuck the shit outta you, but that ain't what this is about. I like you, but first you gotta start liking yourself."

No, he didn't just go there. "What the fuck you mean, liking myself? Hell, if I don't love me, then nobody will."

"What I'm saying is you're a lady, Ma. You can't be sucking niggas off after one date. How're they gonna respect you in the morning?"

Who gives a fuck! As long as they fatten up my pockets and I can go to the mall, who cares? But with Trey I wasn't looking for a payout. I really liked him, and it bothered me more than I was willing to admit that he thought I was playing myself. Hell, I was just trying to give him a freebie. That's what I get for tryna donate to charity.

"Make a nigga earn getting between them thighs. It's one thing when you working the club, but when you tryna get to know a dude on a personal level, you gotta make him earn your respect."

As much as it pained me, I knew some of what he was saying was true, but what he didn't understand was that sex had always been about getting what I could. I learned early on that my pussy was worth a lot of money, and the better I fucked a nigga, the more he was willing to pay to get it. Trey wasn't interested in that. And for that I felt humiliated. I tried to come at him like all them other tricks and the shit backfired on my ass.

I didn't want to hear shit else he had to say. I snatched away from him and went inside and slammed the door. I was mad because I had broken my rule and allowed a man get to me.

17

Monica

"Tell me you're joking," I screeched, hoping that I was being punked and Ashton Kutcher was somewhere in the bushes lurking. But when the man didn't even crack a smile, I knew this was no joking matter.

"I'm sorry, ma'am, but I'm afraid your air-conditioning system needs to be replaced."

This was not happening. It couldn't be. I had bought the house shortly after my divorce with the hope that I wouldn't have to worry about any problems for years. Wasn't that why I paid for a home inspection? Now I was regretting not renewing my home owner's warranty, which had expired last night. "Do you have a payment plan?" I asked with a sheepish grin.

He gave me a look like my question was ridiculous. "No, but we have financing if you're interested."

How in the world would I get approved when I didn't even have a legitimate job? He gave me an invoice and I paid the hundred dollars for his service call, then watched him walk out of my house toward his service truck in my driveway.

I looked up at the ceiling fan overhead, blowing in the foyer. It wasn't doing anything but stirring hot air. There was no way the girls and I could stay in that hot house without air-conditioning. I didn't have fifteen hundred dollars I could just spend. It was two weeks before I would get any more money from Anthony, and what little I had needed to last. Damn. If I had known days ago, I wouldn't have splurged on the trampoline out back for the girls or the new bikes.

It was times like this I got depressed and started hating my life. At one time all I had to do was pull out a gold card or write a check, but not anymore. I didn't have it like that. I took a seat on the couch and thought about what to do. The girls would be home in a couple of hours. I needed to figure out how I was going to be able to keep my babies cool. Putting my pride aside, I did the only thing I could. I picked up the phone and called Anthony.

I stepped into the large building on Coach Road. The floor was gleaming and the white walls were fresh and clean. I walked down the hall to the elevator and pressed the button for the second floor. While I waited, I took in my appearance in the reflection of the door. I was wearing a slamming blue jean jumpsuit with a black belt around my waist and open-toe sandals. I wanted to look my best. With all that dancing I'd been doing, I had lost ten pounds and was in love with my newfound curves.

I stepped into the elevator. The only person in there was a man with a receding hairline and a thick waistline.

"Good afternoon," he greeted me with a smile that was far too eager.

"Hello." I didn't even bother to make eye contact because if I did, he would be hitting all over me. Just as I thought. The second the elevator doors shut, he turned and stared dead at me.

"Excuse me, but you look so familiar."

Was he fucking kidding me? I gave a rude snort and rolled my eyes. That question wasn't even worth answering.

His brow crinkled. "Seriously, I've seen you somewhere before."

"I've been told I have that kind of face."

"I'm Greg, by the way. I own Richmond Investment Fund."

My head whipped around. He was Anthony's new partner. The corporation had grossed over a billion dollars for their clients last year. "It's a pleasure meeting you. I'm Monica. Anthony's ex-wife."

His brow drew, and I could see my announcement shocked him. "Damn, I didn't know you were that beautiful. I'll definitely have to tell Anthony he's a fool for letting a woman so beautiful outta his life."

I put on a fake grin. He took my hand into his, which was slimy and wet. He held it a second too long and brought it to his lips. I tried not to flinch, because he was Anthony's partner and right now I needed to be on my ex's good side.

The doors opened and I said good-bye, then sashayed down the hall. I knew his eyes were following my ass. I glanced over my shoulder, winked, and never broke stride.

At the end of the plush hall, I spotted Melody sitting behind the desk chatting on the phone. The short mousy woman had been Anthony's assistant for over seven years. If anyone knew the gossip of the office, it was her. I think part of the reason was that she started most of it. I was certain she'd been eavesdropping on his conversations for years and knew every painful detail of our divorce.

"Hey, Monica," she chimed as she ended her call.

Smiling, I waved. "Hello, Melody. Is Anthony around?"

I saw her sizing me up, checking out my slim curves and fierce new hairstyle. What? Did she think after the divorce I was going to fall apart and look a hot mess? "Yes. He's expecting you."

After finding out how much it was going to cost to install a brand-new cooling system in the house, I had mustered up the nerve to call Anthony and ask for the money. Instead of belittling and treating me like a child, he told me to come over to his office.

"Go on in."

I nodded and was getting ready to knock when his office door flew open and a handsome black man stormed out. I had seen him with Anthony several times before and smiled up into his angry greenish brown eyes, yet he barely looked in my direction and headed toward the elevators.

Anthony was sitting behind the desk in his large corner office, which had windows for walls. Everything was white from the ceiling all the way down to the bone white marble flooring. He motioned for me to take a seat on a white upholstered chair across from his desk while he finished his call.

I sat down, crossed my legs, and took a moment to take in his profile. Liese had his small pudgy nose, while Arissa got his good hair and beautiful chocolate eyes. Anthony had always been a vain son of a bitch. He knew he looked good. You could see it in his thousand-dollar suits and his expensive wingtip shoes. He finally ended his call and swung around in his seat.

"Sorry about that. You know I'm always in high demand."

"What else is new?" I said with a phony laugh, hoping he didn't notice. He leaned across the desk, staring me in the face. "So what's up? You were saying something on the phone about needing money."

I nodded and put on my little-girl face the way Arissa did when she wanted her way with her daddy. "The central air unit went out. I wouldn't ask you if I didn't really need the money, but I really can't afford it this month, and as hot as the house is, I can't imagine letting the girls sleep in that heat." I knew I was rambling but I had to make sure I put a plug in about the kids so he wouldn't have a chance to say no.

"No problem," he began with this grin like he was about to tell me something good. He reached inside his desk drawer and pulled out a checkbook, then reached for a pen.

I couldn't believe it had been that easy. "I just need fifteen hundred."

"Absolutely," he said, then grinned and quickly scribbled

out a check. I waited eagerly. I had already called the man before I left and told him to come back to my house first thing tomorrow morning. I was off tonight, so the girls and I were going to stay the night at the Marriott. I knew they would enjoy that. Reyna had enough hotel points that the room was free. Thank goodness for best friends.

"Here you go." He reached across the desk and handed me the check.

"Thank you." I started to fold up the check and stick it in my purse, but something told me before I did that to look down at the amount. When I did, my eyes grew large and my jaw dropped. "This is for a hundred thousand dollars!"

"Yes . . . it is."

Before I could question him, there was a knock at the door and I turned to see a beautiful woman stepping into the room. Tall, thin, with a professional weave. It looked almost real, but I knew enough to know a fake when I saw it.

"Hello, you must be Monica," she said, then sashayed her narrow hips over to me and shook my hand.

I smiled up into her gray eyes and realized she was truly beautiful beneath the painted eyes and tinted lips. "Yes, I am, and you must be Rosa. I've heard a lot about you from the girls."

"They're wonderful kids." She moved around the desk and wrapped her arm around Anthony, and he kissed her so passionately, I turned my head for a brief moment to give them some privacy. I couldn't remember if he had ever kissed me like that before. The two of them obviously had something Anthony and I never had.

I was ready to go, but I still had an issue to address. I gave them another five seconds and when I realized they must have forgotten I was in the room, I cleared my throat rudely and said, "Anthony, we need to talk about this check. As much as I would love to keep it, I can't."

"I owe it to you."

Rosa looked at him and they shared a look that passed between them. "Sweetheart. Have you talked to her yet?" she asked with a nervous glint in her eyes.

He purposely avoided looking my way as he replied, "No, I was just getting ready to."

I suddenly had a bad feeling as I looked from her to him. "Talk to me about what?"

Anthony reached over and squeezed Rosa's hand, then replied, "Monica, we would like to spend a lot more time with the girls. I miss them and Rosa adores them."

"That's fine. You know I've never had a problem with you being with them."

Rosa shook her head like I was stupid or something. He patted her hand. "Monica, yesterday I asked Rosa to marry me."

For the first time I noticed the large rock on her finger. It had to be five carats or more. Damn! My ring had barely been one carat.

"Congratulations," I said as she wiggled her fingers so I could get a closer look.

Anthony took her hand in his. "Right now I think . . . we think it's important that you focus on your education and get your nursing career off the ground. I've talked to Rosa, and we would like the girls to come live with us."

What the hell did he just say to me? "Live with you?" I rolled my eyes and lowered my gaze to the check. "Is that was this is all about?" I knew he had been up to something all these weeks. I just had no idea what. Now I knew.

"I want you to have the money so you'll know that I'm willing to help. If you agree, I will give you two more just like that."

"Anthony, you can go to hell!"

Rosa gasped and I watched a tear roll down her painted cheek. "Please, I can't have kids, so I would love to raise your girls as my own." She looked desperate.

"As your own? Excuse me, but they already have a mother."

She got ready to say something but Anthony stopped her. Good move, because I was seconds away from snatching that weave from her head. How dare she try to steal my babies! Anthony leaned back in his chair like he didn't have a worry in the world. "Arissa's been saying you work late and when you're home you're either tired or busy studying. All we want to do is make life easier for you."

"Really . . . and what happens after graduation?" I asked with straight attitude.

Casually he replied, "We'll be more than willing to give you reasonable visitation."

"Reasonable?" I sprung from the chair. "I don't know if you know this or not, but those are *my* girls. They came outta this coochie over here, not hers, and I'll be damned if I sell them to you for a price!"

He leaned back in his seat, then had the nerve to say, "I'm sorry you feel that way."

I snatched my Gucci purse from the chair and tucked it under my arm. "You should be sorry for even bringing something like that to me!"

"I think we provide a more . . . stable home environment. Monica, I hate to get the lawyers involved, but if I have to . . ." He purposely allowed his voice to trail off. I didn't miss the threat.

"Bring it, baby." I ripped the check in two pieces, tossed it at him, then stormed out of the office. If he wanted a fight, then he'd just got one.

18

Robin

I was working the pole when I spotted Trey stepping into the club. Other than discussing who was going to pick Kyle up from school, he hadn't said two words to me about the other night, and that was okay with me. He'd left me feeling cheaper than any of the tricks that paid me.

I removed my bikini top and made sure I was staring straight at him as I did a slow striptease. Just as I suspected, his hazel eyes were glued to me. He was too far away to know for sure, but I was certain he was licking his lips and kicking himself as he saw everything he'd missed out on the other night.

For the next two songs I worked the stage, batted my eyes, jiggling my ass and collecting money along the way. By the end of my set I was sweating and breathing hard, holding a fistful of money.

When I came off the stage Trey was standing there waiting for me. I tossed him a cold look so he would know that after what happened the other night, any possibility of me and him was history.

"Yo, how much for a private dance?" he cooed.

Money was money. It felt good inside knowing I worked the pole so well I had his dick hard.

"Depend on what all you want."

He held up a hundred. "What can I get for this?"

I snatched the money from his hand and walked up to the VIP section. As soon as I reached the balcony, I moved to the couch at the far end and signaled for him to take a seat. The music changed to Nicki Minaj and I moved my body to the beat of the music, swaying my hips and playing with my nipples. Trey sat back on the couch, eyes glued to mine. I could tell when his tongue slipped out from between his lips that he was aroused. I gave him a deep, penetrating gaze, then dropped down to his crotch and started rocking my hips.

"I miss you," he finally said.

He didn't have to tell me. His hard dick was evidence of that. "So what? You missed me."

His hands came and grabbed my hips. He tried to pull me closer but I pushed them away. "There's no touching."

"You know you want my hands on you." Boldly he brought them back to my hips, and his hand moved around to stroke my belly. "Yo, I've got mad respect for you, Robin."

I moved off his lap and swung around and straddled him. My nipples were only inches from his lips and I could feel his warm breath as he spoke.

"I don't wanna be another one of them muthafuckas you fuck . . . I wanna make love."

I ain't gonna lie. His words did crazy things to me. I couldn't remember the last time a man said that to me.

"Robin, I want to be with you . . . not just for sex," he whispered.

He rocked his hips and I followed his rhythm. My eyes were locked on his when he leaned forward and captured a nipple between his lips. I tried not to moan too loud because a bouncer was at the end of the balcony and the last thing I wanted was to draw attention to us. Thank goodness it was dark.

"How about we go to the zoo Saturday? You, me, and Kyle?"

"Okay," I heard myself say. I wanted to stay mad but I couldn't. Not with him looking at me that way. Besides, I liked Trey. I liked him so much it scared me. One thing for sure, I didn't want to lose him.

When the second song ended I climbed off his lap, grabbed my dress, and headed toward the stairs.

"Can I buy you a drink?" Trey asked as he moved up beside me.

I grinned. "Sure."

We were heading down the steps when I noticed Halo standing down there waiting for me. The look on his face said he was ready to start some shit.

Dammit. He spent so much time at Scandalous, who would have known he owned a hip-hop club in Colonial Heights? Club Swag was the hottest club in the city. So why the hell was he always here sweating me? I tried to pretend I didn't see him and walked past him, but he grabbed my wrist and pulled me toward him.

"Hey, take yo muthafuckin' hands off her!" Trey jumped all in Halo's face. He loosened his grip, then moved to stand in Trey's face. The last thing I needed was a fight to break out up in here so the club manager could come down hard on my ass.

"Trey . . . please . . . let me handle this."

He had his hands balled in fists at his sides and was breathing fire like a paranormal dragon. "Then handle your business, but if I see that muthafucka grab on you again, I'm going to make it my business."

Halo laughed. "Yeah, my bad, nigga." Before he could say anything further, I grabbed his arm and pulled him off to the right.

"Halo, what the hell you want?"

"What you mean what I want? Maybe I want a lap dance so I can feel that wet pussy stroking my dick."

I rolled my eyes. "Halo, it's over between us. When you gonna get that shit in your head?"

"Baby it ain't ova till I say it is. Now can I have a lap dance or what?"

I blew out a heavy breath. Sometimes I felt like I was talking to a fucking brick wall when it came to this dude. He just wasn't ready to let go. Damn, I know I got some bomb-ass pussy, but this shit was getting beyond ridiculous. "I said no."

He grabbed my hand and laced my fingers with his. "Oh, so I see how you are. I'm not good enough but that mutha-fucka ova there is."

"Damn, Halo, either leave me the fuck alone or I'm calling security." I snatched my hand and signaled to Trey that I would be right back. I was so sick of Halo thinking I still belonged to him.

I strolled into the girls' locker room and Honey was in back, changing into a short orange dress with high splits on each side.

"Can I bum some baby wipes?" she said.

I nodded and turned the combination to my lock. The whole time I could feel her eyes on me. "What?"

"That dude I saw you wit is so got damn fine!"

Despite Halo's drama, I couldn't resist a grin. "Yeah, he's a friend of mine."

"Friend, huh?" Intrigued curiosity was written all over her face, although I could tell she was trying to hide it. "Well if that's the case, can a sistah get a hook-up?" I guess something in my face told her hell no because her eyes got big. "Oh, hell nah! Is that the dude you went out with the other night?"

I shrugged. "Yeah, something like that." I handed her a wipe, but before she took it from my hand she looked me dead in the eyes.

"Girl, you know Halo will kill you if he finds out somebody else is getting his pussy, right?"

She was joking, but I was starting to think that there was some truth to what she was saying.

19

Monica

I lay in bed with my arms wrapped tightly around Tremayne as I waited for my breathing to return to normal.

That man was an amazing lover, to say the least. After making him wait almost a month before I finally decided to give him some, we'd been trying to steal moments alone together every chance I got. Fridays had become our time to share. With the girls at school and me not having any classes, he usually played hooky part of the morning to come over and make sure I was made love to. And what a wonderful job he did. Anthony had been my first, but thank goodness he hadn't been my last.

Speaking of sex . . . my hands traveled across his hip and down between his legs, where I started stroking him. Within seconds I felt him spring to life. He groaned. "If you wake Joe up, I'm gonna have to put him somewhere."

"That's the plan," I purred.

True to his warning, Tremayne flipped me onto my back and slid inside. He then rose up on his forearms and stared down into my eyes. I loved watching his expressions while we made love. With every pump we stared at one another, and I always knew when he was close to coming. He slowed down his pace and ran kisses along my neck, then traveled down to take one of my nipples in his mouth. While he sucked, he thrust in and out of my body. I rocked to meet each one of his strokes with one of my own.

"Feel good to you?" he breathed against my neck.

"Yes, baby. It feels *sooo* good." I whimpered and then I pulled him even deeper so he was hitting my spot, and within seconds I was crying out his name.

Afterward we lay in each other's arms and drifted off to sleep. The alarm was set for one o'clock, so we had plenty of time for another round and a shower before the girls arrived home from school. I was slobbering on his chest when I heard the doorbell. I tried to ignore it, figuring it couldn't have been anybody this time of the day but a Jehovah's Witness or a delivery, and I wasn't expecting anything. But when the ringing persisted, I finally groaned and got up from the comfortable bed and reached for my robe on the back of the door and headed downstairs. I looked through the peephole and wanted to scream.

It was Reyna.

I swung the door open, ready to give her a piece of my mind for ruining my perfect afternoon. She knew I was spending it with Tremayne because I had called her last night to cancel our weekly ritual. Over the phone I could tell she was pissed off at me because I was putting a man in front of our friendship, but Reyna knew as well as I did a good man was hard to find.

Any thoughts of yelling at her crashed and burned when I saw her red eyes. "Reyna, what's wrong?"

She pushed past me and stormed into the house. "You will not believe what that bastard did," she said, bottom lip quivering uncontrollably.

"What bastard?" I don't know how many times I've told Reyna she has a bad habit of starting at the middle instead of the beginning of the story.

"Monty."

"Who is Monty?" I asked, because for the life of me I couldn't keep up.

"This guy I met a couple of weeks ago." She moved into the living room and flopped down onto a wingback chair, which meant she had no intention of leaving any time soon. Sighing, I decided to play along for a few moments, then I was putting her the hell out. I just wasn't in the mood for relationship drama.

"What happened?"

She had to take several deep breaths just to calm her nerves enough to speak. "Well, after you *canceled* on me last night, I decided that maybe I needed to start spending more time getting to know Monty, so I gave him a call. He was happy to hear from me and invited me to have breakfast with him. You know I never pass up a good meal, so I met him for breakfast. Afterward, he invited me back to his place. I followed him there and one thing led to another and we were in his bedroom."

I kept thinking about Tremayne lying upstairs in my bedroom naked, where I should be instead of down here listening to my girl getting her freak on with another dude she barely knew.

"Anyway, we had sex and I drifted off to sleep, then we had sex again. It wasn't until I woke up with Monty fucking me that I realized there were two of them in bed with me."

My head whipped around so fast, it's a wonder I hadn't gotten whiplash. "What do you mean, two of them?"

"He and his twin brother! I hadn't fucked one man, but twins. They were laughing and talking about how good the pussy had been and then tried to slide back under the covers with me for a ménage à trois."

My bottom lip dropped. I couldn't have even begun to imagine how embarrassed she had been.

She started crying. "I have never felt so violated in my life!"

I felt so bad for Reyna. I wrapped my arms around her and tried to comfort her. I would have thought she was into that kind of freaky shit, but I guess I was wrong.

"I couldn't get out that apartment fast enough. They had even taken digital pictures! It was some kind of sick joke." My heart went out for my best friend. Nothing worse than a man, or in her case, two men making you feel like a whore.

I released her and watched her wipe the tears from her eyes. She then looked down and started giggling. "You really don't have any titties, do you?"

I noticed my robe had fallen open. Frowning, I pulled it tight and adjusted the belt. "*Whatever*. According to my man, I have plenty. Anyway, I'm sorry that happened to you, but you are interrupting our quality time."

She jerked back like she had just been slapped. "You're kidding, right? I just told you I had been used by a couple of perverted twins and you're ready to kick me out?"

"Reyna, I'm not gonna kick you out. You're more than welcome to stay if you wanna, but I got a man who took off to spend the afternoon with me and I plan to do just that. If you want, we can hang out this evening before I head to the club. Maybe take the girls to McDonald's so they can play in the jungle gym."

Her eyes narrowed and she glanced up the stairs. "I thought you were supposed to be my best friend. Where was your man last week when you needed fifteen hundred dollars for a new air conditioner? Whose shoulder did you cry on when Anthony threatened to take custody of the girls? I'm always there for you, but lately you don't seem to have time for me anymore. I thought we were best friends."

I hate it when she's right. After that whole double-team bullshit with Anthony and Rosa, I headed straight to Reyna's boutique and vented. Reyna had even locked the door and put up the OUT TO LUNCH sign so we wouldn't have any interruptions, then she listened patiently to every detail. I still couldn't believe Anthony had tried to get me to sell my kids to him and that fake-ass Barbie. As a result, we were back on our regular scheduled visitations according to the divorce decree. You should have seen his face when I told him he was about to meet the bitch in me. He called, tried to apologize, and even offered the money to fix the air conditioner but I told him to kiss my ass and accepted Reyna's offer. I hated to take it, but it was either that or burn the fuck up, and that wasn't happening. I'm sure Tremayne would have loaned me the money but I didn't even want to go there. I already depended on one man, and I wasn't about to do that again.

"Reyna, I am your best friend."

"Best friends don't let anyone get in the way of their friendships." She was talking loud, but she looked more hurt than angry.

"Sorry, but you can't fuck me like he does," I said, teasing, but she didn't see anything funny.

"Monica, men come a dime a dozen but friendships are forever. You know you're the closest thing I have to a sister."

"And so are you, but I've got a man and needs." I couldn't believe she was even trying to go there. "Damn, Reyna, quit acting like you don't understand."

"It's not that I don't understand . . . I'm just jealous." She playfully stuck out her lip and I gave her a big hug.

"You'll find a good man soon enough." I already had a good man, probably better than I deserved.

Rising, she headed toward the door. "I'm glad you've got faith because I'm starting to wonder if I ever will."

20

Robin

The only reason I was back was because Trey had insisted that Deena needed to talk to me. It would have been better if she had just passed the information on to Trey, but he said she was adamant about talking to me herself.

As soon as I stepped into the visitor's room, she was already sitting on the other side of the glass with the phone in her hand. She gave me a smile that I tried to return, but it's hard when you're the last place you want to be. Besides, I still hated her ass.

"Thanks for coming," she said the second I picked up the receiver. The bags under her eyes were heavy, and I could tell being locked up was starting to take its toll on her. Part of me wanted to say something to ease her mind, but I just couldn't bring myself to do it. I knew I was being stubborn, but as far as I was concerned, she deserved it for forcing her way back into my life.

"The only reason why I'm back here is because Trey told me you really needed to see me."

The last two weeks had been amazing. Trey was such a good man. He taught me so much about relationships and trust, something I've always had a problem with. It seemed like every time I put my trust into someone, something always happened to fuck things up, but Trey taught me that being with someone meant learning to take risks. I don't know how I got so lucky. The only problem I seemed to be having was juggling my relationship with him and servicing the needs of my clients. Don't get me wrong, I was committed to our relationship, but at the same time I had to make my money. I was meeting my regulars at the hotel in the afternoon so I had plenty of time to pick Kyle up from day care.

"I wanted to thank you personally for hiring me the attorney. He's seems committed to helping me. That's more than I could say about that public defender."

I let out a rude snort. The attorney wasn't all that great. He hadn't even been able to get reasonable bail. I didn't have one hundred thousand dollars, and even if I did, I doubt I would have put it up for her ass. Besides, Kyle was seriously growing on me and I wasn't in such a rush to get rid of that little rugrat as I had been in the beginning. I figured he was family, so the least I could do was share my crib with him until whatever was supposed to happen happened. Besides, if Deena was free she would be trying to get together and talk about the past. When it came to her trying to push her way back into my life, I preferred her ass behind bars.

"If that's all you needed, you could have sent that message with Trey." I rose and got ready to leave when I heard her plea.

"Robin, please," she pleaded. "Don't go. I really wanna chance to talk."

I leaned back in the chair and rolled my eyes, making sure she knew she was wasting my time. "Go ahead."

She wrung her hands and leaned across the table. "I want you to know I would never kill anyone. I swear to you."

She was pleading with me. Tears were in her eyes and I felt something stir in my gut. The big sister I knew would never have hurt a fly, but that was a long long time ago, and people changed. "That's between you and God."

"Trust me . . . I've been down on my knees since I got in

this place . . . but I'm scared, Robbie. I really don't think anyone believes me."

I glared through the glass, trying not to look at the fear in her eyes. For some crazy reason it was important for her to know that the only family she had in the world had her back. Well, that was too bad. She'd turned her back on me when I had needed her most.

"Why don't you start by telling me what really happened?"

She looked pleased that I hadn't flat-out rejected her, even though that was exactly what I wanted to do. Deena took a few moments to pull herself together, then took a deep breath and started stuttering nervously as she spoke. "For real, I don't know what happened."

She was already starting off with a lie. "What do you mean you don't know?" I wasn't in the mood for games. If she was going to waste my time, then there was no reason for me to be sticking around.

"I'm serious! I don't know what happened. Mannie and I had been—"

"Mannie? Mannie who?" I hoped to hell it wasn't the Mannie I knew.

"Marvin Hollingsworth. Tall . . . dark skin . . . with an open-faced gold tooth on the right. Why? You know him?" she asked suspiciously. "He worked for this drug dealer they called Dollar."

I tried to nod like it was no big deal, but my hands were shaking because I knew him all too well. *Fuck.* Dollar worked for Halo. *It's a small world after all.* All along we'd been running around in the same circle. "Uh-huh, I know who he is."

"Well, he's the man they *think* I murdered."

I vaguely remembered Honey mentioning Mannie getting smoked, but I tried to ignore anything that had to do with Halo and that life. What was even more fucked up was that Mercedes kicked it for years with Mannie's trifling ass.

"So what happened?" I asked, suddenly interested in hearing her story.

"Well, he had taken me to see that new movie with Zoe Saldana. We were walking across the parking lot when someone grabbed me from behind. There were three of them, and Mannie tried to fight them off but one of them stuck me in the arm with something sharp like a needle and everything went black. The next thing I remembered was waking up in bed with Mannie lying beside me covered in blood. Before I could figure out what happened, the police stormed inside my apartment and carted me off."

I tried to make some sense of what she was saying. Had she been drugged?

"Why would someone try to kill Mannie?"

She hesitated, avoiding eye contact. "Mannie said this dude named Halo thought he was stealing from him."

"Was he?" Shit, I didn't believe in beating around the bush.

She took a moment and shrugged, then looked up at me. "Yeah, he was skimming a little off the top, but Mannie didn't think anyone would notice."

She obviously didn't know Halo like I did. "You ever meet Halo?"

Deena shook her head. "Only in passing."

"Well, let me tell you, he's bad news. Can't nothing get past that muthafucka. He knows what his soldiers are doing at all time."

"How do you know so much?" she asked suspiciously.

I looked down at my freshly manicured fingernails so she couldn't see the truth. "Who doesn't know who he is? Let's just say he's not someone to mess with." I was too ashamed to admit I had once been in love with that psycho. "I'm curious . . . how in the world you got mixed up with someone like Mannie in the first place?" Not that I was one to talk.

"I met him at the mall. Can you believe that shit? The

same place I met him was the last place I saw him alive. He was good to me . . . and Kyle." She was emotional again and I could tell she had really been feeling that dude. I don't know why. Don't get me wrong, Mannie was fine as hell with a Tootsie Roll complexion and light brown eyes, but he was no good just like all the rest of them. I loved me a thug with a bad-boy image, but all them dudes that ran with Halo treated their women like shit.

"I thought he was my ticket out of Virginia. He'd been talking about moving down to Miami, since the real estate was cheap, and buying something close to the ocean. We were all set to leave in two weeks."

"Did he tell anyone he was leaving?"

She frowned. "No, we didn't tell anyone. We were planning to sneak out while no one was watching. He said Dollar would never let him outta the game even if he asked."

She was right. Loyalty was one thing Halo insisted on. If he suspected disloyalty, he would have you killed. Everyone was scared of him and had every reason to be.

"What's your lawyer saying?"

Deena shook her head. "He's trying to do everything he can, but he says things aren't looking too good for me. If they had taken a blood and alcohol sample after I was arrested, then maybe I could prove I had been drugged. What's worse is that there was gunpowder residue on my hands and my fingerprints are all over the gun. But I swear I didn't kill him. Someone is trying to set me up."

I had a feeling everything had been staged. And for the first time, I actually felt sorry for my sister.

We talked a few more minutes before the guard signaled our visit was over. I rose from the chair. "I'll see you around."

"Wait!" she screamed and I brought the receiver back to my ear. "You believe me, don't you?"

I hesitated before I finally nodded and said, "Yes, Dee-Dee, I believe you."

Smiling, she was clearly pleased by my answer. "Thank you, Robbie. That means so much to me." Tears were streaming down her cheeks, and I won't lie, they were burning the corners of my eyes as well; but there was no way I was going to allow her to see me cry, so I pushed them back and walked away.

21

Monica

Liese barely had the paper bracelet around her arm before she jetted off behind her sister. "Slow down before you fall!" I called as they hurried over to a small merry-go-round. While I watched them play, I thought, those were *my* darlings. I would be damned if I let my ex and that skinny-ass bitch take them away from me.

I took a seat at a table close enough to keep an eye on them. They each had a cup filled with tokens, so it would be a while before they were ready to leave, which was fine with me. I reached inside my purse for my anatomy book and got to reading, but made sure I looked up every few seconds to see if the girls were still in my view.

"Deja, is that you?"

My head snapped up in a start. If someone was calling me by my stage name, then that meant they knew I danced at Scandalous. I looked at the woman standing in front of me and felt a wave of relief when I noticed it was Treasure. "Hey," I replied, then looked around to see if anyone had heard her. The last thing I wanted was to put my business in the streets.

Treasure looked fabulous as ever and had me reaching up to comb my fingers through my spikes. She was wearing a pair of low-rise jeans that hugged her small hips and a tight blue shirt that cinched her tiny waist and big-ass breasts. Her long golden hair perfectly framed her face. She was the total package.

"What are you doing here?" I said as my eyes traveled down to the adorable little boy holding her hand. I would have never imagined her as a mother.

"Thought I'd bring my nephew out so he could burn off some energy," she said while stuffing his pockets with tokens. "Okay . . . go ahead . . . and stay where I can see you." Grinning, he nodded and dashed off to join the rest of the kids who were near the front stage, dancing with Chuck E. Cheese.

"That boy is a handful!" Treasure groaned as she flopped down on the bench across from me.

"Tell me about it. I have two." I pointed to Liese and Arissa, who were holding hands and dancing around with all the others.

Treasure glanced down at her phone, then over at my book. "What are you reading?"

I looked up to see if she was curious or just being nosy. I wasn't quite sure which one it was. "I'm in school, studying to be a nurse."

Her eyes lit up and she appeared to be truly impressed. "That's whassup. I've been thinking about going back to school someday but I'm not sure what I wanna be when I grow up." She giggled like a schoolgirl and I joined in with her. "You working tonight?" she asked.

I nodded. "Mmm-hmm, I'll be there."

Treasure leaned back on the bench and I caught her studying me. "I'm curious . . . as smart as you are . . . what made you decide to strip?"

I dropped my head and blushed. "What kind of question is that?"

She shrugged. "I'm just curious. You just don't seem like the type."

I thought about it for a hot second. "Is there really a type?"

"Yeah, actually there is. Most of the girls are from broken

homes . . . with no education . . . been pimped out . . . even abused."

I quickly shook my head. The last thing I wanted was for her to put me in that category. "No no no, it's nothing like that. I've got two mouths to feed, so I'm willing to do whatever it takes to support my family until I graduate and can provide a better life."

"I've got mad respect for ya," Treasure said with a grin. "It takes a lot of guts to do what we do."

Since she was all up in my business, I figured it was a good time to get in hers. "What about you? What's your story? I mean . . . why do you do it?"

"Shit, I don't know how to do nothing else. After my parents were killed in a car accident, I spent several years in foster care. The day I turned seventeen, I hit the streets, got emancipated from the system, and never looked back. It's a way to survive and I've learned how to make it work for me."

I have to admit she was raw, but I liked that about her. "What about your sister?"

Treasure gave a rude snort then leaned back on the bench. "My sister's in jail. I got her son because I didn't want him in the system."

"What?"

She looked uncomfortable, like she had said more than she wished she had. "Girl . . . I'm not even gonna go there, but let's just say . . . it's a tripped-out situation." On cue, her stomach growled. "Shit, I'm starving. I'm gonna get something to eat." She slid off the bench and rose.

"Wait . . . I'll go with you."

By the time we got our food, Treasure and I were talking like longtime friends. It's crazy, because I would never have guessed I would have related to any of those women, but Treasure was as real as it got, and I appreciated that quality in her. She didn't talk much about her personal life, but I figured she was a private person and had every reason to be.

"The girls and I are going to see that new Pixar movie when we leave here, you wanna join us?"

"Hell yeah . . . whatever it takes to wear his little ass out."

We were eating hot wings and talking about the other girls at the club when I spotted Reyna coming our way. She looked adorable in blue jeans, a hot pink top, and matching pumps.

"Hey, girl . . . sorry I'm late! It was packed at the shop. I couldn't even take a second to go pee." I noticed her looking suspiciously out of the corner of her eyes at Treasure. "Don't I know you?"

"Reyna, this is . . ." It was then that I realized I had forgotten Treasure's real name.

"Whassup . . . I'm Robin."

"We *work* together," I offered, hoping I wouldn't have to come out and say it.

It took Reyna a few moments to understand what I was trying to communicate before her eyes got large. "Oh, yeah. *That's* where I saw you at." She took a seat at the table but I could see her sizing Treasure up, taking in her hair and her clothes. Envy was so obvious. Women can be so petty at times.

"So what were y'all talking about?" Reyna acted like she had missed something.

Treasure shrugged and so did I. "We were just talking about the girls at the club." I met her glance and we started laughing.

Reyna looked from me to her. "What am I missing?"

I gave her a dismissive wave. "Nothing you would understand. You'd have to be there to understand."

Treasure wiped buffalo sauce from her mouth, then rose. "I'll be back. I'm gonna go check on Kyle."

I nodded, then glanced over to the girls to make sure they were in sight. They were. As soon as Treasure was far enough away, Reyna kicked my feet under the table.

"Damn, what you kick me for?"

"What's going on? So now you're hanging out with strippers too."

She can be such a bitch at times. "I'm not hanging. I was already here with the girls when she came in with her nephew. What's the big deal?"

"The big deal is you don't want anyone to catch you with that chick. Look at how she's dressed . . . like she's a streetwalker or something. What the hell is up with that?"

"I don't see anything wrong with what she has on."

"She looks like she's getting ready to work the pole in here. Look at the way she's walking. Every man up in here has his eyes on her ass."

"And . . . so what? You jealous?"

"I am chocolate super deluxe . . . why the hell would I be jealous of that bitch?"

Whatever. She was jealous. I could see it in her eyes. "Why she gotta be a bitch? Remember, it was *your* idea I work at Scandalous in the first place . . . not mine."

"Yeah, that was to pay your bills. I didn't say hang with the girls. Come on Monica. You've got a reputation. What would Anthony say if he found out?"

I looked at her and rolled my eyes for even mentioning that bastard name's after that stunt he and Rosa pulled. "Reyna, don't piss me off."

She blew out a long breath and must have seen something in my eyes that said, *Don't even go there with me.* "Fine. Fine," she hissed, then conveniently changed the subject. "You and the girls wanna come over my house and help me make ice cream?"

I glanced up and spotted Treasure returning to the table. Sure enough, some guy with a receding hairline was watching her ass and had almost run into the salad bar. "No, Treasure . . . I mean Robin and I are gonna take the kids to the movies."

"Are you for real?" Reyna looked like I had slapped her in

the face. "I can see you're forgetting who your *real* friends are." She rose. "I'm gonna go and talk to my goddaughters. I advise you to take a few moments and think about what it is you're doing." With that she stormed away, swinging her wide ass, bumping into anyone who was in her way.

I'd dealt with insecurity, but Reyna's jealousy was definitely starting to get out of hand.

22

Robin

"Thank you, boo," I purred, then climbed off his lap, grabbed my dress, and escorted him out of the VIP section. It had been a crazy slow night, so I was thankful for the private dance.

The club was hyped and there were a few stragglers at the stage watching Honey shake her skinny ass. I made my way through the female chatter in the dressing room and moved to the lockers in back. Two dykes were on the bench in front of my locker getting a late-night snack. Chloe was sitting down with her legs spread wide while Diamond was down on her hands and knees, licking the hell out of her pussy. Both of them had men at home.

"Hell nah! Y'all need to take that shit somewhere else!" Without stopping, I moved straight to my locker and pushed them outta my way and turned the lock. Chloe, who looked like she was a second away from having an orgasm, opened her eyes and rolled them at me.

"Damn, Treasure! You coulda at least waited a few more minutes."

"Nah, I ain't got that kinda time." I shooed her like a pesky fly, reached inside for a baby wipe, and started wiping myself off. She rose and I caught that bitch staring at me.

Chloe grinned. "We would love to do a threesome with you." She gazed at Diamond, then leaned over and stuck her tongue down her throat.

"Only if the money is right. Now y'all bitches need to get the fuck away from me." I grinned when I said it, but I was dead serious. I wasn't getting down with that shit unless someone was flashing some real money in my face.

I was changing into another costume when Mercedes sashayed into the locker room. I looked over at the puzzled look on her face.

"What's up with you?" I could tell whatever it was, it was killing her to ask me.

"You got a tampon I can bum off you?"

If she was asking, then chances were nobody else had one. It was Wednesday, and House Mom only worked on the weekends and the club never had any tampons in the machines in the bathroom.

"Yeah, I got you." I laughed, then reached inside my locker. All night I had been trying to think of a way to come out and ask Mercedes about Mannie's death. If anyone knew what had happened, she would. "Hey, you wanna go on stage with me for my next set? That crowd out there has been begging for a sixty-nine. I think if we double-team them with all *this*, they won't know what hit them." I gave her a knowing look and smiled.

I knew she would be surprised by my suggestion. I rarely allowed another woman the chance to go on stage with me, and when I did it was usually for some ebony-and-ivory action. But if I wanted to get any information from Mercedes, I needed to show her we were still cool.

"Hell yeah." I knew she wouldn't turn me down.

She took the tampon and lowered on the bench where Chloe was just getting her coochie eaten out. "Can I bum a wipe too?" she said.

I handed her one, and she slipped down her G-string and started cleaning off. "Hey . . . Treasure . . . that new chick Deja . . . what you know about her?"

I gave her a curious look. "What you mean, whadda I know?"

She shrugged and tossed the wipe in a small trash can in the corner. "I mean I think I know her from somewhere, I just can't put my finger on it." She had that vindictive look in her eyes and I could tell she was still salty over Monica stealing one of her regulars. In fact, Monica had been clocking almost as much as me, and several of the dancers were pissed the fuck off about it. "Do you know if she used to fuck with Dollar?"

Monica with a thug? It took everything I had not to laugh. "I doubt it. She ain't even the type," I replied, then decided that it was as good a time as any to ask. "Speaking of thugs . . . damn, girl, why the hell you didn't tell me someone smoked Mannie's ass?"

"I thought you knew," she replied with her eyes locked on mine like she was trying to figure out why I was suddenly being so nice to her. "Everybody was talking about it. That shit was foul. It fucked me up when I heard about it. I went to the funeral. Yo, that shit was sad as hell! They had to have a closed casket."

She spread her legs and pushed the tampon inside, then removed a pocketknife from a purple Crown Royal pouch, cut the string short, and tucked what was left deep inside her cootie-cat.

I remember when I first started stripping I had gone out on stage, stripped off my panties, and spread my thighs. You should have seen how fast them muthafuckas jetted away from around the stage. It wasn't until I made it back to the dressing room that this chick, Delicious, told me the string from my tampon was hanging out for the entire world to see. I learned the hard way. That's why I tried to school the new girls, so they didn't have to go through the shit I went through. Gutter rats weren't trying to do nothing to help anyone but themselves because they felt threatened. I, on the other hand, knew I was too damn good at what I did to worry.

Mercedes lifted her head and I could see anger in her eyes. "Did you know some bitch killed him in his sleep?"

I don't know why, but I got pissed at her for calling my sister a bitch. I could do it, but let someone else talk bad about family and I was ready to pull off my earrings and grab the Vaseline. "I heard they found him in bed with this chick named Deanna or some shit like that. You know her?"

Her eyes started shifting right and left before she finally looked at me and frowned. "Hell nah, I don't know that bitch. Why should I?"

I shrugged like it was no big deal. The last thing I wanted was for her to be suspicious of where I was going with this. "She's friends with my cousin and she was telling me that Deanna had been kicking it with Mannie. In fact, the way she tell it, they were living together."

Mercedes tried to look like she didn't care, but I noticed the way the muscle pulsed at her jaw. One thing about Mercedes, she didn't want Mannie, but she never wanted anyone else to have his crazy ass either. "He's dead now, so I don't give a fuck where he was laying his pipe."

As I slipped a short yellow sequined dress over my head, then pulled it down over my hips, I noticed her fidgeting nervously on the bench. What wasn't she saying?

"You wearing the hell outta that dress," she complimented me, and I could see the envy in her brown eyes. Like I said, that chick was always trying to duplicate.

"Thanks. You know I gotta keep it cute. As soon as I saw it I had to have it." I tied the side and took a moment before I got the conversation back on track. "Anyway, the rumor on the street is that someone else killed Mannie and then left this chick to hang."

Mercedes' eyes shifted to the floor. I had a feeling she knew something that I didn't.

"Ho, don't even try to hide it. Whatcha know?" I moved in closer so she would think her secret was safe with me.

She was shaking her head. I could see her mind racing a mile a minute. "Nothing, but you heard how they found him, right?"

I nodded, then took a seat on the bench and moved in close like we were two friends sharing gossip. "Yeah, I heard. She was lying in the bed with that dead muthafucka when the police broke down the door. They found the gun on the dresser with her fingerprints all over it." I shook my head for dramatic effect.

Mercedes grinned and had the nerve to look pleased. "Yep, that's how I heard it."

"But she's saying she didn't do it . . . that someone drugged her and when she woke up Mannie was dead."

Mercedes sat there shaking her head and staring off into space. Damn! I wished I could get in that ho's head and see what she was thinking.

"I stopped fucking with Mannie because he was being careless. You wouldn't believe how he started acting . . . like he was going to be taking over Halo's operations. I wasn't having none of that shit. There ain't no telling. If I hadn't gotten out when I did . . . that coulda been me that woke up in bed with Mannie."

"So you *do* think someone framed her?" I asked, maybe a tad bit too seriously.

Mercedes rose and stood there for a second with a suspicious look. "Why you care?"

"I don't . . . I just know how scandalous Halo is."

She glanced around, making sure no one was listening, then moved in close and whispered, "All I know is someone said he'd been skimming off the top for months and Halo found out."

She was telling me exactly what Deena had said. "Well, if he was, I guarantee Halo smoked his ass."

Mercedes stared down at her stilettos for several seconds before she raised her head and met my eyes. "Yeah, you're probably right."

23

Monica

Tonight I just wanted to climb up on that stage and strip off my clothes. And that's what scared me.

The money had been flowing for weeks, and bills were no longer a problem for me. It felt like such a weight had been lifted from my shoulders that my ass was floating. I had a strong feeling it was like a crack addiction. It had to be. No matter how much money I made, I still wanted more, and I knew there was plenty to be made. Never had I ever felt that level of determination, not even after sipping one too many drinks. But at Scandalous, I felt a vibe I had never felt before that seemed to take over, and the high energy just ran through my veins.

I finished my set, collected my money, then climbed off the stage smiling inside. Two of my regulars had come in tonight and had tipped me quite nicely. I was moving toward the locker room when I felt an arm snake my waist. As soon as I swung around and saw who it was, my heart jumped. "Damn, you scared the hell outta me!" I pressed a hand to my chest and tried to pull away so I could run back to the dressing room and hide.

"Sorry, beautiful. I told you I thought you looked familiar. Now I know why."

I looked at the devilish grin on Greg's face. I should have known it was likely to happen again sooner or later . . . that I would run into someone I knew. Only it was even worse this time because it was Greg—Anthony's partner. He had already seen me, so it was too late to hide. All I could do was play nice and see what he wanted.

I gestured for him to come a little closer so I could make sure he heard me over the music. "I guess you caught me. I hope between you and me, what happens at Scandalous . . . stays at Scandalous."

"Absolutely. I wouldn't dream of saying anything. That's as long as you're good to me." He stared at me with this hungry look in his eyes like he thought I was a thick juicy steak.

"Sure . . . what do you have in mind?" I painted on a smile and tried to act like it was all good between us.

"How about a lap dance?"

Greg was the last person I wanted to give a lap dance, but business was business. Besides, as long as his money was green, why should it matter? Reluctantly, I took his hand and led him up to the VIP section and moved to the last couch on the end. I waited until he was sitting down, grinning like a kid who stole something, before I said, "What will it be? One song for twenty-five . . . two for forty, or the deluxe for a hundred."

"What's the deluxe?" he asked liked he was ordering lunch from the drive-thru window. I almost didn't want to respond.

"Bareback."

Grinning, Greg reached inside his pocket and peeled off a crisp $100 bill.

I removed my dress, and for the first time I felt like a whore. And to think I was loving this shit a few minutes ago. Damn that man, I thought as I slid my panties down and kicked them away. He was the reason why dancers left this place feeling like shit. I straddled his lap and started gyrating my hips to the sounds of Ludacris. Greg started rocking his hips with me. "You are so beautiful, Monica."

I hated the way he said my name . . . like I had done something bad. "It's *Deja*."

He released a hearty chuckle. "Whatever you say. Like I said, your secret is safe with me."

I needed to believe he wouldn't say anything for just a little while longer. By then I would have graduated and quit dancing, so it would no longer matter.

When he brought his hands around to cup my breasts, I stilled. "There's no touching."

"C'mon. You can't make an exception for me?" he asked, eyes dancing with amusement.

I guess I didn't have much of a choice, now did I? I continued to gyrate my hips while he caressed and fondled my breasts.

This can't be happening.

I glanced over at the bouncer at the corner of the VIP section, waiting for him to wave his flashlight, but he was too busy talking to another dancer to notice. The only person who seemed to be paying attention was Mercedes, who had the nerve to grin. No doubt she wanted to make sure I knew she had witnessed me in action.

Greg had paid for four songs, so I was either going to give him his money back and take a chance of him telling Anthony, or give him what he wanted and hope he never came back. Anthony's threat to take the girls echoed in my ears, leaving me with only one choice: sit there and deal with it. The only consolation was that he was compensating me for my time.

When he brought his hand around and fondled my pussy, all I could do was rock against his hand and breath heavily close to his ear. "You like that, don't you?" he hissed.

"Oh yeah," I moaned pretending I enjoyed what he was doing.

"I bet Anthony couldn't make you feel this way, could he?" He slipped his finger inside and moved it in and out. *God help me.* As much as I wanted to scratch his eyes out, and knew it was wrong, I couldn't do anything. It was scary and humiliating at the same time. It wasn't until the middle of the fourth song that Gus finally flashed his light over toward the couch and, thank goodness, Greg removed his finger. I wanted to go over there and scream, "What the hell took you so long?" But I know for a fact dancers have been caught fucking up here numerous times. The bouncers knew. They just figured if they didn't say anything, we'd break them off a piece. Well, he wasn't getting shit from me.

I slid off his lap like it had suddenly caught on fire and swung my hair away from my face. Greg just sat there smiling.

"That was nice," he finally said.

I struggled to keep a straight face as I put my clothes back on. By the time I tied my dress on the side, he rose and stood before me.

"I'd like to see you again. What days do you work?"

"Tuesday, Friday, and Saturday." I couldn't believe I was telling him that, but then what else could I do?

"Good . . . I'll see you then." He reached inside his pocket, pulled out another $100 and slipped it inside my G-string, and when his fingertip grazed my crotch, I jumped.

"That's for being so nice to me." Chuckling, he winked, then left the balcony.

I waited until he had gone back onto the dance floor before I followed. Unfortunately, Mercedes was waiting at the top of the stairs. I watched as she blatantly eyed me from head to toe with her lips scrunched up like I had just passed gas.

"You know . . . it's ho's like you got muthafucka coming in here treating us like tricks." With that she spun on her heels and stormed down the stairs.

That was one time I couldn't even argue.

24

Robin

"Let me go in back and see if I've got any extra-skinny on hand," Reyna sneered.

I rolled my eyes and watched as she walked to the back of her shop. *Bitch.* If it hadn't been for Monica, I wouldn't even be in her little boutique in the first place. But Monica had been raving about Reyna's Couture, a shop prominently displayed on Sycamore Street in downtown Petersburg. She had been talking about how cute her clothes were, so when she invited me to go to lunch and insisted we drop by, I agreed.

Big mistake.

I couldn't stand that chick. Reyna acted like she owned Monica, the way she kept jumping into every conversation, making it clear they were best friends for life. From the second we stepped into her little-ass shop, she'd been turning up her nose at me, talking about how skinny I was and that she catered to women with curves. If it wasn't for Monica, I would have cussed her fat ass out minutes ago but I was trying to hold my tongue because I could tell it was important to Monica that the two of us hit it off.

She and I had been hanging out quite a bit—going to the park, movies, and even out to eat. Kyle loved her girls, and I was glad to let him play with them and give me a break because that boy demanded all my undivided attention.

"You're in luck. I found a size *extra-skinny* in back," Reyna commented on her return.

I took the proffered dress from her hand. "Thanks."

I held up the yellow wraparound dress and made a show of examining it. It was the best-looking thing I'd seen so far. It had a cinched waist and capped sleeves, and was perfect to go with these slamming chocolate pumps I had found at Saks. I was definitely planning to buy the dress. I just wasn't ready to let that fat cow know that yet.

"Ooh, Robin! That dress will look perfect on you. Why don't you go in back and try it on." Monica was ooohing and aahing and pointed to the small dressing room to the right.

"I guess it won't hurt to try it on."

Reyna stood to the right looking like she didn't want me to try it on. Too bad; if that was the case then she should have pretended she couldn't find one in a size six.

I moved into the room and within minutes I had the dress on. Just as I suspected, it was fabulous on me. I strutted out of the dressing room and made sure everyone else knew it. "Whadda you think?"

Monica turned from the shoes displayed on the wall and smiled as I turned from side to side. "Dang, girl, you wearing that dress!"

Reyna walked over with arms folded across her chest and scrunched up her face. That woman barely came to my shoulder and was almost three times my size. The way she was looking at me only cosigned everything Monica had just said, but since she was jealous of skinny women, I wasn't at all surprised by her response.

"Hmm, I guess you don't look bad for someone with a flat ass."

"Flat ass? I don't know what you're looking at because I've got plenty of junk in my trunk." To emphasize my meaning, I bounced my ass, then dropped it like it was hot. Monica laughed along with me but Reyna didn't see anything funny.

"Uh, I know this might be hard for you to understand, but, um . . . this ain't no strip club." She then stormed off to assist another customer.

Monica shook her head. "Robin, don't pay her no mind."

"Shit, I ain't thinking about your girl. She's just mad because I make this dress look better than that damn mannequin." Grinning, I turned on my heels and went back to change. While I was slipping on my jeans, my cell phone rang. I glanced down at the screen. "What the hell does he want?" I mumbled when I saw Halo's number on the screen. Ignoring it, I let the call go to voice mail. By the time I had made it back to the front, Monica had a pair of rhinestone jeans in her hands. "Those are cute."

"Well, of course they are. That's why I picked them out for her," Reyna sneered from out of nowhere. "Are you buying that dress or do I need to hang it back up?"

"Robin, you better buy it or I'm kicking your butt," Monica urged.

"I'm buying the dress." I moved up to the counter and reached inside my purse. I hadn't had a chance to run by the bank this morning, so inside I had a stack of one-dollar bills. I could have used my debit card but since Reyna was such a bitch, I decided to make her work for her money.

"That will be a hundred dollars."

I handed her the stack and almost burst out in laughter at the disgusted look on her face.

Monica noticed what I had done and started chuckling. "Reyna, I don't know why you tripping, because I'm about to give you the same thing." Sure enough, she reached inside her purse and pulled out a wad of bills. Laughing, I gave her a high five and watched as Reyna personally counted each bill, barely touching them like the money was diseased or something. Whatever.

"Let's go get something to eat." The sooner I got the hell away from Reyna, the better.

Monica nodded and moved up to the register. "Cool, I'm starving."

"Why don't you wait until my relief gets here, then I can go too," Reyna insisted.

Hell no. The last thing I wanted to do was share a meal with that chick. Thank goodness Monica shook her head.

"Reyna, I'm about to pass out. We're going to run to Louise's for catfish. Just come over and join us when you get lunch."

Reyna nodded with her lips poked out. I didn't care how mad she was. That chick rubbed me the wrong way. As soon as we were alone, I was going to make sure Monica knew how I felt.

"Monica, what is up with your girl?" I asked as soon as our waiter left with our orders.

She shrugged like it was no big deal. "Reyna just acts funny like that. She has a hard time making friends."

"I see why. That bitch wears my nerves. I was ready to let her have it."

Monica reached for her water glass and tried to explain. "She doesn't mean any harm. Just at times she comes off too strong. We've been friends for years, and I guess she's afraid someone else will step in and take her place."

"Whatever, I think the chick has issues."

"No, she's really a sweet person. Will give you the shirt off your back if you need it. You might not believe it, but it was her idea for me to audition at Scandalous."

She was right. I didn't believe it. "I know you lying. That chick acts like she can't stand me because I'm a stripper."

"No, she's jealous because she wishes it was her chunky ass up on that stage. You should have seen her at home swinging around that pole in her basement."

My eyes widened. I couldn't believe what she was saying. "You is killing me!"

She was cracking up. "I'm serious, but don't say anything. She bought some poles and a video. That's how I learned how to do the few moves I know."

I still had a hard time believing that. I sipped my lemonade and glanced down at my watch. I needed to pick up Kyle in another hour.

"She really is a good person," Monica insisted. "Just has a few insecurity issues, but she's like a sister to me."

"I guess that's why I don't have a sister."

Monica gave me a strange look, and it took me a moment to realize what I had said. "I thought Kyle was your sister's child?"

Damn. Okay, I put my foot in my mouth with that one. Now what the hell was I supposed to say? I didn't like talking about my personal life with folks, but I guess I didn't have a choice but to explain. Monica was cool so I felt I at least owed her that much.

"My sister and I are not close . . . we haven't been for years."

I could tell that all I was doing was confusing her even more. "Then what are you doing with her son?"

"While she's in jail I don't have much of a choice."

"Jail!"

At the sound of her annoying voice, my eyes snapped over toward Reyna, who just so happened to make it to the restaurant in record time. "Oh, hell no," I cursed.

For someone who couldn't go to lunch until her relief came in an hour, she sure broke her neck to get to the restaurant in under thirty minutes.

I guess I wasn't the only person who'd noticed. Monica made a show of glancing down at the slender watch on her wrist, and then up at her. "I thought your lunch wasn't until one?"

Laughing, she gave a dismissive wave. "Shana got there early, so since I was starving I thought I would go ahead and eat with my friends."

Friends? I couldn't help but laugh. A friend was the last thing I would ever consider her.

"Did you already order?" she asked as she lowered onto the chair to my right. Monica nodded, and don't you know Reyna had the nerve to look disappointed that we hadn't waited for her needy ass. I didn't understand how Monica's friends with that chick.

My cell phone vibrated and I reached for my phone in my Prada purse and frowned. It was Halo. Why the hell couldn't he stop calling me?

"Stalker on your hands?" I looked up at the smug look on Reyna's face. "Girl, it's okay, I've got one of those myself. They just don't seem to understand when a sistah says she's done, she's done."

I had to smile at that one. I guess she was trying to make up for being a bitch earlier.

Our food arrived and Reyna ordered a salad and then we chatted about the upcoming fashion show she was planning at her boutique.

"Robin, I would really like it if you'd model for me. With a shape like yours, you'd make everything I'm selling look good."

I was stunned by the compliment, being that it was coming out of that crazy chick's mouth. "That's funny, because earlier you said my butt was flat," I replied sarcastically.

"Girl, I was just playing! I had to find something to complain about. For a little chick you got an ass, although Monica's got you beat!"

"Whatever," she mumbled.

We laughed and I was starting to relax a little bit and was thinking maybe Reyna wasn't so bad and I was too quick to judge; however, just as I was considering giving her the bene-fit of the doubt, she had to say something to put up the radar again.

"I happened to walk in while you were talking about your sister. Why's she in jail?"

I looked over at Monica, who was staring down at her salad. Ms. Nosy was leaned across the table waiting to hear some juicy gossip. I decided to let her have it.

"She killed her boyfriend. Shot him in the head twice with his gun."

Reyna's eyes grew large. I guess it was because I spoke so loud I made sure the couple at the next two tables had heard as well.

"How's she doing?" Monica asked between bites.

"About as well as expected."

She shook her head with compassion while Reyna looked amused by the whole thing. "Murder, huh?" She ran her tongue across her lips in a mischievous smirk. "I hope your sis-ter has a good lawyer. One of my customers . . . her brother just got twenty-five years for shooting a man." Reyna acted like we were discussing the weather.

"Actually she does. I hired a damn good legal team."

"It's a good thing she has you in her corner," Monica said. "The last thing she wants is to leave her future in the hands of a public defender."

"I know that's right," Reyna chimed in. "So why'd she do it? Was he beating her?"

I bit into my fish and ignored her question.

Monica cleared her throat and mumbled, "Reyna, quit ask-ing folks their personal business."

"Why? We're all friends, right?" She made a show of throwing her hands up in the air. "If your sister went burning bed on his ass, then I ain't mad at her."

I had to count to three, backward, on that one to resist the urge to punch her in the mouth. Monica looked uncomfortable. "Robin, you know I'm here if you ever need me to watch Kyle for you."

I glanced across the table and smiled. "Thanks, Monica. I appreciate that."

"Yes, she's right," Reyna chimed in, although her tone was anything but supportive. "If you ever need a friend to talk to, Monica and I are always here to be supportive." She leaned in closer and flashed me a coy smile, "So tell me . . . how she kill him? C'mon . . . paint a picture and take me there."

"Get the fuck outta my face!" I pushed my chair back and rose so fast, Reyna fell backward out of her seat and hit the floor. "Monica, I'll holla at you later. If I spend another second with this fat ho, I'ma have to stab her in the eye with this size eight stiletto." I tossed a twenty on the table, then stormed out of the restaurant.

25

Monica

"I can't believe you were that rude."

"Who, me?" She pointed at herself, grinning innocently.

I gave her a very serious look. "Yes, *you.*"

Reyna tried to laugh like it was no big deal. "Seriously, Monica, why the hell would you wanna hang out with someone like that?"

"Like what?" That's what I wasn't understanding.

"Come on, Monica, she's a stripper who obviously grew up on the wrong side of the street with a badass little nephew and a sister who's in prison for murder."

"Kyle isn't bad . . . and you forget, I'm a stripper too."

"Yes, but your situation is different. She doesn't have a choice, you do," she said, all nonchalant.

"Excuse me . . . what choice? If I had another choice, do you think I would be working at that club?" I didn't even wait for her to answer. "Of course I wouldn't be. And might I remind you that it was *your* idea. The only reason I'm dancing is because I didn't have any other freaking choice." She was starting to piss me off. Reyna had this habit of judging folks and thinking she was better than other people, and that shit just wasn't right.

"What I'm trying to say is that she's not even in our class. She's from the streets."

"Reyna, I don't know if you remember, but you grew up on the west side of Chicago. If that ain't the hood, I don't know what is. It wasn't until your mother married a man in the military that you had a chance to experience another way of life. Before that your mother was cleaning toilets at the Holiday Inn."

She rolled her big eyes toward the door and looked relieved the waitress had arrived with her food. For a second I thought she was going to cry. "I guess you're right," she finally said.

"Damn right, I'm right. Robin's really cool people. There's a lot of hating going on in that club, but girls respect her and that's saved my ass from more than a few squabbles."

"Really?"

I nodded, not that I should have to justify myself. "Some of them chicks are treacherous. Ready to cut you with blades and shit, but Robin's different." She was nothing at all like that bitch Mercedes, who I had caught last night sitting in her Camry, watching me leave the club. I swore I saw her writing down my license plate number.

Reyna sat there quietly playing with her food. "I guess I'm just jealous. You and her have been hanging out and I've been working overtime trying to keep the boutique afloat."

"Afloat? I thought business was good."

She shook her head. "No," she said sadly. "Business has been way down. I've been struggling just to make my lease payments. The economy is really starting to make business suffer for me. If things don't change soon, I might have to close the store."

My heart went out to my friend because I knew that boutique meant everything to her. In all these months, she had been trying to loan me money and help me with my bills when she was barely holding it together herself. I felt so bad for her.

I placed a sympathetic hand on her shoulder. "Maybe the fashion show is what you need to pull it together."

Her smile returned. "That's what I'm hoping. You think you can help pass out some flyers?"

"Sure, I would love to, but all that jealousy shit has got to stop." I gave her a look that said I was serious.

"Agreed."

I brought my salad to my lips and chewed before asking, "So . . . have you heard back from the twins?"

Reyna gave me a strange look. "Hell no, and if they have any sense they won't bother. I decided to leave men alone for a while."

"Excuse me?"

She shrugged like she'd just told me she decided to dye her hair red. Not dating was just not something she did. "I decided that I'm looking for love in all the wrong places, and maybe I need to just take some time out for Reyna and learn my own self-worth before I can get some man to see that."

"Have you been watching *Oprah*?"

She shook her head. "Silly . . . *Oprah's* no longer on the air. I've been seeing a life coach, and she's teaching me how to have the best life ever, and that starts by being true to myself."

"Hell to the no! I can't believe what my ears are hearing." I started laughing even thought I could tell she was dead serious. Reyna was finally trying to take relationships to a new level.

"I guess you having a good man in your life is what made me finally realize I want what you have. Now I just need to allow everything to fall into place for me."

All I could do was sit there and shake my head. Maybe there was hope for her after all.

26

Robin

I moved over to the full-length mirror and looked myself up and down. I had on a pair of Lisa Pliner pink snakeskin mules that I had bought in Las Vegas last year. I paired it with a pair of black skinny jeans and a pink corset that I had cinched so tight my titties were standing to attention. I slipped on a black bolero jacket just in case Trey was taking me somewhere fancy. The last thing I wanted to do was look like I was trying to solicit, although as beautiful as I was, there was really no getting around it. After dinner, I hoped Trey was planning to take me back to my place and fuck me senseless.

Trey was the bomb in the bed, and I'm not saying that because he was packing a powerhouse. Because he was in fact so good with that magic stick that I don't know how I was ever a slave to Halo's dick. Trey was everything I could possibly ever have wanted in a man, not to mention he treated me like a queen. From the first time I let him spend the night, that man took his time getting to know every corner of my body with so much skill that by morning, he had a sistah practically turned out.

Trey made me feel like a woman, while all my sponsors were starting to wear me out. I was tryna juggle my time between them and Trey. Even Halo was starting to drive me crazy with his constant calling and showing up at the club. However, now that I had a man in my life I was trying to keep the two worlds separate. At Scandalous I was Treasure, but the second the night ended, I rushed over to Trey's crib to his bed, where he drove every inch deep inside my body, stroking my coochie just right, until I was crying out his name. I had even given up fighting it and started staying the night lying in his arms. I had sex with my fair share of men, but what I felt with Trey went beyond fucking. From his mouth to mine, we were making love.

"Aunt Robin, you look pretty."

I glanced through the mirror at my nephew standing beside my bed with melted chocolate all over his face. "What have you been eating?"

"Nothing," he mumbled and stared down at his feet.

I walked over to him and cupped his chin with my hand so he had no choice but to look up at me. "Nothing? It looks like you've been in my chocolate."

"Uh-uh."

"Yes, you have." I reached out and started tickling him. He tried to get away, but not before I scooped him up into my arms and carried him into the bathroom so I could wash his face and hands.

He was such an adorable kid, and my heart melted every time he called me Aunt Robin. I could see why Deena was so concerned about him. Through this fucked-up ordeal, the last thing I wanted was for the situation to break his spirit, like life had done to my sister and me.

I had him cleaned up by the time I heard the doorbell. Kyle rushed down the stairs and made it to the door before I did. I swung the door open and there he was. Mr. Fine, and I do mean *fine*. Trey was what every woman wanted in her Christmas stocking. I allowed my eyes to peruse a button-down Sean John shirt, dark jeans, and a fresh pair of sneakers. I don't think clothes ever looked so good on a man.

"Hey, little dude." He gave Kyle a high five, or should I say a low five, then his eyes traveled to me. "Whassup, sexy?"

I stared up into his pretty hazel eyes and had to keep from licking my lips. He was definitely tasty. Before the night was over I planned to be straddling his lap.

An hour later, we had Kyle dropped off at his sister's and had just been escorted to our seats. To my delight, Trey had taken me to the Tobacco Company, an upscale restaurant in downtown Richmond.

Within minutes we both ordered a glass of wine and were sipping and grinning at each other like some damn fools.

"I'm glad we had a chance to chill by ourselves," he said.

"So am I." We hang out, but it's always with Kyle. And when we weren't together, I was working at the club or he was at the restaurant. I had even started hanging out at Mama Lee's and had met his whole damn family, and I loved all of them. They even had me behind the counter working in the kitchen.

We had just ordered dessert when I noticed someone getting off the elevator.

Halo.

The last thing in the world I wanted was for him to see me, because the way he'd been acting lately there was no telling how he would react. I'm not trying to say I'm all that or anything, but Halo refused to believe I was no longer interested in him. It didn't matter that he had some hoochie with him, and I wasn't just saying that because she was cute. Her dress was short enough to show the hairs on her coochie if she made a mistake and sneezed. I had never seen her before, so she was obviously someone new as far as the chicks in Halo's life. Don't get me wrong, when he and I were together there was no doubt in my mind he had been true to me. A chick like me had been on her job twenty-four seven and gave him no reason to stray. But I've been in the game long enough to know all the tricks, and this one, I didn't know.

For a brief second, I thought Halo would just follow the

hostess to their seat, but instead he detoured and headed over to my table.

"Looka here," he sneered.

I rolled my eyes and gave Trey a look of apology. "What's good, Halo?" I said like he wasn't just down at the club sweating a sistah two nights ago.

He fixed his eyes on me with this incredulous stare. "I don't know . . . you tell me."

Brow raised, Trey glanced from him to me.

"Trey, this is Halo . . . Halo, Trey."

"Whassup?" Trey looked him over, nodded, then went back to studying the menu, and so did I. I had hoped Halo would have gotten the hint and moved on, but I looked up to see him still standing there. I know it was wrong, but I loved knowing the sight of me with another man was killing him.

"You need something?" I asked while trying to suppress a smile.

Halo stuck his chest out. "Yeah, I need to holla at you a moment."

I guess his date got tired of being ignored because she slinked her long legs in our direction and placed a possessive hand on his arm. "Baby, she's waiting to seat us," she huffed.

"Then go sit the fuck down," he said with enough bass that she retraced her steps and got the hell away from us. Trey's head whipped around.

"Halo, we don't have nothing to talk about," I said and sucked my teeth in disgust. He could play them games with those other chicks, but the days of him controlling me were long gone. Halo looked like he couldn't believe his ears.

Trey look from me to Halo, and I didn't miss the exact moment the light came on in his eyes. "Yo, Robin . . . is this that dude from the club?" I was wondering how long it was going to take him to remember. I nodded.

Trey rose from his seat and towered over Halo by about three inches, looking like a linebacker for the Philadelphia Eagles. "You heard the lady. She said there's nothing for the two of you to talk about." He stared at Halo, daring him to start something.

The couple at the next table started whispering and the hostess gave us a weird look as she headed back toward the elevators. Halo figured out someone was getting ready to call the police because he finally moved to his table. But not before he got in the last word.

"We ain't done with this conversation," he said, and it was clear by the look in his eyes it was a promise.

I watched him walked across the room and over to his seat before I looked over at Trey. "Sorry 'bout that," I apologized.

"No problem. Who's that muthafucka?" Trey asked.

"My ex," I answered with a disgusted sigh.

He nodded and clearly understood. "Who broke it off with who?"

"I moved outta his house and got on with my life."

Leaning back in his chair, he chuckled. "No wonder he's salty. The brotha's not ready yet to see you with someone else."

I rolled my eyes. "Too bad . . . it's over. We haven't been together in almost a year."

"Hey, it takes some of us longer than others to get over a female."

"So you're telling me you're a stalker too?" Goodness, I couldn't bear it if he was.

"Nah, never that, but I have no problems fighting for what's mine."

"Is that so?"

"Serious. If I'm feelin' a woman, I'ma let it do what it do, and if she's not happy I want her to come and talk to me and tell me why, not just pack her shit and leave."

I had to laugh at that one because I knew exactly what he was talking about. "Have you ever had to beg a woman not to leave you?"

"Hell nah. One thing I don't do is beg," he said with confidence. "I believe in communication. I'm willing to put my heart and everything else out on the line to let a female know how I feel about her, but if she still wants to bounce then I'ma help her ass pack."

I was laughing. I liked Trey the more I talked to him. He was funny and he kept it real, and that's all I asked in a man other than to wine and dine, and make love to me on a regular.

As soon as we finished dessert, he paid the check and we rose from our seats. Trey took my hand and I couldn't help but sneak another peek at Halo, who wasn't even trying to hide the fact he was staring at me. He just didn't get it. I wanted no part of him.

Trey stayed in a fourplex in Henrico, which was about ten minutes from my driveway. He parked in the lot on the side of the building, climbed out, and opened the door for me.

His apartment was small, with two bedrooms. One had a desk, weightlifting equipment, and a futon. He signaled me back to his room and I took a seat on a queen-sized bed that took up most of the room.

"You wanna listen to some music?" I nodded. Music always set the mood. He reached for the remote control, turned on his television, and switched to Sirius radio. Monica was singing my jam. "Kick your shoes off and get comfortable."

I smiled and didn't object when he reached down and slipped my mules off my feet. We sat there lying across the bed staring at each other.

"What are you thinking about?" he asked.

"How long it's gonna take you before you kiss me."

He chuckled, then pulled me against him and pressed his lips to mine. His mouth was soft, just the way I believed a man's should be. He rolled me onto my back and moved on top of me and the kiss got deep and nice. I don't know who started pulling their clothes off first, but before I knew it, we were naked and under the covers wrapped in each other's arms kissing and touching.

"Hold up. Let me get a condom." He slipped out of the bed and headed into the bathroom, and I watched as he walked in. Damn, he had a body. And brotha was working with plenty. Trust and believe. When he climbed back into the bed, I was more than ready for him. I wrapped my legs around his waist and he entered me with one push. He stroked me deep, and it wasn't long before I was moaning.

"You like that?"

Was he serious? That sexy muthafucka could fuck. "*Oooh, yeah,* I like that."

Trey brought his lips down over mine and we kissed the entire time we rocked our hips together. He was taking his time, not rushing anything, and moved like he had all the time in the world, and I liked that about him.

"*Ooh, I'm about to come!*" I screamed his name at the top of my lungs, then shortly after he gave two hard pumps and came.

He lay on top of me until our heartbeats returned to normal, then he rolled over to the side. "C'mere, Robin."

I snuggled close to him and he held me the rest of the night.

27

Monica

One thing about being a nursing student . . . I always got the shitty jobs. No pun intended.

"I'm all done," Ms. Carter said with a grunt and a loud fart.

It took everything I had to try to hold my breath as I slid the bedpan from beneath her wide ass.

"Aaaah, I feel so much better." She sighed, then had the nerve to pass gas again.

This shit was ridiculous. Seriously. I was getting ready to leave for lunch when Ms. Carter, a patient in 4W12, rang the nurse's station insisting that she needed to have a bowel movement ASAP. The moment the charge nurse turned and looked at me over the top of her bifocals, I knew I had to handle it.

"Thank you Monica. You are such a good worker," she replied with a sly smirk.

Skinny heifer.

I've been putting up with her shit ever since I started my clinical training. Before I'd started, I was well aware that everyone had to pay their dues, but this shit had gotten beyond ridiculous. Ms. Carter had just used her fourth bedpan today.

"Thank you so much," she said.

I nodded, then carried the pan over to the bathroom and

dumped it in the toilet. She smelled like something had crawled up into her wide ass and died. "Ms. Carter, can I help you with anything else?"

She shook her head and gave me a sincere smile. She really was a nice old woman. I just wished she had waited until I had left for lunch before she called for someone to come to the room and wipe her behind.

"No. I'm just gonna sit here and eat my lunch."

I smiled, then removed the rubber gloves and tossed them in the trash. "Okay. I'll be back later to check on you."

I reached over to the dispenser on the wall and squirted hand sanitizer in my palm and rubbed my hands together. The second I stepped out her room I took a deep breath, thankful for the fresh air.

Karen, another nursing student, was coming down the hall pushing a wheelchair. "Monica . . . there's someone at the front desk asking for you."

"Okay, thanks," I mumbled as I headed to the nurse's station. As soon as I turned the corner, my face lit up when I spotted Tremayne standing there. He looked so good it took everything I had not to run into his arms and lick him up and down. He was wearing a chocolate double-breasted suit that had to be Brooks Brothers because Anthony had something similar. With a tan shirt and matching handkerchief in his pocket, and dark brown leather shoes, he was definitely a sight for sore eyes. "What are you doing here?"

"I got out of court early and I remember you said you had lunch at twelve. Thought I'd drop by and see if I could steal you away for a few minutes."

"Just give me a minute." I went to reach for my purse under the desk and noticed how the other nurses were checking him out and not even trying to hide it. "I'm going to lunch," I announced.

"Don't do anything I wouldn't do," the charge nurse mumbled under her breath. "Then again, if you do, chile, I can't blame you, 'cause he's fine."

I chuckled, then swung my purse strap over my shoulder and signaled for Tremayne to follow me down the hall to a bank of elevators that would take us to the cafeteria.

"Have I mentioned how sexy you look in scrubs?" he whispered and leaned forward and pressed his lips to mine. I felt like the luckiest woman in the entire building as I stepped into the elevator.

"Thank you, baby, but I better warn you . . . the food here isn't that great."

"Doesn't matter. I'm here for the company . . . not the food."

This man always seemed to know how to say the right things. I don't know what it was, but it was like I was waiting for the other shoe to fall. There was no way in hell he could be this perfect. We got off on the ground floor and headed down the long, narrow hall. Tremayne placed a hand to my back and my skin tingled.

"Is the emergency room that way?" he asked, pointing down the other end of the hall.

I nodded. "Yes, the ER's that way, but the cafeteria is down this way."

He stopped walking and grabbed my hand. "Before we eat, how about you showing me where you work?"

"Where I . . . ?" Damn. I forgot I had told him I worked in the emergency room on the weekends. I coughed to hide my mistake, then tried to think fast. "I don't work at this hospital."

Tremayne frowned. "You don't? I thought you said you did."

"Nooo . . . I-I'm doing my *clinical* training here. I work part-time at the Chippenham Medical Center."

He looked confused, and for a second I thought maybe he

knew I was lying before he nodded. "Okay, I must have gotten it mixed up."

"No problem." When he started walking and let the subject drop, I released a sigh of relief. I was going to have to learn how to lie better.

We stepped into the cafeteria, got hamburgers and fries, and found a table in the corner away from all the watchful eyes. It's a damn shame how bold women can be when they see something they want.

While we ate, Tremayne talked about his brother, who was flying in from Phoenix in a few weeks for a wedding. A good friend of the family was getting married. I could tell they were pretty close.

While we finished eating, the conversation shifted and Tremayne told me he'd won in court this morning. I was so proud of him. "We'll have to celebrate."

"Sounds like a plan. Will I see you tonight?"

Liese had swimming lessons tonight, but I was sure I could have the girls in bed by nine so there was plenty of time for some good loving. But I never let him stay the night. Call me old-fashioned, but I wasn't ready to take our relationship to that level. The girls had met Tremayne and adored him, but I was uncomfortable about them seeing another man sleeping in their mother's bed. Arissa mentioned Anthony's girlfriend lived with him, and that was all fine and dandy. What Anthony did at his house was one thing. I had girls that I wanted to raise as ladies, and I didn't want them seeing their mama with different men in and out of her bed—not that I didn't think Tremayne and I had a future, because I did. He was good to me and the girls, but I wasn't just trying to jump into another relationship feet first. I needed to use my head and not rush our relationship. Besides, I had a lot on my schedule between clinicals, working at the club, and the girls. Having a man was hard. "I can't. Liese has swimming this evening."

"I'd love to come and watch."

I felt like he was trying to push his way into our lives and I just wasn't ready for that. I had too much going on as it was, and with the club I just didn't want to slip up and get caught. I felt confident that once I was done with school, I would have plenty of time to maintain a relationship, but for now I just wanted to take things slow. "By the time I get done with practice, I've gotta get them a bite to eat and get them ready for bed." School was out and they were spending the summer at day camp.

"Monica, I know that to be with you I get three for the price of one, and I'm okay with that. I like your girls, and correct me if I'm wrong, but I think they like me too."

I smiled. "Yes, they like you."

"Okay then, why won't you let me help you, because for some reason I thought I was your man?"

"You are," I replied and our eyes locked.

He flashed a pearly white grin. "Then what kind of man would I be if I couldn't help my woman out?"

Anthony believed since he was the breadwinner, it was my job to take care of the home and the girls. So a man who was interested in helping me was just hard for me to believe.

"I'm sure the girls would love to have you come watch them swim."

Tremayne looked pleased. "Afterward, we'll have pizza."

"Thank you."

"You don't have to thank me. I told you before, if a man can't help you, then you don't need him. Money . . . a shoulder to lean on . . . that's what I'm here for."

How did I get to be so lucky? Tremayne leaned forward and pressed his lips to mine and I felt like everything was right in my life. That was before I glanced over his shoulder and spotted someone staring in my direction.

Greg.

I almost jumped out of my seat. What the hell was he doing at the hospital? *Don't tell me he's a fucking stalker.* Okay, maybe I was smelling myself. He might be a coincidence. He could be at the hospital visiting a sick friend. Nevertheless, I released Tremayne and tried to finish my food as quickly as possible when I noticed Greg rise from his seat and head in my direction.

Oh shit! I quickly gathered up my utensils and folded my napkin on the tray. I still had fifteen minutes before I needed to return to the floor, but I was suddenly ready to go back to changing bedpans. "I better go. I've got a lot of charting to do." I rose, and before we could get away from the table, Greg moved up beside me.

"Hello, Monica."

I looked at him and noticed his balding head was shining. "Hey."

"Sorry to interrupt, but can I speak to you for a moment?"

Was he for real? I couldn't believe his audacity. "Tremayne . . . sweetie, I'll see you later?"

"No problem," he said with a kiss. "I'll call you when I get home." He then carried the trays over to the belt and I watched him walk out of the cafeteria.

"What the hell do you want?" I hissed.

Greg placed his hand at my elbow and escorted me out into the hallway. As soon as we turned the corner, I jerked away from his hold.

"I asked you a question. What do you want?"

"Beautiful and talented. And to think I thought you only took your clothes off for a living. With beauty and brains . . . I think I might be in love," he said with a stupid smirk.

"You still haven't answered my question."

"I want to see you this evening."

Was he crazy? "I don't work tonight."

Greg flashed a coy smile. "I didn't say anything at all about the club. I want you to meet me for some quality time."

I couldn't believe he was asking what I thought he was asking. "No way."

"That's too bad. I was talking to Anthony today, and he mentioned he was thinking about fighting for custody of the girls. It would be such a shame to see them go and live with their daddy and new stepmommy." He chuckled.

I felt this sick feeling inside and I wanted so badly to tell him to go to hell, but I couldn't lose my girls. I also needed my job until graduation, and then I could tell Greg to go to hell.

"What is it that you want?"

"Do I have to spell it out? You know what I want. Meet me at the Holiday Inn in the West End at four. Stop at the front desk and I'll have a key waiting. Oh, and by the way . . . make sure you wear the heels." He then leaned forward and kissed me on the cheek. I pushed him away and hurried off to the ladies' room just in time to throw up my lunch.

At four, I was walking toward the elevators wearing dark shades and a long blond wig. I had already stopped at the front desk, given them my name, and prayed there wasn't a key waiting for me, but I'd never had much luck. Ever since I had run into Greg at lunch, I'd been feeling sick to my stomach. The other nurses were going on and on about how gorgeous Tremayne was and asking if he had a brother, but I couldn't even enjoy being the envy of the wing because all I could think about was how the hell I was going to get out of meeting this asshole. I called Reyna, and she agreed to pick up the girls from day camp. I lied and said I had a study group to meet. I thought about telling her, but I figured the fewer people who knew, the better. Besides, what choice did I have? It was either do as Greg said or run the risk of fighting for custody of the girls in court. There was no way I could afford a legal battle, and that's exactly what Anthony would give me.

I rode the elevator to the second floor, then got off and headed down the hall. The closer I got to the room, the tighter my stomach got, not to mention beads of sweat were rolling down my forehead. As soon as I found room 208, I slid the keycard in the door and opened it. The first thing I noticed was Luther Vandross's voice floating through the room. There were also rose petals across the floor leading over to a king-sized bed where Greg was lying on his back, naked, with his dick in his hand.

"So glad you could make it," he said with that stupid smirk I wanted so desperately to knock off his face.

I didn't bother responding. Instead I just stood there waiting for him to tell me what he wanted so I could get it over with and pick the girls up from swimming lessons. Tremayne was going to be waiting.

"I was trying to figure out your taste in music. I sure hope you like Luther." He then rose from the bed and walked over to me. His dick was standing proudly at attention. For a white man, he definitely had something to be proud about; if it had been attached to someone other than him, I might have been impressed.

"Why are you looking so tense? Relax. Let me pour you a glass of champagne." He moved toward the ice bucket.

"Greg, cut the crap! Tell me what it is you want so I can go. I've got more important things to do."

He shook his head. "You sure know how to kill the moment." He reached for an open bottle and filled two glasses, then carried one over to me. "Here, drink this."

I took it from his hands and thought about throwing it in his face, but on second thought I needed something to calm my nerves before we got down to business. Just looking at his soft body made me nauseated.

He took a sip from his glass, then reached over for his pants and pulled out his wallet. "So how much is it going to be—two . . . three hundred?"

"What?"

"Oh, come on. I know you dancers have sex all the time for money."

I was totally shocked. I never expected him to pay me. "Do I look like a ho to you?"

He shrugged. "I figure the least I can do is compensate you for your time because I am certain it's going to be worth every dime." He stared at me, licking his lips, and I felt violated all over again. I watched as he peeled off three one hundred-dollar bills and sat them on the nightstand. He then removed a wad of dollar bills and took a seat on the edge of the bed.

"All right. Go ahead and dance for me."

I stood there frozen in disbelief that one man had so much power over me. What angered me the most was that he knew it. "I can't do this."

"You can't or you won't?" He appeared tickled.

As much as I didn't want to lose my girls, there was no way I could allow this man to blackmail me into becoming his whore. "I won't. You can tell Anthony whatever you want." I started for the door.

"Really?" he chuckled. "Then why don't I call him now and invite him over."

I turned around and watched in horror as he reached for his cellular phone and dialed. He then put the phone on speaker. I heard the receptionist at their front desk answer.

"Richmond Investments, how may I help you?"

Greg looked at me with a wide grin on his face. "Suzan, sweetie, this is Greg. Is Anthony in the office?"

"Sure, one moment, Mr. Stevens. Let me connect you."

Oh shit! I hurried across the room, snatched the phone from his hand, and ended the call just as I heard Anthony come onto the line. Greg just sat there laughing and waving the stack of dollar bills. "You bastard," I mumbled.

"Hey, I've been called a lot worse," he said and waited for the show to begin.

Tears burned the backs of my eyes but I pushed them away. There was no way I was going to let him know I was that easily broken. *Never let 'em see you sweat,* my mother used to say. I reached for the top button on my blouse and unfastened it.

28

Robin

"Mama, when you coming home?"

Deena looked from me to Trey for help.

"Sweetie, I can't come home right now. But I'll be home soon. I promise," she reassured him with a big smile. I hope she wasn't making a promise she couldn't keep. The last I checked, the sentence for murder was twenty to life.

"I miss you," Kyle whined.

I saw her bottom lip quiver and something in me shifted. I dropped my head. The last thing I wanted was her to see any emotion.

"I miss you too, sweetie."

She hugged him, and Trey reached over and ruffled his hair. "Don't worry, dude. Your mama will be home soon. In the meantime, you get to hang out with me and your auntie Robin."

I hated to see his adorable face look so sad. "That's right. How about we go back to Chuck E. Cheese tomorrow?"

"Yeahhh!" He started jumping up and down with excitement. Trey cupped a hand over his mouth, causing him to squeal even more.

"I'm going to take him to the bathroom and meet you out front when you're done. Dee, I'll see you next week."

"Thanks, Trey." She waved good-bye to Kyle and got choked up with emotion. Despite whatever had happened to my sister over the years, I could tell she really loved her son. At least that was a relief.

"How's he really doing?" she asked after they were gone.

I nodded. "He's doing good . . . really . . . you don't have to worry about him."

"Thank you. Thank you so much for taking Kyle in. If you hadn't . . . I don't know what I would have done. That boy is my whole world."

"He's a sweet kid."

"I hate that the two of you met under such circumstances, but it's not like I didn't try to get together before this."

Once again she was sitting there pretending to be the victim in all of this. Here I was trying to be nice for Kyle's sake—it was because of me she had gotten transferred to a facility where we no longer had to visit across a glass wall—and she fucked it all up by bringing up the past again. "C'mon off it. You know why."

"I've been trying to apologize to you for years, and I'm sorry . . . but I couldn't go back to that house. All the abuse, it was just too much! You have to understand that."

I slumped back against the seat. "You weren't the only one being abused. That woman beat me even more after you left."

"But *you* fought back. That's the difference. I never knew how to do that."

"So because you were a coward, you left me? Do you know how many times I thought about running away, but I didn't? I figured despite how many times she popped me up-side my head, at least we were together. Now *that* made it worth the abuse."

Deena stared across the table and her bottom lip quivered. "He was raping me, Robin," she cried.

"What . . . what the hell are you talking about?"

"Her boyfriend . . . Floyd . . . he was raping me."

I looked at her. "Why you lying?"

She brushed tears away from her eyes and continued. "I'm not lying. He used to climb in my bed at night."

Oh my God. The one thing we had liked about staying at Ms. Ernestine's was that after years of sharing rooms with three or four other kids, at her house we finally had rooms of our own to decorate with pictures and posters of our favorite celebrities. But now she was telling me something that I just couldn't stomach.

"Did Ms. Ernestine know?"

Deena snorted rudely. "Oh yeah, she knew. She would knock on the door and tell him to hurry up before you heard anything."

This was just too much. I didn't want to believe what I was hearing. Mainly because deep down I knew what she was saying was true.

I remembered feeling weird around Floyd. I used to find him staring at me from across the room, and one time he had commented about how big my titties were getting and some man was going to love sucking on them. I thought he was giving me a compliment until one time when I was in the kitchen washing dishes, he came up behind me and I felt his dick against my butt. I remember to this day what he said to me.

"Damn, I bet that pussy's tight."

I had a butcher knife in my hand and swung around so fast he fell back against the kitchen table. I leaned over him with the blade pointed at his dick.

"Rub against me again and I swear I'll kill you while you sleep."

Floyd hurried out of the room, mumbling, "That bitch is crazy," and never fucked with me again.

"Why didn't you tell me?"

Deena gave a strangled laugh. "How would I look telling my younger sister that? Besides, Floyd promised he wouldn't touch you as long as I gave him what he wanted . . . so I did, until I just couldn't take it anymore."

I didn't know what to say. All those years I spent hating my sister for leaving me when she had been running away from a rapist.

"I tried telling the social worker what was going on in the house, but when you denied any abuse . . . they said I was causing trouble and to leave it alone."

I couldn't find words because I clearly didn't know what to say.

"I tried, Robin . . . really I did. But after a while I gave up and just sent you letters instead, letting you know where I was."

What the hell was she talking about? "Letters? I never got any letters."

She shook head. "Ms. Ernestine must have taken them. Any time I tried to call, she hung up the phone on me. I just kept calling hoping one time you would answer."

We sat there for the longest time just staring at each other thinking about the childhood we had lost and could never get back. But that girl sitting on the other side of the table was my sister, and all bullshit aside, I missed her.

"So what do we do now?" she finally said.

"We get you the hell outta here so that you can get back home with Kyle. Trey moved all of your stuff outta your apartment and is storing it for you."

"He's a good man."

"Mmm-hmm, he is." I tried to sound nonchalant, but I guess I did a poor job and she saw something on my face.

She pointed an accusing finger at me. "Wait a minute. Is there some kinda love connection going on?"

I shrugged and tried to act like it was no big deal when in fact I was crazy about him. "We've been kickin' it. With Kyle we have to spend a lot of time together."

"Don't try to blame it on my son. I can tell you're really feeling Trey."

"I guess I am." I giggled, and for the first time since I was sixteen, I heard my sister's animated laugh.

"I'm happy for you," she replied, then glanced down at my wrist. "I see you still have the butterfly charm Mama gave us."

I fingered the small piece of jewelry that dangled from a thin chain. The Christmas before her death, Mama had given us both matching jewelry sets. Over the years while being passed around, I lost the earrings, and the necklace broke during a fistfight, but I held on to the charm with everything I had because it was the only connection I had left to my mother. "Yeah, I need to replace the clasp on this bracelet before I lose it," I said, smiling down at it with fond memories. "What about you? You still have yours?"

She shook her head, wearing a gloomy smile. "I did. But I lost my charm the night Mannie was murdered."

29

Monica

"You are lying."

I shook my head at Reyna, who was standing in front of the stove. "Nope. I'm not lying. Greg's been showing up every Tuesday for a private lap dance."

We were in my kitchen. I had invited Reyna over so she could make her famous Ro-tel cheese dip and so we could spend a few moments of girlfriend time before Tremayne arrived for movie night. Between the club and Tremayne, I knew she felt like she was losing her best friend, and I didn't want her to feel that way. Reyna was so insecure. I guess she always had been, but I was too busy being Anthony's wife to notice, which I found crazy because up until recently I thought she was the most confident women I'd ever known.

"I can't believe this shit!" Reyna turned the fire off under the skillet, then came over and took a seat at the table across from me. "How come you didn't tell me?"

How the hell was I supposed to tell my best friend that some bastard was threatening me so he could do what he wanted? Even now I was too embarrassed to tell her I'd been meeting him in a hotel for the last two weeks. "I was too ashamed to say anything."

"Damn, Monica. Do you think he's gonna tell Anthony?" she asked with a worried look.

I shook my head. "I don't think so." I was at least certain that as long as I gave him what he wanted, my secret would be safe with him.

"That's fucked up! Maybe you should quit."

"I can't afford to." Trust me, I was more than ready to hang up my dancing shoes, but the money was just too good for me to let some bastard run me away from my job. Besides, I still had two kids to feed, a mortgage, and a car note. Until I graduated from nursing school and passed my boards, I needed my job.

Reyna tapped her pudgy little fingers against her lip. "Yes, but if he tells Anthony . . ." She allowed her voice to trail off for dramatic effect. The outcome went unsaid.

"Either way I'm fucked," I replied, biting my lip in frustration. "At least right now Anthony hasn't tried taking me back to court for a custody battle." And I wanted to keep it that way.

Reyna rolled her eyes with disgust. "I still can't believe he tried to buy the girls' parental rights! I'm just saying . . . what kind of man does something like that?"

"A man who is used to getting what he wants, that's who." Ever since that incident at his office, I had been keeping our phone conversations brief and only allowing him to have the girls on his scheduled weekends unless it was a special event. I had even contacted an attorney for a free consultation, and she told me as long as I didn't give him any reason to contest the custody agreement, then I had nothing to worry about. That was a relief, although I had a lot of reason to worry.

When Anthony arrived and picked up the girls, he tried to be cordial. At least his Barbie wannabe had sense enough to stay her skinny ass in the car.

Reyna left for a Mary Kay party, and while I waited for Tremayne to come over I pulled out my school books and got to studying. I had a big test on Monday that was fifty percent of my grade, so I'd decided to take the night off and spend some time studying and with Tremayne. Saturdays were big money nights, and I tried not to think about how much money I was missing out on.

By the time Tremayne pulled into my driveway, I had memorized most of my notes and was feeling pretty good about my test.

"Hey, baby." I opened the door and greeted him with my soft lips pressed to his. Instinctively, I wrapped my arms around his neck and held him close. I felt so lucky to have that man in my life.

I stepped aside and escorted him into the foyer and took a moment to admire how well he was wearing a pair of jeans and a red polo shirt.

"Come on in, have a seat. I made us some snacks to eat while we watch the movie." I held up the new release so Tremayne could share in my excitement. It was then I noticed that he wasn't smiling. "What's wrong?"

"Nothing." He shrugged it off, then moved into the living room over to the couch and took a seat. Mama ain't raised no dummy. I knew something was on his mind, but I had every intention of making sure the only thing he was thinking about was me.

I fixed us both some Ro-tel and chips, then we got comfortable on the couch. While I popped in the movie, Tremayne poured us both a glass of white wine. The evening was perfect.

"How was work last night?" Tremayne asked only seconds after the movie began.

Damn, I hope he wasn't planning on talking through the entire movie. We had plenty of time for that later. I didn't even bother to look away from the television screen when I answered. "It was busy as always."

"Really?" He didn't sound convinced.

"Yes, really. Why you ask?" My belly did a flip-flop because I had a feeling I wasn't going to like what he was about to say, and his response confirmed it.

"Because I came by the hospital last night."

I practically choked on a chip. "You did?"

"Yes, I did. I wanted to surprise you with a bouquet of flowers, but unfortunately no one in the ER knew who you were. The girl at the desk was even nice enough to look through the directory and told me something interesting. No one named Monica Houston works at the medical center."

Ain't that a bitch.

I sat there with my mouth wide open. I was straight busted. My brain didn't work that fast, so I didn't know what to say.

"What the hell's going on, Monica?" Tremayne reached for the remote, pausing the movie, and the entire room went deathly quiet. I could tell by the serious look on his face that this was no joking matter.

"Okay . . . I lied."

He shook his head and looked totally confused. "Why? Why would you lie about working at the hospital?"

I looked down at my plate, over at the television, and out the window. Everywhere except at Tremayne. "Because I was ashamed to tell you the truth."

"The truth? The truth about what?"

"About what I really do for a living." Oh goodness, this was worse than I thought it would be.

His expression seemed to soften. "Baby . . . what could be so bad that you couldn't tell me?"

I took a long breath. "My job. I didn't lie about working at the hospital. I lied about working in the ER." I took a moment to catch my breath. I couldn't even look him in the eyes anymore, and prayed the Lord didn't strike me down for this one. "I work in housekeeping cleaning patient rooms." I took a deep breath and leaned back against the couch cushions. Oh God, I couldn't believe I had let that lie fall from my lips. "I'm employed through a temporary service."

I guess I must have looked pathetic because Tremayne draped his right arm across my shoulders. I released a deep sigh of relief for thinking fast on my feet. "You know how hard it is trying to raise two girls on minimum wage."

"Hey, baby. You have nothing to be ashamed of." Leaning over, he planted his sweet lips to my cheek and squeezed me tight. Damn, I didn't deserve this man. Genuine tears spilled from my eyes. I just wasn't used to anyone being this good to me.

"You know how embarrassed I would be if anyone found out I was scrubbing toilets?" I tried to laugh it off, but it was no use. A sob caught in my throat and I brushed the tears away. How in the world had I suddenly become such a liar?

"Hey, we all have to do what we gotta do. Would you believe I used to flip burgers while I was in college?"

"Yes, but I'm a grown-ass woman with two kids." He had no idea how embarrassing it was being my age with almost nothing going for myself.

"It doesn't matter. You're going to school and trying to make a life for yourself. No one can fault you for that." He cupped my chin and tilted my lips upward and kissed me with so much passion my toes curled.

"Thank you." I was seconds away from bawling. Like I said, I don't deserve someone as good as him. "Can we watch the movie now?" I was more than ready to end this particular conversation and get back to the action flick, especially since I was feeling guilty as hell, but Tremayne wasn't ready to let it go.

"Listen, Monica . . . I hope you realize by now I am an all-or-nothing man. When I have a woman, I'm committed to her." He sighed and dragged a hand across his face and I waited, giving him time to collect his words. I'd never seen him look that serious before. "What I'm trying to say, Monica . . . is that I love you and at some point when we both feel we're ready I want to make you, Liese, and Arissa a permanent part of my life."

My heart was pounding so hard I couldn't even speak. He loved me. That fine, educated man loved me . . . a woman with secrets and excess baggage. His words meant so much my hands started to shake.

"But we gotta be honest with each other. As your man I should be able to accept you for you, and you should be able to do the same. No secrets."

"You're right," I said, and it was the perfect time to be honest with him and tell him what I was doing. Only I couldn't.

"Do you need money? If you do, baby, all you have to do is ask."

I cut him off. "I've got too much pride for that."

"You're my woman. I'm supposed to help you." He gave me a huge grin. "Now let's finish watching the movie, then I'm taking you to bed and show you how much you mean to me." He lay back against the couch and I settled between his legs and rested my head on his chest and tried not to think about the lies that were starting to become second nature.

30

Robin

I had just finished giving a dude a lap dance and was strutting across the club in nothing but a pink G-string, titties and ass bouncing. This was half-price night and the brothas had flooded the club. Just in case they hadn't received the memo, I wanted to make sure they all saw what I had to offer.

Dudes started hollering trying to get a sistah's attention and I grinned and added a little extra *umph* to my sway. I was almost to the dressing room when I spotted Halo sitting at a small table. Any other time I would have gone the long way to avoid him, but I had important matters to deal with, like finding out how to get my sister out of this mess.

"There's my treasure chest. Yo, come holla at me a second." He signaled with his hand for me to move closer. I faked like he was bothering me and sucked my teeth in disgust.

"Damn, Robin, give a nigga a break."

I dragged my feet over to where he was sitting. As soon as I was close enough he snaked out an arm and pulled me against him.

"Halo, what do you want?" I said through gritted teeth.

"I wanna know who that nigga was you were tryna make me jealous with?" He actually sounded upset.

"Jealous? How the hell was I trying to make you jealous

when I didn't even know you were coming there?" Goodness, men could be so stupid at times.

"If you were tryna hurt a brotha you succeeded, no doubt," he whined. "Robin . . . I miss you. Why won't you let a nigga prove it to you?" He stared at me with those green puppy-dog eyes of his. It didn't make any sense for a man to look that good. Thank goodness I already knew behind those fine qualities was a fuckin' lunatic. If I wanted information, I needed to play this shit right, because one thing I could say about Halo, he wasn't stupid. If all of a sudden I acted like I was interested in him, he would know something was up.

"C'mon, Halo. Why don't you just give it up?"

" 'Cause I can't. I miss that good-ass pussy you got," he said with a grin.

I allowed myself to smile just a little. "Yeah, my shit *is* the bomb."

He hugged me close, laughing. "I know, that's why I want you back in my life. C'mon, can't you just give a brotha a chance to prove he's changed?"

I sighed. "You just not gonna give up, are you?"

"Not when I want something as bad as I want you."

Ever since I had visited Deena in jail, all I could think about was what she had told me. Floyd raping her for God knows how long. After all she had gone through, there was no way I could stay mad. All my fight and anger was now pointed at finding out who had framed my sister, and that meant getting close to Halo again. I knew it was just a matter of time before the truth was revealed.

I acted like I was giving his suggestion some consideration when in reality I had already made up my mind and knew I was going to see him again. I had to, but it was going to be on my terms and just long enough to find out what I needed. But I had to play it safe, otherwise I would have to deal with a lot more than just Halo's fist.

"How about we try being friends? Wait . . . let me finish. Let's start with being friends and see where things lead."

Halo clearly didn't agree, but he didn't argue either. I gave him a look that said *either that or nothing* and he finally lowered his shoulders and grinned. "Yeah . . . a'ight. I'll take what I can get for now."

I grinned. "Now we're getting somewhere."

"How about dinner on Sunday?"

I had planned to spend the evening at Trey's place curled up on the couch, watching a new DVD release, but helping Deena was just too important to pass up the opportunity.

"Okay, but dinner only."

"How about we let it do what it do?"

I could see the look in his eyes. He thought he was going to dip into my treasure chest. Well, he was in for a few surprises. "Cool. Call me tomorrow." I then wiggled out of his grasp before he could try to kiss me, and made it back to the dressing room. The whole time I kept wondering if maybe I was making a big mistake.

31

Monica

"For a second there I thought maybe you weren't working tonight."

The hair on the back of my neck stood up. I turned around and found Greg sitting at a small table close to the stage with a beer in his hand. It took everything I had not to ask security to escort his ass out of the building. What the hell was he doing at Scandalous on a Saturday night?

All of a sudden my head began to hurt. It was bad enough he was still showing up at the club every Tuesday like clockwork for a private dance that felt more like being violated. Not to mention I was still meeting him at the hotel on Wednesdays. He even had the nerve to request the same room every time and was now calling it our love nest. I wanted to refuse but I couldn't, because so far he had been a man of his word and hadn't said anything to Anthony.

Reluctantly I walked over to him with a hand propped at my hip. "Greg, when are we going to stop playing this game?" My voice was cold and serious. I was far beyond annoyed.

"Well let's see . . . Hmm . . . probably not until I've had my fill of you, and as good as you feel that's a *long* time coming." He chuckled, then boldly reached out and pulled me close until I was standing between his legs. I leaned back as far as I could, but it didn't stop him from kissing the side of my neck and whispering in my ear, "Have I told you how good you taste? Next week I plan on tasting that sweet pussy."

Men at the club grabbed and touched me all the time, but it was different when Greg did it. As soon as I felt his clammy wet lips, I flinched. "Would you please let me go!" I gave him one hard push, putting some distance between us.

He shook his head wearing a nauseating smirk. "I don't know why you keep playing this game with me when you know you can't win."

I was so tired of him hanging the custody of my girls over my head. It had to stop. I couldn't keep having sex with this man and letting him use my body at his own discretion. I was starting to have a hard time performing for Tremayne because I felt so used by the time he tried to touch me. Not to mention the guilt was starting to take its toll. I sighed unhappily. "Don't you have any compassion? Goodness! All I'm trying to do is raise my girls and graduate nursing school."

"Which is why I always tip you generously. I know it's hard out here for a single parent, so I'm trying to do everything I can to help you. You wash my hands and I wash yours. I think that's a fair enough trade, don't you think?" Greg gave me this look like my response really mattered. As far as I was concerned, the sick fuck could kiss my ass. "How about my lap dance? Did you know it's the highlight of my week?"

Did he know that every week I imagined plunging a knife through his heart? "I was just getting ready to change for my next set. Why don't you have a seat? I'll be right back."

"And I'll be right here waiting."

I did an exaggerated eye roll and hurried back into the dressing room. I don't know what I was going to do with Greg. I couldn't think straight and had barely scored a B on my last test. My irritation was even starting to rub off at home with the girls. And when Tremayne tried to make love to me last night, I pretty much told him I had a headache. As much as I didn't want to lose custody of my girls, something had to give because I couldn't keep living like this.

I was slamming my locker shut when Treasure stepped into the locker room. I eyed the Wilma Flintstone costume she was wearing.

She gave my face a once-over, then asked, "What's wrong with you?"

I wasn't sure how much I could say without getting myself into trouble. But I didn't know where else to turn. All I knew was I needed help. "Did you see that guy I was just talking to?" She nodded. "He's a friend of my ex-husband who's been blackmailing me." I then told her everything, I guess because unlike Reyna, Treasure wasn't one to judge me. She understood.

"Deja . . . Deja . . . Deja." She wagged a perfectly manicured fingernail in my face and actually looked disappointed. "Girl, you shoulda come to me a long time ago. I coulda already gotten rid of his ass."

"You can?" I was so excited, I hugged her. "Treasure, you're a lifesaver! How are you going to do that?" I didn't want to get ahead of myself.

"All you need to do is turn the table on his ass," she replied like it was really that easy.

"How can I do that?" One thing I loved about Treasure was that she knew how to handle her job. I really needed to start taking notes.

"Think about it. I learned to find out everything you can about your clients because you never know when you might need to use that bit of information." She looked me straight in the eye. "What do you know about him?"

I leaned against the lockers with my arms crossed. I had to think about that one for a minute because Greg Stevens started working at Richmond Investments right around the time Anthony and I were separating.

I pressed my trembling lips together, then exhaled. "I know he's married to this rich chick whose father is the dean of medicine at the University of Richmond."

She snapped her fingers. "Bingo! There you go. You know more than enough. C'mon."

I was totally confused but that didn't stop me from following her into the dressing room, where her eyes scanned the area.

"Tequila! C'mere a minute," she called.

A pretty white girl stopped brushing her hair and without hesitation strutted her long legs over to see what she needed. I loved the way when Treasure spoke, girls just jumped to attention.

"Yeah, girl, what's up?"

"Remember that time we helped Ginger out?"

"Hell yeah, I remember," Tequila said with a mischievous grin.

"Well, Deja's got the same problem." I swiveled my head back and forth between them as Treasure started chattering away, telling her only what she needed to know.

Tequila shrugged like it was just another day on the job. "No problem, but it's gonna cost you your half."

Hell, I would give her every dime I had earned tonight if it meant getting that sleazeball off my hands. "No problem."

Her eyes sparkled with dollar signs. "Okay, go back out there and tell 'em you wanna do a private in the hot tub room."

"Hot tub? I didn't even know we had one of those."

She nodded her blond head. "It'll cost him a hundred and fifty. Seventy-five goes to the house and the rest to me. Get him in there and act like you down for fucking him and we'll handle the rest."

After first I hesitated but since I didn't have much of a choice, I nodded and went back out to the dance floor, taking several deep breaths. *You're a survivor. You can do this.*

I found him still sitting, waiting eagerly for my return. He gave me that devilish grin when he spotted me. All I wanted to do was kick him in the dick with my stiletto heel for being such an asshole.

In one swallow, Greg finished his beer, then rose from his table. "You ready to go upstairs?" he said all too eagerly.

"Actually . . . how about we get into the hot tub instead?"

My approach worked because he seemed caught totally off guard. "Hot tub?" He looked at me suspiciously like I might be up to something. I was, but he didn't need to know that. "How much is that?"

"A buck fifty." I could see he was getting ready to decline, so I leaned in close and rubbed his receding hairline. "It's in a private room in back. There'll be no one in there but you and me," I purred. The thought of being alone must have gotten his attention because he quickly reached for his wallet.

I took his money and walked over to the floor manager and gave him his half and waited while he went in back and unlocked the door. I then grabbed Greg by the hand and led him inside. I thought, Treasure better know what she was doing, because the second I saw him pulling off his clothes, I was ready to run out of there.

The room was warm and the tub quite inviting. If it had been anyone else I might have looked forward to slipping inside. As I was reaching for the zipper of my short royal blue dress, there was a quick knock. The door swung open and Tequila came in wearing a red bikini and matching come-fuck-me shoes.

"Oops . . . my bad! I didn't know anyone was in here."

"Hey, Tequila," I said, pretending that I hadn't been hoping she would walk in at any moment.

She winked, then walked over to Greg with this hungry look in her eyes. "My, aren't you delicious. Deja, who's your friend?"

I looked over at him with a phony smile. "This is Greg."

"Mmm, Greg . . . you mind if I join in the fun?" She smiled seductively, her eyes locked on him. She then had the nerve to reach down and squeeze his crotch. Greg's eyes grew large and for a second I thought he was going to flat-out refuse.

"I-I'll never turn down a t-two for one," he sputtered nervously.

I was so relieved. Tequila slipped off her shoes and climbed into the hot tub and purred. "Oooh, Greg, baby! This water feels *soooo* good. Hurry up and join me." She moaned like she was having an orgasm.

Greg forgot all about me. He practically dived inside. Tequila patted the spot beside her. I shook my head. Maybe he wasn't used to beautiful women throwing themselves at him. Whatever it was, I was thankful.

I was taking off my shoes when Tequila climbed over and straddled his lap. Within seconds she started tonguing him down. Greg was groaning and moaning and making all kinds of noise. It was almost comical.

"Deja, why don't you go and get the massage oils from Treasure." She then tossed her bikini top onto the floor and guided a large rosy nipple into Greg's mouth.

"Massage oil?" I mumbled because I had no idea what she was talking about, yet I turned on my heel and left her alone with that freak. I stepped outside the door to find Treasure standing on the other side grinning.

"What?" I asked, because she was clearly amused.

"Girl, relax. Tequila is a straight-up freak! She'll have that muthafucka feinin for her ass."

I released a heavy sigh of relief. "Good . . . anything . . . as long as he leaves me the hell alone."

"He will," she replied confidently, and I prayed she was right. "Here . . . take this."

I looked down, and when I saw what she was holding, it finally started to make sense to me. I smiled. "This is gonna be good."

"Just wait three more minutes and go back in."

My teeth were chattering with excitement and I was also nervous as hell. I counted to one hundred and stepped back into the room and found Greg had Tequila bent over and was ramming her from behind. Her breasts were bouncing all over the place and he had the biggest grin on his face. His eyes were rolled so far back in his head, he hadn't even noticed I had stepped back into the room.

I started snapping pictures like crazy on Treasure's cell phone. She had one of those that took beautiful pictures. Greg was so into what he was doing he didn't even stop until he came, and by then I had taken a dozen photographs.

"Deja . . . did you get that?" Tequila asked nonchalantly.

"Yes, ma'am . . . you know I did," I replied loud enough for him to have heard me.

Greg, who was breathing hard, looked over at me and finally noticed the phone pointed in his direction and the light flashing. It took a few moments longer before realization sank in. "What the hell are you doing?"

"This is my insurance policy." I snickered. The grin fell from my face the second he jumped out of the tub. Oh shit! I padded over to the other side of the room and moved behind a small bar in the corner, which meant I was trapped. You just don't know how happy I was when Treasure stepped into the room.

"Well, well . . . this must be Greg Stevens," she purred, eyeing his dick appreciatively. Like I said before, God had definitely blessed the wrong man.

He gave a suspicious look. "How do you know me?"

"Actually . . . I know Lauren . . . your wife."

He practically jumped out of his skin as he turned and reached for a towel. "Y-you are mistaken. I'm not married."

"Hmmm . . . really? Because you look a lot like the picture I found of the two of you on the Internet."

"Deja, let me see that." She signaled for her phone and I hurried over and handed it to her. She flipped through the pictures, shaking her head. "You should be ashamed of yourself. Lauren would be so hurt."

Greg started fumbling with his clothes as he tried to put them back on. Tequila leaned back in the water, laughing and splashing her toes. "Greg, you need to give me your wife's number so I can tell her how good her man was," she purred.

"I know that right, girl." Treasure started laughing, and for the first time in weeks I let out a thankful sigh. It felt so good finally being in control again.

Greg looked like Treasure had him terrified. "P-please don't tell my wife. I'll do anything you want. Anything."

She stood defiantly with her arms crossed. "Of course you will. Well . . . for starters, we'll take everything you have in your wallet."

He quickly reached inside and pulled out several large bills. "Here, you can have it all." He practically threw the money at her.

"Also, you are to never touch Deja again," she demanded in a threatening tone. "If I hear that you've come by her job or said a word about this to her ex-husband, I swear your wife will see these pictures and I'll make sure to CC a copy to her daddy."

I don't think I ever heard anyone sound so serious. Greg realized Treasure meant every word. His eyes landed in my direction, and if he'd had a gun I would have been dead. I forced myself to remain calm.

He hesitated before speaking. "I swear to you . . . Monica won't see my face again."

"Good. Now get the hell out of here before I count to three and change my mind," she ordered with a wave of the hand and gestured toward the door.

You would have thought Greg was trying out for the Olympics the way he sprinted out of there, leaving his shoes behind.

32

Robin

I was in my bedroom, standing in front of a full-length mirror primping in a Baby Phat strapless jean jumpsuit with red pumps and a wide matching belt. I looked delicious. It was the type of outfit I would have picked out for myself if I had seen it at the mall. Only I didn't buy it. Halo had.

A delivery man had appeared at my door with a box for me to sign for. As soon as I looked inside I saw the outfit and a card that read, *Look forward to seeing you tonight.*

The gift had made me nauseated because that was the type of shit Halo did after he got done whupping my ass. He'd buy me something like it was supposed to make things all better. At first I was tempted to take a pair of scissors to the outfit, but then thought better. Halo would expect me to have it on, and tonight I didn't need any drama. I was supposed to meet him at the Hard Shell, a seafood restaurant located in historic Shockoe Slip, at eight, and I needed him smiling and the drinks flowing if I wanted to get any information out of him.

Thank goodness Monica was able to watch Kyle for me. I didn't feel right asking Trey to babysit while I was stepping out with another man. Not that it was *really* a date. I was just anxious to get the evening over so that I could slide over to Trey's. I'd called him earlier and told him I had cramps and was going to lie down and I would give him a call later. It was the first time I ever felt guilty about lying to a guy, which was how I knew I cared a lot about him. I wasn't sure if he would understand, so it was easier just to not tell him what I was doing. I tried to tell myself I was doing it for Kyle so I could get my life back, but I knew it was more than that. I just wasn't ready yet to admit it.

I slipped on a pair of diamond drop earrings and tossed my keys, money, and ID in a small clutch and was heading to the kitchen when I heard my doorbell ring. When I saw who was on the other side, I was ready to scream. It had to be a mirage. But even after I yanked open the door, he was still standing there in black jeans and a white button-down shirt.

"What are you doing here?"

Grinning, Halo stepped into my town house as if he had every right to be there, glancing around, admiring my place. I'd done everything in my power to keep him from finding out where I lived. "Halo, I asked you a question . . . what are you doing here?"

"You know I like to pick my women up."

I had to apply pressure to my temple to keep from screaming. "But I thought we agreed to meet at the restaurant."

"And I decided to come and get you instead. Relax." He walked around the room admiring the décor and the African-American art I had on my walls.

"You got a nice place here."

"Thank you." I watched him strutting around the room like he owned the place. Touching this and that, being nosy. "How'd you know where I lived?"

He glanced over his shoulder and laughed. "Believe me . . . it wasn't that hard. You've known me long enough to know nothing gets past me."

Yeah, that's what I was afraid of. I didn't know why I felt violated having him in my private space, but suddenly I was anxious to get out of there. "I'm ready if you are." I grabbed my purse off the couch and headed toward the door, only Halo wasn't following me.

"What's the rush? How about showing me around first?"

I hesitated because the last thing I wanted was for Halo to see where I slept at night, yet if I didn't show him around Halo would know something was up and I couldn't risk that. Damn, the games we have to play.

I did a big sweep of my arms like I was a game show host. "Well, this is the living room."

Grinning, he looked around the room, admiring the décor again like he hadn't just been checking it out a few minutes ago.

"The kitchen is in here." I started toward the next room and signaled for him to follow, but what he said next almost made me break the heel of my pump.

"Since when do you have a kid?"

My eyes zeroed in on the action figures lying on the floor beside my couch, and I cursed under my breath. In my haste, I had forgotten all about Kyle's toys. "Oh . . . uh, I've been . . . uh . . . babysitting for a friend while she's looking for day care." Nodding, he seemed to accept my explanation, and I sighed with relief.

He followed me into the kitchen, stopped, turned, and looked at me, admiring my outfit. "You look sexy, but then you always do." Halo reached out an arm and pulled me against him so fast I barely had a chance to breathe before he pressed his lips down against mine.

It took everything I had to remain still when what I wanted to do was kick him in the nuts. But what I realized while we were kissing was that I felt nothing for him anymore. No more coochie purring and nipples getting hard. I couldn't believe it, but my body had finally caught up with my brain. I had Trey to thank for that. The whole time Halo was kissing me, I pretended it was Trey.

When I felt his fingers squeeze my breast, I decided I had done more than enough to make this shit seem believable and pushed him away. I stood there breathing hard and glaring at Halo. He was trying to keep a straight face but I could tell he was fighting a grin. *Bastard*. He loved making me feel uncomfortable. It was his way of keeping the upper hand.

"Robin?"

"Yes." I didn't mean for it to, but my voice shook just a little.

He winked. "Relax. All I wanna do is have a good time tonight. We straight?"

I shrugged and tried to act like it was no big deal. I hurried through the tour and when we reached my room, I watched him lick his lips as he stared down at my comfortable bed. If he thought the evening was going to end with my legs in the air, he was sadly mistaken. It ain't that kind of party. I wasn't lying earlier when I said I had cramps. At least when I told him I was on my period, I wouldn't be lying. Trust me . . . Halo ain't no vampire.

As soon as we returned to the living room, I moved toward the door. "I'm starving. Can we go now?" I was so relieved when he followed me. Hanging out at my place was not even an option. I had locked the door and we were on our way out to his SUV when I spotted Trey coming across the lawn.

What the hell?

Halo turned and was the first to greet my guest. "Well, well . . . we meet again."

Trey stormed up the sidewalk and looked from him to me, looking clearly confused. "Robin, what the fuck's going on?"

"Homeboy, what it look like? I'm taking my girl out." I desperately wanted to knock that cocky grin off Halo's face.

"Your girl?" Trey stepped up to Halo and was all in his face. The two of them were staring each other down, and if I didn't do something soon there was no telling what was about to happen.

"T-Trey, what are you doing here?" I was nervous.

"I thought I would see how you were feeling." There was no mistaking the heavy sarcasm in his voice.

"Trey . . . I . . ." I didn't know what to say. With Halo standing beside me there was no way I could tell him the truth. I had to find out who really killed Mannie. Despite everything that had gone down between Deena and me, she was still family, and family had to stick together because at the end of the day, all we really had was each other.

The two of them were in each other's face and I could tell they were seconds away from setting it off out here. Knowing Halo the way I did, he was strapped and I definitely didn't need any bullets flying.

"Trey . . . I wish you had called first." At this point, I didn't know what else I could possibly have said.

"Obviously," he snarled and I didn't miss the hurt in his eyes. "I come over here to check on you only to find you stepping out with this cat?" Oh, he was angry. "What's really fucked up, Robin, is . . . how you gonna go out with another muthafucka in the outfit I bought you?"

His words hit me so hard my jaw hit the concrete, and trust me, I felt the blow. I couldn't even answer him because I was in shock and lost my breath. I had just assumed the outfit was from Halo. It never occurred to me that maybe Trey had bought it.

Neither of us spoke for a long time. I stood there in the grass wondering what was going through his mind. "I'm sorry," I said, like it was gonna soften the blow, but I think it only made matters worse.

Shaking his head, Trey stormed off, but instead of leaving, he sat in his SUV and watched as I climbed into the QX56 beside Halo. I hadn't expected it to hurt so much. As he pulled off, I started to wonder if my sister was really worth losing the best thing to happen in my life in a long time.

33

Robin

I was heading toward the dressing room when I heard the club manager calling my name. "Yo, Treasure. There's a bachelor party upstairs. Grab another chick and get yo ass up there."

Cha-ching! I loved doing bachelor parties. I hurried through a cloud of cigarette smoke to my locker. Monica was slipping on her shoes. "You just getting here?"

She nodded. "My study group ran a little late."

I stripped off my costume, then reached inside my locker and started wiping myself down. "You ever do a bachelor party?"

Monica gave me a nervous look, then shook her head. "No."

"You wanna do one? It's big money. The house pays us as well as we get tips."

She hesitated before finally saying, "Okay."

"Just follow my lead. Everything goes . . . short of fucking. If you feel uncomfortable, then just let me know and I'll handle them."

"Will I ever get comfortable doing this shit?" She rolled her eyes and made me smile.

"Depends on how long you plan on investing in this career." She frowned, and I knew if Monica could afford it, she would quit tomorrow. As long as it wasn't tonight. Right now I needed her to help me make it a big moneymaking night. "Put on something pink. We're on in ten minutes."

Nodding, she rose and moved to her locker. As nervous as she looked, I wouldn't be surprised if she came back to change her mind. She was definitely not cut out for stripping. What she didn't realize was the customer could tell when a dancer's heart was in it, and that affected the bottom line. Unlike her, I knew how to turn that shit off and on and played the role.

I was putting glitter on my ass when Honey came around the corner grinning like a damn full. "Girrrl, money's in the house. You should have seen them fine muthafuckas that went up to the VIP lounge. Money, money, money, *money!*"

"You stupid." I sprayed my body with a tropical scent and grabbed a slinky pink dress while she flopped down on the bench in a white nightie.

"What you getting ready to do?"

"I'm doing the bachelor party."

"Hell yeah! I knew they chose you. Give me five minutes and I'll be ready." Before I could open my mouth, she jumped up and was heading to her locker when Deja came around the corner dressed in a bad two-piece outfit held together only by two slipknots on the sides.

"I'm all ready."

Honey looked from her to me with her hand on her hip.

"Honey . . . Deja's doing the party with me."

"What?" she said with attitude. "Whassup with that shit? We *always* do the parties together. We're supposed to be two peas in a pod, so how the hell you gonna change up the game?" Damn, I knew she would be mad, but I never thought she'd be that mad.

"Girl, quit tripping! Deja never did one, so I asked her. Besides, I'm doing that party with you for Lil D if they ever decide when they're gonna let his ass out. Damn! Quit being so fucking money hungry." Her eyes lit up the way I knew they would since I was finally confirming doing that coming-home party for Lil D. Nobody was sure when he was being released since the date had already been changed twice. Although I'd rather not do the party, I really didn't have much of a choice. After that fiasco with Trey last Sunday, I had to follow through before I changed my mind.

I still hadn't been able to forget the hurt on Trey's face when he watched me pull off with Halo. I wanted so badly to tell him to stop the damn vehicle and let me out. But I couldn't until I found out what Halo knew about Mannie's murder.

Usually I loved me some crab legs, but I had lost my appetite and all through dinner I kept thinking about Trey and how in the hell I was going to explain this mess. One thing about Trey, I couldn't treat him like one of my sponsors because he definitely wasn't listening to no okeydoke. I was just gonna have to keep it real. But that's hard to do when someone won't talk to you. Ever since that night he'd been blowing me off.

"Robin, unless it's about Kyle, I don't wanna hear shit you gotta say," was all he said before the phone went dead. Damn, how was I supposed to know he liked me to keep it cute and had bought that outfit for me?

"Treasure . . . Carl said you need to get yo ass upstairs ASAP!"

As soon as I heard Sunshine's loud ass, I exhaled a deep breath and got back in character. I'd figure out what to do with Trey later.

I quickly slipped into a new pair of white platform shoes, then slammed my locker and my eyes landed on Deja. "C'mon, girl. It's show time."

34

Monica

I would be lying if I didn't tell you I was nervous as hell. It was one thing to be at the center of a stage in the middle of a large room, but doing a bachelor party was altogether different because the focus was on two people—Treasure and me.

I was on the small stage in the center of the room, twirling around a pole, while Treasure was giving the groom-to-be a lap dance. Most of the crowd of men were more interested in what she was doing, because she did it so freakin' well, but there were a few surrounding my stage waving money. I kept my head low. They thought I was trying to be mysterious with the platinum blond wig all in my face, but actually I was so nervous I couldn't look any of them in the eye.

They definitely weren't ballers or some of the lowlifes I've seen in Scandalous. Most of them seemed to be older, so I thought that meant they wouldn't expect as much, but I soon found out I was wrong.

"C'mon, make that booty clap!"

"Take off that top and show me them little-ass titties!"

I smiled, and ignoring their outbursts, I finished the first song. Thank goodness I had two shots of vodka before I stepped onto the stage. I was starting to feel the effects of the alcohol and was beginning to relax.

By the time the music changed to Usher's "Love In This Club," I was untying my bikini top and moving over to the best man. He was making it rain five-dollar bills, so there was no way I was passing that up. I dipped low enough for my nipples to brush his cheek and took another crisp bill from his hand. By the end of the next song, I was relaxed, half-naked, and my garter was filled with money.

"Deja, come help tame this fool!"

I looked over at Treasure and laughed. The groom needed a two for one. I stepped off the stage in five-inch silver platform shoes and swung my hips over to where she was gyrating her naked butt in his face. I lowered onto his lap and was laughing and having so much fun, I brushed my hair back away from my face. I had risen and was lowering my little skirt when I heard four words that stopped me in my tracks.

"Monica . . . is that you?"

I felt like I was in a trance as I turned my head in horror. My eyes collided with the last man I ever wanted to see me like this.

Tremayne.

He was sitting at the table with three other dudes with money in their hands. He had been shouting "Spank that ass!" just like the others were. Oh my goodness! I suddenly remembered him mentioning that his brother was flying in for their best friend's wedding.

"You know him?" Treasure asked, not missing a beat.

I nodded and rose from the groom's lap. Even under the dim lights I could see the hurt on his face. Never had I regretted anything in my life like I did hurting him. I had deceived him in the worst way.

Tremayne rose from his chair, walked over to where I was standing, then took my arm and led me over toward the side of the room. Several of the men were watching us, and I was so embarrassed, but he didn't seem to care. Luckily, Treasure had my back. She started dancing, and within seconds, all eyes were on her again.

"What the hell are you doing here?" he barked over the loud music.

I tried to get my lips to move but for some reason I couldn't get the words to come out. I mean, seriously, what could I really say at this point except, "I work here"?

Tremayne stared at me for a moment like he had expected me to say something other than what I just had. Believe me, if I could have been anywhere else at that moment, I definitely would have.

"You're a stripper?" he said with disbelief. Obviously he was having a hard time digesting the news.

"Yes . . . I'm a stripper."

His eyebrows went up. "And when were you planning on telling me this?"

I paused. Did he expect me to lie? "I wasn't."

He shook his head. "Of course you weren't. Instead you were going to allow me to think that I was dating a divorced nursing student with two little girls."

Okay, he was starting to piss me off. I placed a hand on my hip. "And this mother has two little girls to feed."

Tremayne scrubbed a hand across his face like he was counting to three. Part of me understood his anger. I probably would have reacted the same way. I mean, come on. I lied about how I earned my living and was shaking my naked ass in front of his brother and their friends. Hell, I would have been pissed as well. I just thought he would never find out. I guess the joke was on me.

"I have never been so embarrassed in my life. I've had women lie to me before, but this . . . this here takes the cake. First you worked in the ER . . . then you're scrubbing toilets . . . now this."

I wanted to say something but I honestly just didn't know

what was left to be said. *It is what it is.* I was stripping to make a living.

Tremayne paused briefly, glancing around the room at the bachelor party that was in full swing before returning his eyes to me. "Enjoy the party. I'm out."

I watched him walk back to his table long enough to tell his friends he was leaving, then he stormed out of the room, leaving me standing there, more upset and humiliated than I ever imagined.

Treasure hurried over to where I was standing. "You okay?" she asked.

I shook my head. "No, I'm not. I-I can't do this. I need to go home."

She nodded, understanding. "No problem. I'll get Honey to slide in. Go handle your business."

I had to come up with an excuse about having bad cramps and bleeding too heavily to be dancing around in a thong before the club manager would allow me to go home. Only I didn't want to go back to my place. The girls were with Anthony. So I went the only place I knew to go.

"Monica, what's wrong?" Reyna said as she swung the door open and found me standing on the other side. I could tell I had interrupted her sleep. She had on a sleep shirt and her hair was all over her head.

I stepped into the living room and was bawling so hard I couldn't even get my words together. Reyna took my hand and led me over to the couch and made me sit. "Monica, you've got to slow down and talk to me. You're scaring me."

She handed me a box of tissues and I took a few deep breaths and tried to explain. "Tremayne . . . He came into the club tonight."

Her eyes grew round. "You're shitting me."

I wished it wasn't true, but it was. I started crying again. Reyna wrapped her arms around me and rocked me the way I did the girls when they were upset about something. It wasn't fair. I had finally met a guy I really liked—okay, I loved, and just like that, I had lost him. I guess I couldn't blame anyone but myself because I should have been honest with him in the first place, but after I realized I loved him, I couldn't even imagine telling him, "Hey, guess what, I'm a stripper."

"It's going to be okay," Reyna said soothingly.

"Reyna, I've never been so humiliated in my life!" I told her about doing the bachelor party and dropping it hot in the groom's lap and Tremayne recognizing me. I could tell Reyna was trying to keep a straight face, and the next thing she was falling back on the couch laughing.

"What the hell's so funny?" How could she be laughing at a time like this?

"Monica, you have to admit it *is* kinda funny. Your big ass tryna give a lap dance and your man just *happens* to be there."

Hell, I didn't see anything that was funny.

She suddenly stopped laughing. "Oh my goodness! Monica . . . you're really hurt, aren't you?"

"What the hell you think I've been crying about since I got here?"

"I'm sorry. I didn't mean to laugh. It's just . . . I never thought you would *really* strip, and once you did, you got so into your work you were taking it way too serious. At the same time you were trying to live a double life with this man who loves you. Sweetie, you should have known it was liable to backfire on your ass."

Sometimes she can be so insensitive. I brushed the tears away. "Okay, so maybe I should have been honest, but would you have?"

"Hell no. I would have done the exactly same thing, but by doing that you have to be willing to accept the consequences."

I know what she was saying was true, but that didn't mean I wanted to hear it. "I guess you're right."

"Of course I am, sweetie," Reyna said with a hug. "So what are you gonna do now? You quitting the club?"

"No."

Her brow rose. "What do you mean, no? I thought you just said you were humiliated."

I rolled my eyes in her direction. "I was, but that doesn't change the fact that I have two mouths to feed."

"Yeah . . . but . . ."

I cut her off with a wave. "But nothing. I don't have a choice." Believe me, if I could, I wouldn't step foot in that place again.

Reyna reached up and brushed a tear away from the corner of my eye. "What about Tremayne?"

I shrugged. "What about him? He got pissed and walked out on me. It's over."

"But aren't you gonna try and talk to him?"

"For what? Nothing has changed. He would still have a girlfriend who's a stripper. And it was quite clear that's something he can't accept." I started crying again and felt like a fool for even thinking I had a chance to start over new with an amazing man. My life was exactly what it was, a constant struggle. I was just going to have to forget about Tremayne and focus on graduating and taking care of the girls. That in itself was enough to occupy my time.

Reyna made us both a cup of tea and we sat at the table and talked until my eyelids drooped. She insisted that I stay over, and I was glad because I just didn't have the strength to drive home.

Feeling dirty, I took a shower. As soon as I was under the spray of water I closed my eyes and the entire event kept flashing through my mind. I still couldn't get past the humiliation, and the worst part about it was I had brought in on myself. I'd had every opportunity to tell Tremayne the truth and yet I kept lying to him, even after he had confronted me about working at the hospital. I thought I could keep the stripping a secret until I graduated. But not once did I stop to think what might happen if he found out the truth.

What the hell was wrong with me? I should have seen this coming, especially after that mess with Greg. I guess I just never thought of Tremayne going to a strip club. My mistake was, I forgot he was a man.

I lathered my body and rinsed off, then climbed out of the shower determined to stop thinking about Tremayne and get some rest. I crawled under the covers in the spare room and must have fallen asleep the second my head hit the pillow.

I dreamed about Tremayne watching me dancing in that club. It was so crazy because the next thing I knew he was pulling me into his arms, carrying me off to bed, and making love to me.

He stripped my clothes and slowly kissed me down my chest past my belly button, where he latched onto my clit and sucked until I was bucking and whimpering on the bed. He then slipped inside my kitty, and I rocked my hips meeting each stroke of his crafty tongue. I don't know how many times he made me come. Instead I savored every second, afraid I would wake up and the moment would be lost.

Tremayne slid up on the bed and positioned himself between my thighs, and I sighed as he slid inside. Oh, he filled me perfectly, and I gasped as he stroked in and out of my kitty with long, deep thrusts. I rocked my hips and called out his name, begging him to fuck me harder.

"Yeah, baby. Tell me, whose pussy is it?"

As soon as I heard those words, my hips stilled and my mind began to register. That wasn't Tremayne's voice. I opened my eyes and had to blink several times before the horror registered.

Reyna was on top of me.

"What the fuck?"

Slowly, she opened her eyes, then she stared down at me with this sickening smile on her face. "Monica, come on . . . tell me it's my pussy."

With one hard shove, I pushed her off me, and that bitch fell onto the hardwood floor.

"What you do that for?" she screamed and had the nerve to look hurt. I leaned over the side of the bed, and it was then that I realized she was wearing a strap-on dildo.

Something in me snapped. I sprang off that bed and punch her dead in the mouth. Then I kept hitting her until she stopped trying to fight back. "You're sick!" I screamed. "Sick!" I finally climbed off her and reached for my clothes.

Reyna just stayed on the floor, crying and wiping blood from her nose. "I love you, Monica! There is nothing sick about that. I've been in love with you for years, waiting for you to get over that bastard Anthony and notice me. But instead you decided to date that other dude and started hanging out with those strippers. I thought they would help you realize there was nothing wrong with being with another woman, but instead they were trying to taste your pussy, and I just couldn't have that."

I shook my head and was tempted to hit her in the face again, but she was already bleeding. I was certain I had busted her lip and nose. "Bitch, I thought you were my friend!"

"I don't wanna be your friend. Don't you see? I wanna be your lover."

I grabbed the lamp, yanked the plug out of the wall, and threw it at her head. "If you ever come around me again, I'll kill you!"

I stormed out of the house and out to my car, then peeled out of the driveway with tears streaming down my face. And to think I thought my life couldn't possibly get any worse.

35

Robin

It had been almost two weeks since that fiasco at my house, and Trey still refused to talk to me. He helped with Kyle with no more than a few words and then was out the door. No more staying over, watching movies, and hanging out. Damn, I missed him.

Halo was picking me up in an hour so we could go to the Richmond Funny Bone. Eddie Griffin was the headliner.

By the middle of the show I was laughing my ass off and having a good time. It felt good clearing my head and forgetting about my problems. On the way out we spotted Mercedes and Dollar. Ain't that some shit. She went from one friend to the other, but then again we were talking about Mercedes, and she'd do anything for a dollar. No pun intended.

We ended up all going to Denny's off Temple Road. I was glad for the diversion because Halo had hinted throughout the evening he planned on tapping that ass. I'd been stalling, but tonight was it. We had just gotten our food when Mercedes said something that made me choke on my omelet.

"Hey, Treasure, did ole girl get released on bail yet?"

Halo stopped chewing and gave me a weird look. "What girl?"

Mercedes's eyes danced with amusement like she knew

something I didn't. "You know . . . that chick who shot up Mannie."

I didn't look at Halo because I was afraid he might be able to read my mind. Instead, I focused on Dollar and saw the smirk on his face just before he and Halo shared a look.

Halo swung around on his chair. "How you know that chick?"

"I don't. She's a friend of my cousin's," I said quickly.

His fork stopped in midair. "What cousin? I thought you didn't have any family."

Shit. I forgot that Halo knew I grew up in foster care. It was one thing we had in common. "Really she's a *play* cousin. This chick named Tangie I grew up with. I ran into her at the store and she told me what happened." I went back to eating my food as I continued. "Tangie said her girl didn't kill Mannie . . . that someone set her up."

Halo chewed his food, then looked at me like he was still trying to read my mind. "I guess that means she musta been in the wrong place at the wrong time."

"Or in the *right* place at the *wrong* time." Dollar chuckled at his own joke, and Mercedes laughed along with him.

"What?" I asked because I wanted to know what was so fucking funny.

Dollar gave me a weird look, then pointed his fork at me. "You know . . . I never noticed this before . . . but you kinda look like that female Mannie was fucking with. Yo, Halo, man, don't you think?"

It took everything I had to keep a straight face with all eyes on me.

Halo barely glanced my way. "I don't remember nothing about that bitch except that she threw up all over my got damn bear rug."

"Really?" I tried to play it cool. "I hope it wasn't the expensive one I bought you?" I said with attitude, but I really was shaking with anticipation.

"Hell yeah."

I couldn't believe it. If Deena had thrown up on his rug, then that meant she had been in Halo's office. How come my sister never mentioned being at Club Swag? While we were still living together, I had bought Halo this ugly bear rug he had wanted for his office.

"Did you get it cleaned?"

He answered between chews. "Nah . . . some things can't be cleaned. I threw that muthafucka out."

Dollar started laughing like a hyena and Mercedes was looking to the left, right, everywhere but across the table at me. I was starting to think that maybe Halo wasn't the only one who knew what had happened to Mannie.

I went back with Halo to his place and was still thinking about Deena. I was going to have to go and see her and find out why she hadn't mentioned anything about being at his club.

"So, Ma, what's it gonna be?" Halo pulled me into his arms and I forced a smile.

"I'm getting ready to show you what you've been missing," I cooed near his ear.

He looked pleased by my answer. "Now, that's what I'm talking about."

There was no getting around it, so I might as well give him what he wanted. I wasn't sure why, but I felt guilty. I'd been sleeping with men for years for money, so what was the difference? Trey. That was the difference. I missed him. While I was with him I didn't think about sleeping with anyone else.

Halo turned on the music and I made him take a seat while I danced. I let the music and the alcohol take over, and it wasn't long before I had forgotten who I was with. Halo made it rain with dollar bills and I wiggled my ass and dropped to my knees and crawled over to him.

When we were together I gave him head without hesitation. But that time was over. So when he tried to guide my head down to his crotch, I removed his hand and reached for his zipper instead. "I missed this," I purred and whipped his dick out of his jeans and wrapped my fingers around it, causing Halo to groan.

"Then quit bullshitting and show me some love."

Grinning, I reached inside the nightstand where he kept the condoms and grabbed one. Halo was just as afraid of having a baby as I was. I slipped it on, then straddled his waist and dropped down onto his length.

Back in the day you couldn't have told me my man wasn't slinging some good dick. But I can honestly say I didn't feel a thing fucking Halo except for regret. I missed Trey, and I was going to do whatever it took to get him back.

36

Monica

I finished early at the nail salon and headed over to a small Italian restaurant on Old Street in historic Petersburg. I was supposed to meet Robin for lunch.

It had been a week since Tremayne ended our relationship, and my heart still ached for him. Despite my determination not to quit dancing, I hadn't been to the club since. Instead every evening I went out into my car, so the girls wouldn't hear me, and cried until I had no tears left. Tremayne had been my rock, and I really thought we had a chance to have something together, but I had blown it but not giving him the one thing he had asked of me—honesty. It was crazy, but in one day I had lost my man and my best friend. It was so unreal. I don't know how I made it to school, and when I did, I didn't even remember half of what the instructor was saying. Luckily, I had sense enough to bring a tape recorder with me. We were studying for boards and the last thing I needed was to start failing this late in the game. Eight more weeks and my hard work would finally pay off.

I had ordered a cup of coffee by the time I saw Robin stepping inside the shop. As soon as she spotted me, I waved and watched as she moved my way. As usual, she looked like she had just stepped out of a salon. Her hair was laid, her clothes were not only fashionable but tasteful. She was wearing skinny jeans, pink stilettos, and a pink and gray shirt that hung off the shoulders. On her eyes was a pair of rhinestone-studded pink-tinted shades that looked perfect for her round face.

"Hey," she said and slid onto the bench across from me.

"Your hair looks good," I complimented her. I loved the way it had been flat-ironed to curl around her shoulders. It had body and not a split end in sight.

"Thanks. I had her squeeze me in this morning."

I loved that her hair was all hers. Unlike me; I stuck a wig on my head every night to disguise my wholesome looks. But with Robin what you saw was what you got all the time. "I called you because I felt I owed you an apology for the other night."

"I was wondering what whassup? The way you ran out the club the other night I knew something was wrong, and then when I tried calling you, I figured you decided stripping was just too much for you to handle."

I shook my head and sighed. "No . . . it's more to it than that."

The waitress arrived and Robin ordered a lemonade and a turkey melt. I ordered iced tea and a chef's salad. I waited until she returned with our drinks before I continued.

"Remember that guy at the bachelor party I was talking to?"

She nodded. "Yeah, he seemed heated."

"That was my man."

Her brow rose like she wanted to say something more, but instead she waited for me to continue.

"I never told him I was dancing."

"You're kidding!" I could tell she was trying not to laugh.

"I'm afraid not. I know it was wrong and I should have been honest with him in the first place, but I kept thinking that I would graduate and quit the job long before he ever needed to know." I had gone over it in my head again and again. It was a stupid idea and I know that now, but it was too late to do anything about it.

"Damn, girl. So what happened?"

"I haven't heard from him since."

She seemed surprised by my response. "Have you tried to call him?"

I sucked my teeth in disgust. "For what? As pissed as he was when he found out, there's no way I'm gonna call a man and beg him to forgive me for not being honest."

"Good for you. That's why I don't let men get close to me," she commented between sips.

"What about that cutie you've been spending time with?"

She rolled her eyes. "Yeah, I kinda fucked that situation up, which sucks because he really cares about my nephew. And as long as my sister is locked up, he and I still have daily contact." She explained to me how the two of them were sharing responsibilities.

"Is that a bad thing? Your sister needs the two of you in her corner. I'm sure she appreciates it."

"Yes, she does." There was something in her eyes when she mentioned her. It was almost sadness.

"Do you think she's guilty?" I had to ask.

She waited until after the waitress put our food on the table before she answered. "I did at first, but now I believe she's innocent." She sighed. "I guess I should have always known. The sister I knew would never hurt a fly."

I didn't wanna be nosy because I could tell she wasn't used to talking about her family, so I waited for her to continue.

"Before Trey showed at my door with my nephew, I had never seen him before."

"What?" She had totally lost me. "Girl, you need to start at the beginning."

37

Robin

By the time I got done telling Monica about our parents being killed and growing up in the system, I was sure she thought my family was straight-up dysfunctional, and guess what, I couldn't blame her. We were.

"Did your foster parents mistreat you?" she asked.

"Mistreat me!" I barked. She didn't know the half of it. "They beat me every which way with whatever they could find, extension cords, tree limbs, and belts . . . but the last one, that big cow, she liked to use her fists." I didn't even bother to hide the bitterness.

"That's terrible! Did you ever tell anyone?"

"I tried, but no one seemed to believe me. She had them all thinking I lived in this imaginary world of make-believe all the time." Part of it was true. "Life was so bad I used to pretend I was some white girl living in Chesterfield, with the big house and parents who took me to ballet recitals and Girl Scouts instead of some cast-off who got her ass beat just for having rusty elbows," I said with a laugh, trying to hide some of the pain. I don't think I would ever get over what I went through growing up. "Sometimes Ms. Ernestine's hand would come out of nowhere for no apparent reason except that I was in the room and she needed to lash out at someone. After

Deena abandoned me, it only got worse." Monica sat there shaking her head, picking at her food. I bet she never heard anything so fucked up before in her life. "I spent years hating my sister for leaving."

Monica looked up from her salad. "Don't take this the wrong way . . . but your sister was young herself. You can't *really* blame her for wanting to leave. You said so yourself, your foster mother tried to beat the black off you. If the roles were reversed, you think you would have stuck around if you didn't have to?"

"No, I probably would have left a month before my eighteenth birthday and hid out in the streets until I was too old for them to take me back." I could see her point.

"How long did you live at her house?"

I gazed across the table at her and smiled as I remembered my last day there. "For almost five years. I ran away a few weeks after Deena and was sent to another foster home. It was right after Ms. Ernestine had fallen down a flight of stairs."

"Oh my goodness. Don't tell me you pushed her?" Monica asked with this incredulous look on her face like she wouldn't have blamed me if I had.

"No, I was too scared of her for that, although I used to imagine her getting hit by a car. The carpet was loose at the top of the basement steps. I always had to be careful when I needed to go down to get something out of the freezer. I remember hating going down there, mainly because it was where Ms. Ernestine put us when she really wanted to teach us a lesson. The dungeon was what she called it. I remembered being locked down there all weekend with nothing to eat or drink. She had cut off the lights so I was left sitting in the dark shivering like a damn fool. There were mice down there, so I always climbed to the top step and huddled close to the door, hoping they wouldn't come up there and bother me. Deena used to try and sneak me food when Ms. Ernestine left for the store, but she figured it out and started padlocking the door and kept that key tucked away in her bra. After a few times down there I learned what not to say or do."

"Damn, girl!" Monica was still shaking her head. The last thing I wanted was pity, but I must admit it felt good talking about it.

"One day while I was at school she must have tripped on the carpet because when I got home, I heard her calling out for help. At first I thought it was a trap to get me down in the basement but when I saw her lying down there with her leg twisted beneath her, I knew she was hurt."

"What did you do?" Monica was leaning across the table, practically holding her breath.

"Nothing. I just stood there looking at her, wondering if I left her there would she eventually die. Then one of the other foster kids came home and called the police. After that she didn't bother me as much. I guess she realized that I wanted to kill her and if I ever got the chance I would do it."

"And you blame your sister for leaving?" Monica gave me a look like I was the one who was wrong.

"No, I don't blame Deena for leaving . . . I blame her for leaving me there. I would have gone with her in a heartbeat."

"I'm sure she knew that, but if she didn't have anywhere to go, why would she take you with her?"

"Because we're family. That's why. Family should stick to-gether."

She thought about it a moment, then shrugged. "That's true. I guess she could have at least called DFS."

"She said she did."

"Then that's all you can expect any eighteen-year-old girl to do."

I know part of what she was saying was true, but after blaming someone and hating her for over ten years, forgiving her wasn't going to happen overnight. All I could do was take it one day at a time.

"I always wished I had a sister. I was lonely being an only child. That's why friendships mean a lot to me."

"You and Reyna seem to be real close."

Monica rolled her eyes then stabbed her salad with her fork. "Whatever," she mumbled under her breath. I couldn't resist asking.

"What's wrong?"

"Let see . . . how should I put this . . . me and Reyna are no longer friends."

About damn time. I never understood how they were friends in the first place. "Why? What happened?"

Monica paused, almost as if she was trying to choose her words carefully. "Reyna . . . she made a pass at me."

My eyes widened. "A pass?" I laughed. "What she do . . . try to kiss you?"

"I wish that's all that it was." She looked embarrassed for even bringing it up. "After I left the bachelor party, I went to Reyna's house because I knew she would understand. We talked and I stayed the night in her guest room. Next thing I know, I wake up with her on top of me."

I choked and fell out of my chair.

38

Monica

"Hell nah!"

Robin got up from the floor and returned to her seat, and I was so embarrassed I regretted even mentioning it. Just thinking about waking up and finding Reyna on top of me fucking me with a dildo was still too unbelievable for words. It had been a week, but I was still having flashbacks. Last night I even woke up in a sweat, thinking Reyna was trying to slide up under the covers. I can't tell you how relieved I was to find it was only Liese climbing in next to me after waking from a bad dream. I was a bundle of nerves because of that woman and even had my locks changed since I had been stupid enough to give her a key. All I could think about was her over at my house when I wasn't there, in my room, sniffing my panties. The whole thing was so sick, there was no way in hell I was gonna admit she had fucked me with a dildo. The worst part about it was that before I had realized it was her on top of me instead of Tremayne, I had actually been enjoying it.

"So what did you do when you found her in the bed with you?" Robin asked, trying to keep a straight face.

How do you tell someone your best friend raped you, because that's what happened. I had been raped by a woman wearing a strap-on dildo.

"Shit, what you think I did . . . I tried to kick that bitch's ass." It still puzzled me, because I guess the signs had always been there. I had just been too stupid to notice them.

"Hell nah! I've heard it all." Robin took a bite of her sandwich, but I could still see her eyes on me. "Sooo . . . did you like it?"

"No!" I said and tried not to blink because I was lying, sort of. I'd liked it up until I realized it was a woman fucking me. "There ain't nothing a woman can do for me."

She chuckled and pushed for more details. While we ate, I told her about Reyna creeping under the covers and eating my pussy, but I left out the dildo because it made me feel dirty and violated. I was tempted to go down to her shop and beat her ass again, but it just wasn't worth it. The farther I stayed away from Reyna, the better off we'd both be.

I arrived back at home at three. I was getting ready to lower the garage door when a gray sedan pulled into my driveway. Suspiciously, I waited until the door opened and an elderly white man climbed out. He looked like a bill collector. I made a quick scan in my head, trying to remember if all my bills were paid, and was pleased to say that for once, everything was in order.

"Is there something I can help you with?" I asked and walked toward him.

He gave me a sweet smile, like he was one of my neighbors just dropping by to tell me my rosebushes looked beautiful. But I knew he wasn't a neighbor because I personally knew all of their names.

"Are you Monica Houston?"

I hesitated, then nodded.

"Wonderful. I have something for you." He handed me a

clipboard to sign, and as soon as I scribbled my signature, he pulled out a large envelope and I took it from his hand. "You've been served," he said, then walked back to his car.

Stunned, I opened the manila envelope, pulled out the document, and as I read the petition, my knees buckled.

Anthony was suing me for full custody of the girls.

39

Robin

After I left the restaurant, one of my regulars started blowing up my phone. I agreed to meet him at the Holiday Inn at four. The entire ride over there I had this sick feeling in my stomach and when I stepped into the room, I seriously started having doubts.

"I've been waiting all day for this," Marty said as he pulled off his clothes. I looked down at his dick standing straight up and found myself comparing it to Trey's. Marty's looked like a hot dog that had been left in the microwave too long.

"I plan to make it worth your wait," I replied and forced a smile that I wasn't feeling. The sooner I got this shit over with, the better.

A stack of crisp twenties was already on the side table. Eagerly Marty leaped his skinny behind in the bed and rolled onto his back. What the hell? Some men were so pathetic.

I made a show of peeling off my clothes, and under his lustful stares I felt so violated. Why in hell was I doing this when I really didn't want to? I knew why: because I had never allowed a relationship with a man to stand in the way of me and my money no matter how much I was feelin' him.

I straddled his waist, slid on a condom, and rode Marty. He was moaning and panting like a wild animal until he finally cried out my name. It felt like forever, but one look at the clock confirmed that it had taken less than ten minutes. I usually lingered and worked to double my money, but not this time. I climbed off, went into the bathroom, and showered.

"Where you going?" he asked when I stepped back into the room.

"I gotta go." I couldn't even look him in the face. Just the thought disgusted me because I was disgusted with myself.

"But you *always* stay at least an hour," he pouted, then had the nerve to slide off the bed and walk over to me.

I quickly moved out of his way and reached for my clothes. "Not today. I've got somewhere to be."

"But I paid for an hour."

I gave him an evil look. "No . . . you *paid* for a nut. You got it. Now I'm gone."

He stood there speechless as I got dressed, and by the time I had put on my shoes, I knew this was going to be the last time I ever slept with a man for money. It didn't matter to me anymore. I had found something—correction—someone who'd brought meaning to my pathetic life, and guess what? I wanted him back.

"Consider this your lucky day. For once you'll leave here with money still in your wallet." Because any other time I would have taken him for everything he had.

I was in love. Can you believe that shit? I swore I would never feel that way about a man again, yet I did, and now I had to make things right between us.

I snatched the money off the nightstand and made my way out into the parking lot, and as soon as I reached my car, Halo pulled up beside me.

"Yo, what the fuck you doin' here?" he barked at me, then sniffed the air like he caught a whiff of another's dude dick lingering around me.

I had to come up with a lie quick. "Hollering at a friend in housekeeping, why?"

"What friend? You know all I gotta do is go to the front desk and ask which room you was in." He gave me this look like he was daring me to lie. You gotta get up pretty early in the morning to catch my ass in action.

I shrugged. "Go ask and they'll tell you none." Hell, I wasn't stupid. I never put a room in my own name. "Why you following me anyway?"

"Just keeping track of what's mine."

Let me just say being back with Halo was taking its toll on me. He needed to know my whereabouts every hour on the hour and was constantly popping up on me. I was starting to think he had planted a tracking device that I had yet to find. "I'm not yours."

"See . . . why you even have to go there? I thought we were letting it do what it do?"

"Yes, but on my terms. Your way doesn't work for me, re-member? And if you keep following my ass we're never gonna get back together." My head and neck were twisting with straight attitude. I wasn't about to be on no short leash.

"A'ight. But you know a nigga like me ain't tryna rent or lease it, I'm tryna own it. You feel me? I don't have a problem doing things on yo terms, but if I find out you're fuckin' around on me, I'll kill you," he said with a grin that said he meant what he said, then peeled out of the lot with Lil Wayne bumping from his stereo.

My hands were shaking by the time I had put my key in the ignition. This situation was getting so out of hand. But nothing was going to stop me from talking to Trey. I had to try to make him understand.

I drove over to the Southpark Mall, dipped into Dillard's, and called a cab. While I waited, I bought a large T-shirt and a new pair of shades, then pulled my hair back into a ponytail. It was a damn shame the changes I had to go through to dodge Halo, but I had to talk to Trey and there was no way I could get within twenty feet of him with Halo sniffing behind me.

I had the driver meet me over near the food court. I jumped into the back, slid down low in the seat, and gave him directions to the restaurant. The dinner hour was getting started, so this was as good a time as any to talk to Trey before he would be too busy for me to get even five minutes of his time. And with what I needed to say, I didn't need any distractions.

"Ma'am, that'll be twenty-two fifty."

I noticed the driver gazing at me all hungry and shit through the rearview mirror. *Whatever*. I tossed three ten-dollar bills in the front seat and hopped out of the cab and into the restaurant. As soon as I stepped through the door I could smell Ms. Ethel's sour cream pound cake.

"Chile, come on over here!" she cried the second she spotted me coming through the door. I slipped off the designer frames, grinned, and moved toward the register. "I almost didn't recognize you. Where you been hiding?"

I really liked his mother. She was a short, round woman with long dark hair and the biggest smile. She kinda reminded me of Loretta Devine with a little voice packed with power.

"Hi, Ms. Ethel, I've been busy." Since that mess with Halo, Trey and I had been avoiding each other as much as possible. With Kyle being at day care all day, it made that easy because one of us dropped him off and the other would pick him up. The weekends, he just stayed at Trey's.

"Go on back and help yourself to some food. I just turned off a pot of black-eyed peas."

I didn't have much of an appetite. I was too nervous. "That sounds delicious. Uh . . . is Trey around?"

She nodded. "Yes, he's in his office."

I turned and walked away before I lost the nerve. I waved at everyone in the kitchen, then moved down the hall, knocked, and without waiting for a response, I stepped into his office. Trey was sitting behind his desk in a shirt and tie, looking so delicious. I missed him being in my life.

"What do you want?" he said the second he spotted me coming through the door.

"Just hear me out," I begged. Seeing the anger in his eyes made me want to just say fuck it and move on. But I refused to react like I typically would, especially since that man made me feel something I had yet to discover with any other. "Trey, listen . . . I'm really sorry about how things went down."

"Is that all you came in here to say?" He glared at me like I had a lot of nerve showing up at his job, giving him some lame-ass apology. I'll give him that. I deserved it.

I stepped boldly into the room. "No . . . I also came to explain."

He laughed. "Yeah, this I gotta hear because I still haven't been able to figure that one out." Leaning back in his chair, he folded his arms, across his chest and gave me a hard look that said he didn't have all day. I stepped farther into his office, expecting him to stop me at any time, and was glad when he didn't. "How about I get this conversation moving . . . are you and that muthafucka back together or what?"

From the tone of his voice, it was obvious he was still hurt about it. I looked down at the black mules on my feet, trying to figure out how to answer that question. "No."

"Okay, if you're not together, then why were you with him? Because the way that dude was grinning, there's a lot more going on than you're admitting."

I moved closer to his desk and tried to make eye contact with him, but it's hard when someone avoids looking at you. "I think he's the reason Deena's in jail."

Hazel eyes snapped in my direction. "What?" I finally had his attention.

"The dude she was kicking it with worked for Halo."

"How do you know that?"

"Trey, I lived with Halo for two years. Trust me. I would know." He didn't look too happy at my answer. "Anyway, Dee told me Halo thought Mannie was skimming his product, and knowing Halo the way that I do, if he really believed that, then he woulda had him smoked."

I stared at Trey waiting for him to say something. He was quiet, thinking about what I said before he shook his head with disbelief. "How you know he ain't just talk? I'm mean . . . I've threatened to kill someone before, but that didn't mean I was serious."

"You don't know Halo like I do. He doesn't just say something unless he means it," I tried to explain. I had enough bruises upside my head to prove Halo didn't play. "I remember this one dude used to work for him, right, and he wasn't nothing but a dime-store hustler, but it didn't matter to Halo what level you were at. Anyway, dude came up short with his money. One minute he was hopping in the car with Halo, and an hour later he was found in a Dumpster a few blocks away, dead. Nobody had to tell me Halo killed him because I already knew the answer to that."

"So what you're saying, you think he killed dude and framed Dee?" he said with this incredulous look on his face.

"I don't think . . . I know. I just need to prove it."

"And how the hell you gonna do that?"

I took his chin in my hand and lifted it so he could see my eyes. I wanted to make sure he knew I was sincere and not spitting game. "Trey, the only reason I went out with Halo was because I know the only way I can help Dee is to find out what really happened that night."

"So fucking that nigga is the answer." It wasn't a question because being a man, he already knew the answer. That was a cheap blow and he knew it, but I didn't even try to deny it. Trey started cussing, then pushed my hand away and sprang from his chair. "Dammit, did our relationship mean anything to you?"

"Oh course it did . . . does. I miss being with you." Probably more than I even realized until I walked in and saw the hurt in his eyes. "Please understand . . . I gotta help Dee."

He shrugged. "I want to help her too, but I'm not about to be fucking around for the answer."

"That's not fair!"

"No, what's not fair is making me think we had something that we really didn't. I'm crazy about you and I respected you for keeping it real with me, but playing me with that nigga, that shit was foul."

"I know and I'm sorry. I wanted to tell you what I was tryna to do, but I didn't know how." I was practically pleading with him to understand, and begging was just not something Robin Douglas did, but for Trey I·was willing to make an exception to the rules.

"Secrets are a muthafucka. You being wit that nigga, I just can't stomach that shit." He stared pacing around his office. I didn't come here to piss him off, but it seemed that was exactly what I had done.

"So where does that leave us?" I asked, waiting for him to say something or to give me some kind of sign we still had a chance.

There was silence for a good thirty seconds before he finally shook his head and replied, "I don't know. You tell me. You still wit him or what?"

"I told you . . . I'm trying to find out what happened that night." Was he not listening?

"So in other words, you plan to keep fucking the nigga until you get some answers?" By his tone he was clearly annoyed. Why was it men always have to be so damn territorial?

"Please, Trey . . . try to understand I'm doin' it to make everything right in my life. I finally got my sister back and I want a chance for us to try and fix our relationship. I also don't want to see Kyle go through what we went through. Growing up without my mama was hard."

"I understand all that and I'm willing to do whatever it takes, but if you want to be with me, you need to leave dude alone."

"I can't do that. At least not yet." I saw the frown on his face. "Damn, Trey, don't make me choose between you and my sister."

"I'm not . . . you are." He sat back down at his desk and reached for a pen, putting an end to the conversation. "Go ahead and handle yo business."

I headed to the door feeling worse than I had before I arrived. Before I exited the room, I heard him call after me. "Yo . . . Robin?"

I swung around and met his eyes.

"Be careful."

All I could do was nod and walk out the door.

40

Monica

"What are you doing at my house?" Although he was whispering, his voice was cold and serious.

"Why the hell you think!" I retorted. "How dare you tell Anthony? We had a deal."

Nervously Greg closed the front door and stepped out onto the wide front porch. "Please lower your voice before my wife hears you."

I didn't give a fuck about his wife. "We had a deal!"

"I didn't say anything, Monica. I swear," he pleaded. His eyes kept darting over his shoulder. I didn't give a fuck who heard us. I had tried to do everything I could to keep Anthony from finding out I was stripping. I was too close to graduating for some fool to ruin everything.

"I don't believe you!" My finger was in his face, stabbing at his chest.

"Please, I swear on my mother's grave I didn't tell Anthony a thing."

Something in his eyes said he might be telling the truth, but a man could lie through his teeth and I'd never know.

"Here, take some money . . . just go!" he said, then reached inside his wallet and pulled out everything he had. He was handing me almost $200 when the door swung open.

"What is going on out here?" I glanced up at the woman with long brown hair and blue eyes who was standing at the door, a hand at her hip. She looked from her husband to me, then down at the money in his hands. "What's going on?"

He hesitated. "Nothing, my sweet."

"Nothing." She put a hand on his arm, drawing his attention. "It sure doesn't look like nothing. Why are you giving this woman money?"

I folded my arms defiantly against my chest, waiting to see what lie he'd come up with. He'd ruined my life, so I was going to ruin his.

"Listen, Monica . . ." he said and dragged a frustrated hand across his face. "I haven't been at the firm in two weeks! You wanna know why? My youngest daughter has just been diagnosed with leukemia."

"Leukemia?" I felt my face crack.

"My wife and I have been at the hospital with her waiting for them to find a bone marrow donor. So the last thing I'm worrying about is Anthony finding out his ex-wife's a stripper."

I heard his wife gasp. "Stripper? How the hell do you know she's a stripper?" She pivoted on her heel with a hand still planted at her hip. She expected an answer right away and was pissed when she didn't get it. "Oh, okay . . . I get it now. You've been hanging out at the strip clubs again, and she's here for payment."

He didn't even bother to deny it.

"You bastard! Pack your shit and get out of my house!" she snapped, then stormed into the house, leaving him standing there.

"I'm so sorry." And I meant it.

Greg stared at me silently for a few seconds before he replied in a chilly voice, "It's too late for sorries. You're gonna to regret coming to my house. I swear to you . . . if you ruined my marriage, I'll . . . I'll kill you." He then walked back into the house, slamming the door in my face.

I left his house feeling that maybe I had made a mistake. I rode around for a while crying and feeling sorry for myself until I thought about one other person who might have wanted revenge. I pulled into the parking lot, then took the elevator up to the seventh floor and stormed down the hall and past his secretary.

"Wait, he has someone in his office!"

Ignoring her protests, I pushed the door open and stepped into the office. Everyone at the table looked up.

"Did you do it?" I demanded, looking him dead in the eyes.

Tremayne rose from the small conference table. "Monica," he said and had the nerve to look surprised to see me.

"I need to know if you told Anthony." I looked around and everyone at the table was staring up at me.

Instead of answering me, he turned to the other three sitting at the table across from him. "Will you excuse me?"

I put a hand to my hips and waited as he walked them to the door and closed it behind them before he turned around and faced me.

"I asked you a question," I snapped, growing angrier by the second. "Did you tell Anthony what I did for a living?"

"I can't believe you would even ask me that question."

Why not? He was a man. "After lying to you, I could see you trying to get back at me by telling him," I said, folding my arms and staring angrily over at him.

"I'm sorry you think so little of me."

"Just answer the question, dammit!" I ordered. I felt like I was about to lose my mind. Someone had told Anthony, and I was going to ask anyone who had reason to get back at me.

"No . . . no Monica, I did not," he finally replied, and I didn't miss the look of disappointment on his face. The second the words came out of his mouth I believed him.

I unfolded my arms and felt ashamed for even accusing him. But if he didn't do it, then who did?

I started crying because I didn't know where to go. I no longer had my best friend's shoulder to cry on I had even texted Reyna to see if she knew anything about Anthony finding out and she said of course not, but she was there if I wanted to talk. I just couldn't bring myself to talk to her on the phone, let alone see her again. My life was a mess. What in the word was I thinking, working at a strip club? I couldn't hold on to my emotions and I started bawling right there in the middle of his office. Tremayne came over and put a soothing arm around me, but when he held me it was nothing like the way he used to hold me in the past. "Why don't you have a seat and tell me what happened."

I stepped away from his grasp and wiped the tears from my eyes but kept standing. "What happened is my husband found out I was stripping and now he's suing me for full custody of the girls."

"I'm sorry, but I swear I didn't have anything to do with that," he said with finality.

I nodded. There was really nothing else to do at that point except leave, go home, and figure out what to do next. As much as I needed the money, I didn't dare show my face at the club anymore. Which meant my girls and I would be struggling again.

Without a word I headed toward the door.

"Do you have a lawyer?"

I swung around look at Tremayne and shook my head. "No, I don't."

"What about your divorce lawyer?"

"I never had a lawyer. Anthony's lawyer handled everything."

He stood there and didn't say anything, but I could see it in his eyes and knew what he was thinking. Stupid. I mean, who in their right mind allowed their husband's lawyer to handle the terms of a divorce without hiring a lawyer of their own? Anthony had all the money. He controlled it. Before he even announced he wanted a divorce, he had already transferred almost all the money out of our joint account. So there was no way I could have afforded a lawyer of my own.

"One of my junior attorneys will handle the case for you," Tremayne said with certainty.

I looked him in the face and said, "Why are you helping me?"

There was hesitation in his voice. "Because despite how you lied to me and didn't trust that my feelings for you were real, I care about those girls and I know it would tear their hearts if they were torn away from their mother. Now if you'll excuse me, I'll have my secretary contact you with an appointment."

Nodding, I stepped out the door, then swung around. "Tremayne . . . I'm sorry."

"So am I," he said as he closed his office door behind me.

41

Robin

It was an All White Party and Club Swag was packed with everyone in their cleanest gear, but I expected as much. Whenever Halo had a private party, everybody wanted to be a part of the excitement. Free liquor, DJ Phenomenon spinning the hottest hip-hop, and some of the baddest strippers working the crowd, what more could a nigga ask for?

Honey, me, and this dancer named Cherry had been working the club for almost two hours, and I was ready to take my ass home. Don't get me wrong, the money was damn good, but I was starting to think that I wasn't gonna find any evidence regarding Mannie's murder. I was tired of riding Halo's dick, trying to get information that he wasn't giving. At the same time I was trying to keep him from popping up at my house and finding out my nephew was living with me. All that shit I'd been feeding him about not being ready for him to spend the night was only gonna work for so long.

I sauntered over to Honey, who was standing at the bar in the far corner with an apple martini in her hand, swaying her hips to the beat of the music.

She stopped dancing when she spotted me coming her way. "Hey, girl. I'm making out like a bandit tonight. What about you?"

"No doubt." I grinned and held up a clutch purse that was hanging from a strap around my wrist. I hadn't bothered to count my money but I was sure I had already made at least five hundred, and that didn't include the money Dollar was paying me.

"*Shit*, tomorrow I'm going to get my hair done, and then Jordan and I are driving to Virginia Beach for the rest of the weekend to do some shopping."

"Shopping? Hold up . . . I thought you were going to spend this money getting a decent place so Sophia could come home?"

She rolled her eyes. "Girl, I got plenty of time for that. I'm tryna do something for me for a change. Hell, it's hard out here for a pimp!" She started laughing at her own joke, but I didn't see shit funny. Like I said before, seeing is believing, and that chick had a long way to go before she'd finally got her shit together. By then Sophia would have forgotten about her ass. I reached inside my purse, pulled out a cigarette, and lit up. To get through this night I was probably going to smoke an entire pack.

I was getting ready to dip to the bathroom when the music stopped and we all whipped our heads around to see a large cake being pushed onto the center of the dance floor. Halo walked over holding a microphone in his hand and everyone got quiet. Despite the fact he was starting to wear my nerves, that man looked good in all white.

"Yo, I just wanna thank all y'all for coming out to celebrate my boy coming home. Everybody raise your glass for Lil D!"

I was standing in the corner taking a few puffs. Smoking was against the law in public places, so as soon as I filled my lungs, I dropped it to the ground and put it out with my foot before someone said something. Hell, everyone was doing it. I'd smelled weed floating around the room all night.

I listened to cheers, then the music started with that sexy new Beyoncé joint and then like a jack-in-the-box, someone jumped from inside the cake and the niggas went wild. My jaw dropped when I realized who it was. It was Mercedes dressed like *I Dream of Jeannie.*

Honey and I exchanged looks. "Did you know she was coming?"

She shook her head. "I swear. I thought it was just the three of us."

Frowning, I watched Mercedes wiggle out of the cake, then gyrate over to the man of the hour, who was sitting in a chair at the center of the dance floor wearing a big shit-eating grin.

"She's fucking Dollar now, so she probably begged him to be a part of the show," Honey spat over the crowd.

I watched in disgust as Mercedes wiggled her skinny ass all up in Lil D's face. Most of the moves she was doing were mine. I rolled my eyes, headed over to the bar, and ordered a cos-mopolitan.

"Yo, you having a good time?"

I almost jumped when Halo came up behind me and wrapped his arms around my waist, pulling me against him. "Yeah, it's cool," I said and forced a grin. It's hard to believe that at one time the mere touch of him made my panties wet. Now all I wanted to do was get away from his ass and throw up.

"You coming home with me tonight, right?" he cooed.

I nodded even though I had no intention of going with him. As soon as he wasn't looking, I planned to dip out the back door. "Of course," I purred.

"That's whassup." He was grinning like a damn fool as he ordered a bottle of beer. As soon as he had it, he took my hand. "C'mere, I wanna show you something."

Reluctantly I followed him away from the crowd and

down the hall. I'd been in there enough times to know we were heading to his office. Shit, at one time I was second in command in that bitch. I glanced down as he punched in the code to the door and noticed he hadn't changed it. It was still 919—his birthday. He stepped in and I followed, and as soon as he turned on the light, I gasped.

"Wow!" One entire wall was a mural of him sitting at a table covered in piles of cocaine. The picture looked so real, a dope fiend would have picked up a straw, ready to take a hit. Only a cocky muthafucka would put on blast how he really made his money. That's because Halo had it in his head he would never get caught.

"You like it?"

"Hell yeah." I said what he wanted to hear. He looked pleased by my answer, then put his beer down and pulled me into his arms and leaned me back against the desk. He started kissing my neck, lips, and cheeks while his fingers traveled down underneath my minidress to my clit, where he stroked. "You look sexy as a muthafucka in that dress. Remember when we used to sneak back here and fuck on the floor?"

I moaned while I tried to think of a way to get away from him. Speaking of floor, I turned my head and looked down and noticed the bear rug wasn't there. "What the fuck? You really did throw out my rug." I pushed him away and dropped a hand to my waist.

"Yo, I told you some bitch threw up on it."

"Whatever. See if I ever buy yo ass anything again." I faked like I had attitude.

"Awww, don't be like that. Come on and show Big Poppa some love." He reached for the zipper of his pants, lowered it, then pulled out his dick. I tried to resist, but he wasn't having any part of it, and the last thing I needed was to make him mad. Besides, if I worked his ass now, there was no way he would trip when I dipped out later.

When he guided my head down, I dropped to my knees and was getting ready to put his dick in my mouth when something under his desk sparkled under the light, drawing my attention.

"Yo, Halo! I need to holla atcha."

Thank goodness there was a knock at his door. Halo cussed, fixed his pants, then walked over to answer the door. I reached down and picked up the object from under his desk, and as soon as I took a closer look my pulse began to race.

It was Deena's butterfly charm.

"Babe, we gonna have to finish this later. I gotta make a quick run."

All I could do was nod as I rose to my feet, clutching the charm in my hand so he wouldn't notice. I followed him out of his office and slipped into the bathroom, then moved into a stall and took a seat.

I lost it the night Mannie was killed.

I ain't gonna lie, my heart was beating so hard, I felt like I was going to collapse at any second. Deena and Mannie had to have been at Club Swag the night Mannie was killed. When Halo said she threw up on the rug, it never dawned on me that he was talking about the exact night Mannie had been murdered. No wonder Deena didn't know nothing about it. She was too drugged to remember.

I slipped off my bracelet and put her charm on next to mine. We were sisters, and these charms were all we had of our past. The rug was gone as well—the only proof I had that she had even been in his office. I wasn't ready to give up hope just yet.

I went back out onto the floor and found Honey sitting on some dude's lap. I sat down at the table with them. "Girl, you missed it. Mercedes was dancing and her wig fell off her head!"

Damn, I always missed the good shit. "I would love to see an instant replay of that shit." I laughed and then suddenly I stopped and my breathing became shallow as I gazed over at the hidden camera in the corner. Halo taped *everything*. If Mannie was killed at Club Swag, it would be on a video in the panic room behind Halo's office. "Where's Halo?" I asked.

She pointed toward the door. "He and Jordan stepped out for a second."

He had a run to make, which didn't leave me much time. "Honey, c'mere, I need to talk to you for a second." I practically yanked her off his lap and into the ladies' room, where I locked the door.

"What?" Her brown eyes were large with anticipation.

I checked all the stalls and made sure the two of us were alone before I said, "I need you to do something for me."

"Yeah girl, anything, whassup?"

I took a deep breath before finally saying, "I'm gonna sneak in Halo's office, but I need you to make sure he doesn't come back there until I'm finish."

"Girl, what's going on? You know he'll kill you if he catches you."

"I know, that's why I need your help. I'll tell you later when I have more time, but you gotta promise me you'll keep him away."

She hesitated and looked nervous before she finally nodded. "You know I got your back." She hugged me, then returned to the table. I stayed in there long enough to take a few puffs on another cigarette, then I opened the door, made sure no one was looking, and moved down to his office, punched in the code, and slipped inside. Back when we used to date, Halo had given me the code to his panic room. He said if the club was ever raided, he wanted me to have a place to hide while everything went down. I walked over, punched in the code— the day we met—and sighed when it opened.

Inside were cameras showing every corner of the club, including the parking lot, and to the right were rows of recorded video. *Shit.* I had to rack my brain and remember the date Mannie was killed, and as soon as I did, it only took me a minute to find the DVD. I slipped it inside my panties and just happened to glance over at the monitor and almost peed on myself when I spotted Honey giving Halo a lap dance. *He's back!* I hurried out of the panic room, shut the door, and tripped on my stiletto as I made my way across the room and out into the hall.

"Where's Halo?"

I jumped when I spotted Mercedes. She was standing outside the door, with her hand raised like she was just getting ready to knock.

"He's not in there," I said, then pulled the door tight behind me.

"Then what are you doing in there?" she said with a mischievous smirk.

"I'm his girl, or have you forgotten?" I sucked my teeth and turned on my heels. "By the way . . . your wig is crooked."

I made it into the club and saw Honey pulling on Halo, trying to keep him distracted. The last thing I wanted was for him to see me. I weaved around the crowd and out the door of the club. As soon as I reached my Camaro, I texted Honey to let her know I was gone. I didn't know what was on that video, but I needed to find out fast before Halo realized what I had done.

I don't know why, except that I was afraid to go home, but I headed over to Trey's apartment. Kyle was with his sister, so that gave us a chance to be alone and hopefully talk. I rang the bell and started having second thoughts about just showing up. But as soon as he opened the door, my entire body began to tingle. He almost looked happy to see me.

"Hey, whassup?" I was shaking and he noticed. Trey took my hand and escorted me into his place.

"What's wrong?"

My teeth were chattering but I felt safe there with him. Ever since I had left Club Swag, I'd been watching over my shoulder, expecting Halo to pull up beside me at any second. "I think he killed him at the club."

He gave me a strange look. "Who are . . . What did you just say?"

I started babbling and knew I wasn't making any sense. I walked over to his entertainment center, stuck in the DVD, then lowered onto the couch and laced my fingers with his. Without saying a word, I hit Play. Together we sat there watching and waiting. My cell phone started vibrating and I was sure it was Halo wondering where the hell I had gone, but I didn't dare look. I was sure that by now he'd realized I had left, or even worse, Mercedes told him she saw me leaving his office.

"How you been?" Trey asked.

I glanced away from the screen. We stared at each other silently until I said, "I'm cool."

"I wish I could say the same. I've missed you." He leaned over and pressed his juicy wet lips to mine.

"So what are you saying?" I hoped it was what I thought he was saying, but I didn't want to get ahead of myself.

"I'm saying . . . I hope you are through fooling wit that knucklehead."

"Yeah . . . I'm done." Even if there wasn't anything on that video, I was through messing with Halo.

"That's whassup." Trey lifted me over onto his lap and I wrapped my arms around his neck. We sat there kissing and rubbing. I had a feeling that everything was going to be all right between us. Trey must have felt it too because he was playing with my nipples and getting my coochie all wet. He had just slipped his hand underneath my dress when I heard Halo's loud voice coming from the television. I turned toward the screen and saw Deena, semi-conscious, being dragged into Halo's office along with Mannie. I didn't move until I watched the entire tape.

Halo had shot Mannie, and I now had proof.

42

Monica

The next two weeks went by and my head felt like it was in a cloud. I was so out of it that I failed my first exam, but my instructor was nice enough to allow me to retake it. The second time, I at least managed to get a passing grade. I still couldn't believe Anthony and that skinny bitch were trying to steal my babies away. It wasn't fair, and unless I could prove that I was a good mother, I was going to lose them.

"What are my chances?" I asked, staring across the desk at Bernard Robinson. The man was sharp and seemed to know his stuff. And I was truly thankful he was representing me.

"According to his petition, he's claiming child endangerment."

"Child what?"

"He says you have men in and out of the house. And the girls are living in an unsafe environment."

Was he serious? "Men? I was seriously involved with one man, your colleague, Tremayne."

He appeared truly uncomfortable with his next question. "Has he been revealing himself to the girls?"

Oh God. This was so unreal. Before Tremayne dumped me, I bent the rule and allowed him to stay the night. Unfortunately, I had forgotten to lock the door, and the girls had barged into the room like they did every morning. We were making love with the covers off and they saw Tremayne's naked booty in the air. "This is crazy."

"No . . . I'm afraid this is serious. Your ex-husband's determined to show he can provide a stable home life. Stripping is only a part of the problem."

This was all like a bad dream.

Bernard was quiet for moment before he asked, "Have you stopped dancing?"

I looked away. "Yes and no. I'm dancing this weekend. I'm sorry, but I can't afford not to unless he plans to give me more child support. There's barely enough money left for gas. Hell, I haven't even figured out yet how I'm gonna to pay for you."

"You don't have to worry about that. Tremayne is covering my fees."

"What?"

"It's covered," he assured me.

I wanted to refuse, but I was in no position to do that. "Since I can barely make my monthly expenses each month, I am in no position to object."

He gave me a puzzled look. "That's another thing. As much as your ex-husband's firm is worth, I would have expected your financial support to have been much more substantial."

Shit, I would too.

Bernard lowered his pen then leaned across the desk. "I think we need to hire a private investigator to check into your husband's finances."

"Is Tremayne paying for that too?" Hell, I had to know. Like I said, I couldn't afford it.

"Yes, I don't think we'll have a problem. Don't worry . . . I plan to counter for all of your legal fees." He discussed a whole lot of other legal terms that made no sense to me, which was probably why I got screwed in the divorce settlement.

"Just be straight with me. What are my chances?"

He glanced up from his notes and gave me a reassuring smile. "You have a good chance. We just have to show the judge your girls are being raised in a safe and loving environment."

I nodded, feeling a little more hopeful, but I had a long ways to go before I would feel as sure as I should. "Thank you." I rose and shook his hand then headed out to the lobby. I had to be in the hospital in an hour for clinical rotation.

I was walking through the reception area when I spotted Tremayne coming out of his office. I stopped, yet I wasn't sure what to say. Thanks goodness he spoke first.

"Hello, Monica."

"Hello." I couldn't help but stare.

"I trust Bernard is taking good care of you."

"Yes. I don't have any complaints." *Except that we aren't still together.* Saying he looked good was an understatement. He was wearing a blue pin-striped suit that looked designed just for him. I stared up into his beautiful chestnut-colored eyes and we both just stood there staring at each other, waiting for the other to say something. I figured it was now or never. "Tremayne, I'm . . . I'm really sorry that I lied to you. I never meant to deceive you."

He looked like he was considering my apology when a woman sauntered into the lobby, drawing his attention.

"Tre . . . you ready to go?"

Tre? No, she didn't. She was beautiful with long hair like I used to have, light brown eyes and the prettiest complexion, and a big ghetto booty, but there was nothing ghetto about her. She had a professional demeanor, wearing a white sleeveless dress that complemented every curve and expensive peach pumps.

Tremayne drew his eyes away from her long enough to give me a sympathetic smile. "It was good seeing you, Monica."

And on that note, he walked off and out the door with another woman, leaving me to pick my jaw up off the floor.

43

Robin

I had been hiding out at Trey's place when Monica called and asked if I'd mind watching the girls so she could work at the club. I was so happy to have an excuse to get out of the apartment. Don't get me wrong. I was in love with Trey and appreciated everything he was doing for me and Kyle, but I was starting to feel smothered with him hovering over the two of us. If I didn't get out of his cramped-ass apartment soon, I was going to lose my damn mind.

Ever since we took that video down to the police station, he'd been right up under me. He'd hardly been at the restaurant at all, and when he was, he spent more time on the phone, calling and checking up on us. Every time my cell phone rang I was ready to jump out of my skin for fear of who was calling. Halo was out there somewhere, watching and waiting for the right moment to break down the door and beat the crap out of my ass. My nerves were so on edge that every time Trey asked are you all right, I wanted to bite his head off. What the hell did he think? Hell no, I wasn't all right. I had some crazy muthafucka out looking for me.

I guess Trey saw how much I needed to get away because he finally agreed as long as he dropped me off and picked me up. I also had to give him the number to Monica's house so he could call me every hour on the hour and check on me. I was so relieved to get away that I gladly gave him the number.

The kids and I had a ball. We played with Liese's Wii games, which was more of a workout than swinging around on a pole all evening. Not that I even dreamed of going back to Scandalous until Halo was behind bars. We also made chocolate cupcakes and Kyle even helped. I loved Monica's kitchen. Hell, I loved her whole damn house. It was huge with plenty of room to disappear if she wanted.

After I stuck the cupcakes in the oven, I sent the kids upstairs to play while I turned the television on in the family room and took a seat on a huge wraparound couch. I'd been having a bad feeling all day that something was seriously wrong and hoped it was just nerves.

I wanted to see if there was any mention yet of Halo being arrested, so I turned on the ten o'clock news. I still couldn't figure out why it was taking so damn long, especially when everything they needed was right there on that damn tape. But according to the officer, they had been trying to build a case against Halo for years and they needed to make sure they did everything right. In the meantime my ass had to keep hiding out and looking over my shoulder.

I turned to Channel 12 News and leaned back against the couch just as the telephone rang. I glanced down at the caller ID, gave a playful roll of my eyes, then grinned.

"Hey, babe. How's it going?"

I wanted to say the same as it was the last time I talked to you, but I couldn't bring myself to do that. Trey cared about me, and that's more than I could say about any other muthafucka I'd dated. "We're good. We got cupcakes in the oven and the kids just went upstairs to play."

"Make sure you save me one of those cupcakes," he said in a low voice. He had this deep baritone sound that was like he was stroking my kitty, because every time I heard it I immediately got wet.

"Okay, I'll make sure to do that."

There was a brief silence before he said, "You sure you don't want me to come over and sit with you?"

"No no no, I'm fine. Just hang out with your boys and have a good time." He was supposed to be at some sports bar with his boys, instead he was worrying about me.

"Well, if you change your mind . . ."

"I won't. I'm okay, Trey, really I am. This is gonna be over soon."

"I don't like it, but I've gotta respect it." He then went on to say something else, but my eyes were suddenly on the television screen. The news reporter was standing in front of a gas station on Temple Avenue that I knew quite well.

"Trey, I need to go and check on the kids. I'll call you later." I hung up the phone without even waiting to for him to respond and turned up the volume on the television:

"Less than an hour ago, the body of a woman was found in a Dumpster behind this Exxon gas station. According to the police, her neck was slit and she'd been badly beaten. The identity is being withheld until her family has been notified."

I suddenly had a terrible chill as the reporter zoomed in on a neighbor who said she got suspicious when she walked by and saw a white Toyota pull up to the Dumpster and several people climbed out. She waited until they were gone before she sent her brother over to look inside, and that's when they found the body.

I had a sick feeling, because if Halo had found me, that could have been my body in that Dumpster. Suddenly I wished Trey was there with me.

I flicked the channels trying to find out if there was anything about Halo, but everyone was talking about the woman's murder.

I had the kids get ready for bed and then we had cupcakes and milk and I read them a bedtime story. Liese and Arissa shared one twin bed and I put Kyle in the other. After I finished the book, I stuck the movie *Tangled* in the DVD and turned out the light. They were so worn out it would be just a matter of minutes before all three were sound asleep.

I stood by the door watching them and thinking how much my life had changed since Kyle had stepped into my life. I loved that little boy so much, and that was something I didn't even think was possible. He had me thinking of someday having a child of my own.

I went back down to the family room and turned to TVOne and caught *Hairshow* with Mo'Nique and dozed off. I wasn't sure how long I was sleep before I heard a crash followed by someone running down the hall.

I sprang from the couch, grabbed the poker near the fireplace, and ran behind the door. Then I thought about the kids and started to panic. They were upstairs. *Please don't let him go upstairs*, I kept saying to myself as I waited, my heart beating fast as the footsteps grew closer. As soon as I saw a shadow step into the room, I jumped out from behind the door and swung but missed. We both screamed at the same time.

"Are you crazy!" Monica shouted.

"Sorry, I heard a crash and thought someone was breaking in!" I explained through ragged breaths.

"That's what I have a security system for." She placed her hand to her heart and stepped away from me and the poker.

I'd forgotten all about that. Monica had instructed me to set it after the kids had gone to bed. If someone had broken in, the alarm would have sounded.

"You scared the crap outta me. I was sound asleep." Monica didn't realize how scared I really was since I hadn't bothered to tell her anything regarding Mannie's murder.

Monica gave me this sad look, then moved around the couch and took a seat. "Robin . . . it's so sad! I can't believe what happened," she said.

Something in her eyes made me scared. I don't know what, but it just told me that what she was about to say, I didn't really wanna know. I hadn't had that sick a feeling in my stomach since the day Deena told me she was leaving Ms. Ernestine's house and wasn't taking me with her.

I dropped the poker. "What happened?"

"The club was a zoo today. I think we spent more time in the dressing room taking about the murder than we did on stage. Everybody was talking about how they weren't surprised . . . that she lived a shady life and prostituted on the side, so it was likely to have happened anyway."

"What the hell are you talking about?" I hated when someone starts talking about something as if you already know what going on. Well, guess what? I didn't have a clue what she was talking about. "Monica . . . who got murdered?"

Her eyes got round as she suddenly realized I had no idea what she was talking about. "Did you watch the news tonight?"

I nodded and took a seat beside her. "They found a woman in a Dumpster behind a gas station."

I watched her facial expressions, and when she ran her hand over her short curls and her nostrils flared, I knew something wasn't right. "It was Honey."

"What?" There is no way I heard her right.

She gave me a long sad look and whispered, "That was Honey they found in that Dumpster."

My head started to spin and then everything went black.

44

Monica

The last thing I had expected was for Robin to pass out. I lay her back on the couch and started patting her hand. "Robin . . . girl . . . you okay?" I had no idea she would react that way. I knew they were cool and all, but they were like day and night. Friends, dancers, but not close friends. "Robin, sweetie, wake up." I started slapping her lightly on the cheek, trying to get her to snap out of it, and eventually she started mumbling something under her breath. For a moment there I thought I was going to have to call an ambulance to see about her. She scared the hell out of me.

"Tell me it ain't true," she kept mumbling over and over under her breath with her eyelids still lowered. I didn't know what to say except for the truth.

"It's true. She's gone. I heard Honey's been missing since yesterday."

Robin started shaking her head in disbelief, and next thing I know she was screaming at the top of her lungs. "No!" I tried to calm her down because the last thing I needed was for her to get hysterical. Besides, the kids were upstairs and I didn't want her to wake them.

She was crying hard and my heart went out to her. I hugged her and whispered in her ear, "I'm sorry." Honey wasn't one of my favorite dancers, but she had at least been nice to me. The person I'd hoped had been in that Dumpster was Mercedes—then I saw her skinny ass sashaying into the club like she didn't have a worry in the world. The bitch. Ever since she caught me in the VIP room with Greg, she had been watching me like she was waiting for the right moment. To do what? I couldn't figure it out.

I patted Robin on the back and tried to say a few soothing words to calm her down. I had never been good with death, but I did the best that I could. Eventually the cries turned to sniffles. I released her, stared at her tearstained cheeks and swollen eyes.

"Do you know what happened to her?" Her voice cracked.

I shook my head. "No, other than she was at the club last night and was seen talking with this one dude and was scared to leave alone, so she got one of the bouncers to walk her to her car and was last seen pulling away . . . but no one knows what happened after that."

Robin pulled her legs up to her chest. She looked so fragile, like one of my girls, sitting there on the couch rocking back and forth.

"I'm really sorry."

I watched as the tears rolled slow and steady down Robin's cheeks before she reached up and brushed them away with an angry fist.

"This shit is fucking unbelievable. I just talked to her on the phone yesterday and everything was fine!" She threw an angry fist in the air. "She and her dude, Jordan, were going out to dinner yesterday before she worked at the club."

"Do you think that guy could have something to do with what happened to her?"

Robin took a moment to think about my question and then she shrugged. "Shit if I know. Those two were always getting into it. I tried calling her this morning but I didn't get any answer. I figured she was still sleeping off last night." She closed her eyes and leaned her head back again the couch, and for a long time neither of us said anything.

Her cell phone rang and I watched as she reached for it and looked down at the number on the screen. Her eyes grew large with fear.

"What's wrong?"

She shook her head like it was no big deal then slowly brought the device to her ear. "Hello?"

I couldn't hear what they said, but whatever it was I don't think I've ever seen a light-skinned chick turn that white before. She closed the phone and sprang from the couch, then moved over to the window.

"What's wrong?" I asked because she was beginning to scare me.

"Monica . . . I need to go. I should have never come to your house."

"Why? What's going on?"

She peeked out between the curtains, looking for something, then looked over at me. One thing I never expected to see from Robin was fear. As far as I was concerned, she was the strongest woman I had ever met.

"Somebody is after me."

"Somebody like who?"

She paced nervously from one end of the room to the other, and I was ready to scream at her to tell me when she finally spoke again.

"Remember the guy who comes into the club all the time asking for me . . . Halo?"

It took a moment to think of who she was talking about, then my eyes grew wide with recognition. Ever since the first time I had spotted him in the club, there was something about him I had found familiar. But that wasn't the reason why I was suddenly seriously worried. "I know exactly who you're talking about." I paused because there was more, I just didn't know how to say it. But Robin could see it on my face.

"Monica, what is it?"

I hesitated. "He was in the club tonight . . . asking about you."

45

Robin

I didn't know whether to laugh or cry, because this entire situation was like something out of a freaking movie, and all because I wanted my sister back in my life. The sister who for years I pretended no longer existed. I walked around the room and took a seat on the couch because I wasn't sure how much longer my legs were going to be able to hold me up. I was a nervous wreck.

"Halo came by asking about me?"

Monica looked afraid to nod her head. "He came up and asked me if I had seen you, and when I told him you weren't working tonight, he said to tell you he was looking for you."

I tried to force myself to remain calm. "Please tell me you didn't tell him where I was?"

"No . . . why in the world would I do something like that? He gives me the creeps. I know him from somewhere, I just can't figure out where."

The police still hadn't arrested him. Why was it taking so long? I just couldn't understand that. As long as he was out on the street, I wasn't safe. Neither was anyone who was around me.

"Monica, I shouldn't have ever come to your house. He's looking for me, and he might have followed you home."

She tried to put on a strong face, but I could see her lips

shaking as she spoke. "Nobody's getting through that security system. If they do, the police will be here the second they step through the foyer."

I tried to smile. I know she was trying to make me feel better, but it wasn't working. Nothing would until this entire ordeal was over.

"Do you know what happened to Honey?" It was more of a statement than a question. I know she wasn't accusing me of anything, but the look in her eyes said she knew I knew more than I was admitting about the whole thing.

I nodded. "Yes. I think I know what happened to Honey." I just didn't want to believe my asking her to get involved in my mess could have gotten her killed, but I had a sinking feeling it had. "Halo probably killed her."

She gasped and there was more silence. Enough to make me nervous. "But why?"

"Remember when I told you my sister was in jail?"

She nodded, waiting for me to finish.

"Well, she was arrested for murdering one of Halo's crew."

She flinched and looked even more confused than before. I quickly explained. "She didn't do it. Halo set her up."

"Oh my goodness! But how can she prove it?"

"Well, that's where me and Honey came in." I went on to tell her about my suspicions of Halo and how he acted paranoid all the time. "Anyway, as soon as I saw my sister's charm, I knew whatever happened to Mannie, happened at the club. I had Honey distract Halo while I snuck into his panic room and stole the video for that night."

"This is crazy!" she said, shaking her head in disbelief.

"Worse than crazy. I watched the video, and sure enough, his murder was on that video. On Monday morning, Trey took me down to the police station so I could give it to the police."

"Oh my goodness. You really saw him get murdered!" She took a deep breath. "Does Halo know that you know?"

I nodded. "Unfortunately yes. When I left the panic room I forgot to secure the door. Not to mention Mercedes caught me leaving. I received a text message from him the next day letting me know he knew. That was him that called a few moments ago. He tried to disguise his voice but I know it was him."

"That was him! What did he say?"

I couldn't even bring my lips to form the words. He was trying to scare me and he was doing a damn good job. "He said, 'you're next.'"

"Oh no! Should we call the police?"

I shook my head. "There isn't much they can do. I already gave them the video. All I can do now is wait for them to arrest him or for him to come after me."

She sat there, eyes traveling around the room, thinking of something she could do to help me. "I hope you kept a copy just in case."

See, that's one thing I liked about Monica, she was smart. "Of course. Matter of fact, I got it right here in my purse. Would you like to see it?" It took her all of two seconds to think about it before she nodded. "You got a computer?"

I followed her down the hall to an office on the other side of the gourmet kitchen. We stepped into a huge room with books lining one wall and a massive desk at the center of the room. She moved behind the desk and took a seat in front of a large flat screen and logged on. As soon as the desktop was up, I reached inside my purse for the thumb drive and stuck it into the USB port on her computer. After a few moments the video started. I fast forwarded it to after the club was closed, when Halo and two other dudes stepped into his office. After that everything happened so fast that Monica was shaking, and by the time Mannie had been shot, she had run out of the room.

Damn, I should have known the video was going to be a

little more than she could handle. I was getting ready to pull the thumb drive out of the modem when she stepped back into the room. "Wait! Let me see that again."

I couldn't understand why she wanted to see Mannie being executed, but I pressed Play again, and before Halo pulled his gun out of his desk drawer, Monica leaned forward and pressed Pause.

"I know that man," she announced.

"Who . . . Mannie?" She shook her head and tried to pull her words together. "No, *that* man there." She pointed at the tall, good-looking dude who had stepped into the room with Halo.

"You do? Who is that?"

Monica reached inside her desk and riffled through some papers in search of something. I had no idea what she could possibly be looking for, but I was anxious to find out. She finally found a picture and handed it to me. She was right. The picture looked just like the man on the video with Halo. Again, I asked, "Who is he?" What she said blew me away.

"That man is my ex-husband, Anthony."

46

Monica

I stepped into the conference room with my lawyer and took a seat. A mediator was already sitting at the head of a long table, looking anxious to get the proceedings started. So was I. Like clockwork, the door opened and Anthony and his attorney stepped in. My lawyer, Bernard, had decided that before we went to court, we should schedule a friendly discussion with Anthony and see if with a little persuasion, he might drop the custody suit. Anthony's eyes said he was ready to make my life hell.

I guess we'd see about that.

I knew there was something about Halo that I recognized, I just couldn't figure out where I had met him before and now I knew. I had seen him at Anthony's office that afternoon I went over to beg for money, and once while Anthony and I were still together, we had run into him and a female at dinner. Anthony had introduced him as a client. The woman had been Robin. Talk about a small world.

Anthony took his seat with his lawyer, and his eyes traveled across the table to me. He had a cocky look on his face and was trying to intimidate me. At one time it would have worked, but not anymore.

"We are here today to discuss the custody of Liese and Arissa as well as an increase in financial support, but before we begin we would like to show you something." Bernard reached inside his briefcase and handed copies of the document to Anthony and his lawyer, as well as the mediator. "After some digging, I discovered something quite interesting. Mr. Houston owns property in two countries and also has over three million dollars in an overseas account that was never entered in the original divorce settlement."

Anthony jumped out of his seat. "That's my money!" he shouted. We waited while his lawyer urged him back into his seat.

Bernard then went on to explain how I had a right to part of those assets and gave an impressive argument that made me sit up taller in my brand-new black pantsuit. "As for the custody of the girls . . . before we get started, I would like to show a short video. I think after Mr. Houston sees it, he might decide it's in his best interest to drop his lawsuit."

Anthony looked at his lawyer with a questioning gaze. He simply shrugged and signaled for him to relax. That didn't last long. The moment the video started and Anthony realized what was on that recording, his eyes looked like someone had stuck his foot in an electric socket. When he glanced over at me, I couldn't resist a grin. *Gotcha!* I wished I had a camera to capture that moment because by the time the video was over, Anthony was hanging his head low. The room grew quiet and I noticed his lawyer wiping beads of sweat from his brow.

"My client is asking for one million dollars and full custody of the girls," Bernard said, then looked at me and winked.

"Mr. Boone . . . what does your client have to say to that?" the mediator asked after another prolonged moment of silence.

Anthony's lawyer started shuffling papers and suddenly lost his confidence right along with his client. And I didn't think things could get any better until the door opened and a man stepped into the room.

Bernard looked over and acknowledged him with a nod. "This officer is interested in asking Anthony a few questions about that video."

Anthony looked scared, and for a split second, I almost felt sorry for him. I didn't want to see Anthony in jail, but at the same time, I was willing to do whatever it took to keep my babies at home with me.

Anthony had a word with his lawyer in private and after a few minutes, which felt like forever, his lawyer finally faced the table. "Bernard . . . go ahead and draw up the papers and send them over to my office."

The two lawyers shook hands, and while the detective spoke to Anthony, I turned to Bernard. "So . . . what happened?"

He winked. "Don't worry. You're going to be able to keep the girls and get the money. The last thing he wants is a fight."

I was so happy I sprang to my feet, clapping my hands like a little girl. I was going to be able to take care of my girls. My days as a stripper were finally over.

I gathered my things and watched Anthony out of the corner of my eyes. The detective said something and Anthony gave a gloomy nod as he watched him walk out of the room. My ex-husband had a lot of explaining to do.

I walked over to where he was standing. Anthony looked down at me and I wanted so desperately to hate him, but I couldn't. "Thanks for dropping the fight."

He shrugged. "I didn't have much of a choice, now did I?"

I should have known he wasn't doing it out of the kindness of his heart. Bernard already said if he refused, we would be going to court and try to take every dime of the three million. Those assets would probably be frozen for a long time if the police discovered it to be laundered drug money.

"Tell me one thing . . . how did you find out I was dancing?"

For the longest time he just stared at me before he finally

took my hand and led me over to the corner, away from eavesdroppers. I glanced at the door and spotted two detectives out in the hall waiting impatiently for Anthony to exit the room and come with them. They were probably taking him down to the station for further questioning.

Anthony took a deep breath. "I don't even know why I'm telling you this, but I guess the only thing that's going to help me at this point is honesty." His voice was low and shaking. I had never seen Anthony so scared before. I figured whatever he was about to say was going to change his life forever. "I had come by the club to discuss business with Halo when he murdered that man," he whispered. "Then this chick pulled up and Halo demanded she let him load the body in the trunk of her Camry, wrapped in this bear rug. Everything happened so fast, and I must have dropped my wallet into the trunk while I was helping load the body. She showed up at my office a few weeks ago to return it. When she told me she recognized you in a photo I still kept inside of you and the girls, I paid her for the information."

"What chick?" As soon as he said the name, I gasped.

"She works at Scandalous . . . her stage name is Mercedes."

47

Robin

"There she is."

Kyle rushed off my lap and ran to greet my sister as she was finally released from jail. Immediately, Deena scooped him into her arms and spun him around.

It had been a long few weeks. Halo had been arrested for the murder of Mannie, and Mercedes and several others were charged as accessories. When Monica told me about her involvement, I couldn't wait for them to cart her ass off in handcuffs. Monica's ex-husband had agreed to testify against all of them in court for a lesser sentence.

I stopped dancing at Scandalous. After Honey's funeral, I couldn't bring myself to return. It was just too sad, and I kept thinking about her dead body being lowered into the ground. That could have been me. Two weeks after her funeral, Jordan had been arrested for Honey's murder. I guess he finally followed through on his threat.

I decided I no longer needed that life and enrolled at J. Sargeant Reynolds in their pharmacy technician program. It wouldn't be the money I was used to making, but anything was better than swinging around a pole, waiting for the next Halo to step into my life.

Trey squeezed my hand as we watched Kyle and Deena.

He was such a good man to me. Last week we'd moved in together. He said it was to keep me safe from Halo's boys, but I
knew he was ready to take our relationship to the next level
and I was okay with that. Men like him only came once in a
girl's life, and I was no fool.

"That boy's gonna talk her to death." He chuckled.

I couldn't resist a smile. "I know that's right."

Deena walked over to me with tears in her eyes, and as
soon as I rose, she wrapped her arms around me. My arms
moved of their own free will and before I realized it, I was
hugging her back. "Thank you so much, Robbie," she said between sniffles.

"Dee . . . that's what family is for." And then I was crying
as I held on to her. I had so much to be thankful for and even
more to look forward to. Not only did I have my sister back,
but now I had a family.

"Why are they crying?" I heard Kyle ask.

"Because that's what girls do," Trey replied.

Deena and I released each other, looked over at them, and
started laughing. I was certain that everything from that moment on was going to be all right.

48

Monica

"Monica Houston."

I rose from my seat and strutted over to the professor, standing at the far end of the stage, grinning proudly at me.

"Congratulations."

"Thank you," I said as I shook his hand. I accepted my degree, pausing long enough for the photographer, then moved back to my seat. I was so proud. After a year of sacrificing, I had finally graduated.

I glanced into the audience at Robin who was sitting with Liese and Arissa. They were waving proudly at me. I was beaming from ear to ear because I had finally given my girls a reason to be proud of me.

The last few weeks had been crazy. The investigation had been all over the news. Richmond Investments had been laundering millions of dollars in drug money. Anthony's partner, Greg, denied knowing anything about Anthony's dealings with Halo and apparently several others, but the jury was still out on that verdict. All I knew was Anthony was in a lot of trouble and could possibly serve some jail time, although the prosecution seemed more interested in Anthony helping them put Halo away for the rest of this life. I wished him all the luck in the world, but I had my girls to worry about. Thank goodness they didn't seize his overseas assets—I now had over a million dollars in my savings account and no one was ever going to try and take my girls away from me again.

As the rest of my classmates went up to the podium one by one, I allowed my eyes to travel around the room, and who I saw sitting to the far left of the room made my heart leap to my throat.

Tremayne.

I had invited him to my graduation way back when we were still together, and I hadn't expected him to show up. But he had.

After the private detective discovered Anthony's involvement with Halo, Bernard revealed that Tremayne had been instrumental in discovering Anthony had been hiding assets. I had planned on thanking him when I got a chance. I guess I finally had the perfect opportunity.

As soon as the ceremony was over and all of us finished hugging and promising to keep in touch, I made my way off the stage. Liese and Arissa raced into my open arms.

"Mommy, you look so pretty!"

"Mommy, does this mean you're now a nurse?"

"Yes, it does." It felt good. Nurse Monica Houston. I still had to pass my boards in two weeks, but I had already tentatively landed a job at Southside Medical Center. Robin had given me a pair of purple scrubs as a graduation present.

"Congratulations," she said as we hugged. She had been such a good friend through all of this. It was still amazing how much we had both gone through in the last few months. However, we were proof all things prevail. She had enrolled in school, given up dancing, and I was so proud of her.

"Did you notice the sexy man in the third row, staring at you?" she whispered as she released me.

I nodded because I knew she had also noticed Tremayne. "Yes, I guess I better go over there and thank him."

"Yes, I guess you better, and don't do anything I wouldn't do." She gave me a saucy grin.

"That leaves my options wide open," I said with a wink and headed down the aisle. As soon as Tremayne noticed me, he rose from his chair and walked down to the end, meeting me halfway.

"Congratulations," he said.

"Thanks for coming." I grinned.

Shaking his head, I watched him take in my cap and gown and black four-inch pumps. "There was no way I was missing your graduation."

That meant a lot to me, considering we were no longer together. We stood there not saying anything. I could tell he wanted to say something, and I found it weird for a lawyer to be at a loss for words.

"Bernard told me you won your case."

"I did, but it never would have happened without your help. Thank you. I don't know how I will ever be able to repay you."

"How about letting me take you and the girls out to dinner to celebrate?"

My jaw dropped. I couldn't believe he wanted to spend time with me. "Why would you wanna do that?"

"Why not? Today's your big day. Besides . . . I miss you."

My heart was beating so hard it took me a few moments to pull it together. "I miss you too." He appeared relieved by my response. "Listen . . . you never gave me a chance to explain before, so I want to apologize for deceiving you. I should have been honest in the beginning."

"I would be lying if I said I wasn't pissed off to find my woman stripping. But what pissed me off the most was not that you were dancing, but that you didn't trust me enough to tell me the truth. All that time I thought you loved me."

"I did . . . I do. I just didn't know how to tell you I was

shaking my ass three nights a week." Even now it was hard to admit.

Tremayne reached down and clasped his fingers with mine and stared in my eyes for a long time before lowering his lips and kissing me. "The only man I want you shaking your ass for is me. Can you do that?"

"Yes." Was he saying what I thought he was saying? I didn't want to get ahead of myself.

He was staring at me, looking so serious. I couldn't have looked away if I had wanted to. And I didn't. "I love you, Monica. My feelings haven't changed."

My heart was pounding so hard I don't know how I found the words to speak. "And I love you." And then we were kissing like there was no tomorrow until I heard someone whistling. I guess we were making a scene.

Laughing, I finally released him. "Come on. Let's go and get the girls." Tremayne took my hand, and together we went to join the others. I looked over at Robin and she winked. Yeah, everything was working itself out, and both our futures were starting to look even brighter.

DISCUSSION QUESTIONS

1. Put yourself in Monica's shoes. What would you do if you had no other means to support your family? Would you consider stripping? Did Monica really have no other option?

2. Do you feel that Robin was a product of her environment? Was she stripping by choice or by chance? Since she was sleeping with men for money, would you consider her a whore, or are there exceptions to the rule?

3. Was Reyna living vicariously through Monica? Was she needy or just a good friend?

4. What would you do if Trey showed up on your doorstep with a little boy, claiming he was a nephew you knew nothing about? Would you take him in even though you didn't want anything to do with his mother? Was Robin wrong for hating her sister?

5. Deena said she did everything she could to try to help Robin get away from Ms. Ernestine. Do you agree?

6. Deena and Robin hadn't seen each other in years only to discover they had been hanging in the same circle all along. Robin left Halo and no longer wanted to be a part of that life. If you were Robin, would you have gotten involved with Halo again in order to help Deena clear her name?

7. Do you feel that Anthony was mentally abusive to Monica during their marriage? After he found out she

was stripping, do you feel that he had every right to try to take the girls? If they had gone to court, who do you think would have won?

8. How would you feel if you found out your best friend was bisexual? Do you think Monica would have been more accepting if Reyna had just been honest about her feelings for her? How would you have handled that *awkward* situation?

9. Trey was pissed that Robin starting seeing Halo again. Should she have been honest with him? Do you feel that she has trust issues when it comes to relationships?

10. Monica believed she had no choice but to sleep with Greg. Do you agree? When it comes to men, does she come across as weak or a survivor?

11. Was Tremayne wrong for ending the relationship when he discovered how Monica was really earning a living? If you were Monica, would you have just been honest in the first place?

If you enjoyed *Scandals*, don't miss

Taking Care of Business

by Lutishia Lovely

In Stores Now!

Turn the page for an excerpt from *Taking Care of Business* . . .

1

All was quiet on the West Coast front. And all was cozy in Bianca Livingston's world as she lay cuddled up next to Xavier Marquis, her husband and the love of her life. Had it been only seventy-two hours ago when she thought she'd go crazy?

Just three short days before this moment, Bianca had stood in the center of TOSTS—her pride and joy—ready to pull the hair she'd decided to grow long again right back out of her head. The chic, quaint eatery on Los Angeles's west side, formally named Taste of Soul Tapas Style, was two days away from its one-year anniversary celebration. The place had been in chaos. The truffle, caviar, and special champagne shipments had all been backordered, the cleaners had destroyed the new waitstaff uniforms, and the chef had been called away due to a death in his immediate family. The stress had brought on the unexpected arrival of Miss Flo, Bianca's monthly, complete with bloating, cramps, and a pounding headache. What was a sistah to do?

Put on her big-girl panties and make it happen, that's what. What other choice was there?

Forty-eight hours ago, Bianca had huddled with her assistant and the sous-chef, who'd then called all over America until they found last-minute supplies of truffles, caviar, and bubbly. After reaming the cleaners a new a-hole, Marquis had called in a favor from a designer friend and had ten new uniforms whipped up posthaste. Finding a selfless bone in her weary body, Bianca had had flowers delivered to the funeral home that housed her chef's brother and had quieted Miss Flo and Company with some prescription-strength pain pills.

Twenty-four hours ago, Bianca had finished her day at the second L. A. Livingston Corporation establishment, the increasingly popular soul food restaurant, Taste of Soul. She'd spent two hours on a conference call with her brother, Jefferson, and the finance department at corporate headquarters, overseen a fiftieth birthday luncheon for a party of twenty-five, and soothed the soul of a hapless vegetarian who'd been losing her mind because she'd eaten the cabbage and *then* realized that this particular selection was seasoned with smoked turkey legs. Bianca had found it convenient that sistah-girl had eaten the entire plate before making this observation, demanding her money back and threatening lawsuits. Not to mention that she'd somehow missed reading the ingredients to the Chaka Khan Cabbage side dish clearly listed on the menu. Bianca was furious but had too much work and too little time to argue. She'd given the emoting customer a gift certificate for two free dinners and a menu to take home so that she could study it before placing her next order. With a bright smile to hide her frustration, Bianca had asked Ms. I-Haven't-Eaten-Meat-In-Twenty-Years to pay particular attention to the items with a small *v* beside the name, identifying them as vegetarian dishes.

Eight hours ago, Bianca had linked arms with her husband and officially welcomed the guests to TOSTS' one-year anniversary. Tickets for the evening's event had been steep—two thousand dollars—but the price included an all-you-can-eat buffet, a champagne fountain (filled with the double-priced bubbly that had to be rush-ordered and FedEx'd to the event), and an intimate evening with the night's entertainment, Prince.

As if pleasing the palate and the auditory senses weren't enough, the tickets were also tax deductible, with part of the proceeds benefiting a soup kitchen. Following in the footsteps that the Taste of Soul founders, Marcus and Marietta Livingston, had set, the establishments Bianca managed did their part in making the communities around them a better place.

An hour ago, Bianca had kicked four-inch-high stilettos off her aching feet, slid a Mychael Knight designer original off her shoulders, separated herself from a Victoria's Secret thong, and eased into the master suite's dual-head marble shower. Seconds later, Xavier had joined her.

"*Mon bien-aimé de chocolat*," Xavier murmured as he eased up behind Bianca and wrapped her in his arms. "You are the chocolate on the menu for which my heart beat all night long." He took the sponge from her hand and began soaping her slender body from head to toe.

"Mmm, that feels good," Bianca said. She leaned back against her husband's wide, firm chest. Moments before, she'd been dog tired, but now her husband's ministrations were filling her with new, lusty energy. She wriggled her soapy body against his and was immediately rewarded with a long, thick soldier coming quickly to attention. They made quick work of the cleaning process before Xavier lifted Bianca against the cool marble wall and joined them together in the age-old dance of love. The contrast of the cool marble, hot water, and even hotter desire swirled into a symphony with a melody known by Xavier and Bianca alone. This was their first time together in almost seventy-two hours. Ecstasy came quickly, and then they climbed into bed for an encore.

Five minutes ago, Bianca had screamed in delight as her body shook with the intensity of a seismic climax. Xavier, the quieter of the two lovers, had shifted rhythms from second to third, before picking up speed and heading for his own orgasmic finale. He hissed, moaned, squeezed Bianca tightly, and went over the edge. Too spent to move, Bianca had kissed

Xavier on the nose, turned herself to spoon up against him, and vowed to take a shower first thing in the morning. She smiled as Xavier kissed her on the neck. *That man knows how to rock my world,* she thought as she looked at the clock. It was early morning: 4:45.

At 4:50, a shadowy figure crouched along the buildings on Los Angeles's west side. He stopped, looked both ways, and walked purposefully toward a door on the other side of the alley. It was the back door to TOSTS—Taste of Soul Tapas Style. In less than one hour, Bianca Livingston's world would get rocked again.